Lights in a Western Sky

BY THE SAME AUTHOR

*Murchison's Fragment
and Other Short Plays for Stage and Radio*

From Higher Places

Lights in a Western Sky

Roger Curtis

Copyright © 2018 Roger Curtis

The moral right of the author has been asserted.

Apart from any fair dealing for the purposes of research or private study, or criticism or review, as permitted under the Copyright, Designs and Patents Act 1988, this publication may only be reproduced, stored or transmitted, in any form or by any means, with the prior permission in writing of the publishers, or in the case of reprographic reproduction in accordance with the terms of licences issued by the Copyright Licensing Agency. Enquiries concerning reproduction outside those terms should be sent to the publishers.

Matador
9 Priory Business Park,
Wistow Road, Kibworth Beauchamp,
Leicestershire. LE8 0RX
Tel: 0116 279 2299
Email: books@troubador.co.uk
Web: www.troubador.co.uk/matador
Twitter: @matadorbooks

ISBN 978 178901 476 1

British Library Cataloguing in Publication Data.
A catalogue record for this book is available from the British Library.

Printed and bound by CPI Group (UK) Ltd, Croydon, CR0 4YY
Typeset in 11pt Aldine401 BT by Troubador Publishing Ltd, Leicester, UK

Matador is an imprint of Troubador Publishing Ltd

For my grandsons Elias and Finley
in their later years

A staircase spiralling
Through generations
Chimney-like
In brick and stone
But measured in time
In its wall, vertically
Apertures, permitting
Glimpses
Of emanations
From men and their affairs
Lifting from the earth
Becoming
Lights in a western sky

CONTENTS

Preface	ix
The Physic Garden	1
Snow in Winter	13
Chemosit	34
Shep Stone	56
Johnny's Ride to Town	69
The Two Nuns	82
Dawn Light	92
Trexler's Orchid	101
Dust to Dust	115
Intercity Trains	125
Muntjac	134
The Chapel of Antonis Stavros	144
Window on the Mind	156
The Tunnel	168
A Jerusalem Trilogy	
Lazarus	192
Judas	202
Judas Thomas	211
The Runners of Afton Jail	236
The Widower	247
Enduring Light	259
Notes on *A Jerusalem Trilogy*	265

PREFACE

The twenty stories presented here are from the same stable that produced *Murchison's Fragment*, a collection of short plays on the theme of trial and tribulation, with most having a twist at the end or an unexpected denouement. If they contain a message at all it is of the frailty and waywardness of the human condition, where what we do is seldom determined by a clear concept of good and evil but instead is influenced by the situations in which we find ourselves and the people that we encounter.

Most of the stories are original and unpublished, but four of them were precursors of plays in the above collection – three under different titles – and appear here because, in the author's opinion, they sit more comfortably in the present format. They are: *Snow in Winter* (*The Pagoda*), *Chemosit* (*Murchison's Fragment*), *Johnny's Ride to Town* (same title) and *Judas Thomas* (*The Gospel of Judas Thomas*). Notes accompanying the plays are to be found in *Murchison's Fragment*.

Three of the stories included here are based upon events surrounding the last days of the biblical Jesus. To those adhering strictly to the authenticity of the New Testament stories they may not be appealing. But for others uncomfortable with supernatural explanations for the miracles and the resurrection of Jesus they are attempts to show that rational explanations are possible, though no claim is made that they are more than illustrative. Since some background information is necessary for their full appreciation additional material is given in an appendix to the main text.

Although some of the stories may owe their origin to situations or incidents experienced or observed by the author, all characters are treated fictitiously. With the exception of brief mentions of publicly known figures no characters are identifiable with real individuals, living or dead. Similarly, existing or pre-existing places and locations mentioned in the text are treated fictitiously.

THE PHYSIC GARDEN

It was a rare Sunday in June, in the year 1781. The oppressive heat of the previous day had carried over into the bright morning and brought forth an abundance of winged life to populate an air already thick with heady perfume. Clutching his stick, and with Rosa, his nurse, supporting his elbow, Dr Pentarius steadied himself at the entrance to the garden and raised the trembling fingers of his free hand to halt their progress. He stood framed within the arch of box, staring and still, allowing the garden to play with his damaged senses.

'I told you summer had come,' Rosa said, squeezing his arm. 'You didn't believe me did you?'

Dr Pentarius smiled, dimly remembering her promise.

They followed the gravel path to a point where the vegetation grew highest, forming a bower from within which neither the house nor noises from the Thames – in fact no other trace of human activity besides the creation that was the garden itself – could be perceived. Grasping Rosa's arm, Dr Pentarius lowered himself into his cushioned wooden chair. His eyes followed the path leading across to the fountain and became fixed upon its bright and convulsing column.

'Call me if you need me,' Rosa said, picking up a little

bell lying on the table and shaking it close to his face. 'I will bring your drink and a pastry at ten.' Then she added, 'Amelia is coming today – you'll like that, won't you?'

Dr Pentarius' eyes widened at the mention of the five-year-old child who now came often to play in his garden. 'Yes,' he replied, incorporating her image into the tapestry of floral colour, buzzing insects and sparkling water spread out before him.

On another summer morning six years earlier, the garden – or, rather, what was to be a garden within a garden – still existed only in Dr Pentarius' imagination and on scribbled plans scattered amongst his papers.

Seen from the river, the house on Mortlake Terrace stood back, square and regular, behind iron railings. Its fashionable symmetry had become softened by the twenty-year-old birches planted on the very day that the newly crowned George III married Charlotte-Sophia. The greensward in their shade swept around the side of the house, encompassing a miscellany of younger growths, fresh and bright in the sunlight.

There was a familiar commotion around the steps leading down to the water's edge. There, a decorated barge, pennants flying, lay ready to depart on the high tide. Oars waved aloft were challenged by antenna-like poles, their bearers barely visible beyond the parapet.

From the window of his study beside the front door, Dr Pentarius observed this activity as an entomologist might scrutinise the waving appendages of a captured insect. He noted with satisfaction the tall and handsome figure of Charles, third son of Lord Somerset, looking on impassively while the bulky figure of his mother – Pentarius' patient – was coaxed into the barge. A little apart now, Margaret, his comely daughter, stood deep in thought. Minutes earlier he had watched the young man's hand hover within an inch of her waist, battling against its owner's better judgement, while she had turned her head away, demurely, flushing pink. With a *third* son Dr Pentarius considered that his own indeterminate status and his daughter's youthful beauty might yet render a social barrier surmountable.

On top of that, it seemed that at last Lady Somerset's acne was improving; and goodwill, too, was important in the equation. On this occasion he had prepared the tinctures with his own hand, releasing Margaret from the routine chore in the dispensary. The thought prompted him to wander into the adjoining room, where the walls were fronted by row upon row of jars and bottles, tidily arranged, their labels mostly in Margaret's neat hand. On the central table an array of blocks, mortars, pestles and flasks flecked and smeared with diverse plant residues emitted a complex bouquet which Dr Pentarius sniffed as he might a rare and cherished wine.

Margaret had followed him, unnoticed, and now stood at his elbow. He turned and they exchanged wry smiles. But the implications of their complicity were for the future. Just now there were more immediate matters to attend to.

Side by side they looked out into the garden beside the house. The bare earth square of twenty-five paces might have been the foundations of a new building, were it not for the lines of tiny box plants marking its margin. Within its confines, Kingsland, the gardener, was raking the earth of beds whose irregularity contrasted with the geometric precision of the perimeter. Towards the far side a ragged hole suggested a pond under construction; nearer, a raised circle of bricks and mortar anticipated a statue or sundial. Only the previous day, from this same position, Margaret had been amused to see her father standing motionless on this very pedestal, eyes skyward, one hand clutching a herbal to his chest, the other grasping a lapel.

'It was fortuitous, Margaret, that with the appointment of Forsyth as Gardener, the Chelsea Physic Garden adopted a more liberal approach to the release of plants.'

'Your list *was* rather long.'

'We'll see what comes. When is the boat due?'

'Around three.'

'So we could start planting before dinner at five.'

'Patience was never one of your virtues, Father.'

Two hours later Dr Pentarius and his daughter were standing on the steps leading down to the water. They saw a black speck separate from the flotsam of craft towards Hammersmith and transform itself into a skiff with a single oarsman rowing with power and regularity. As the boat drew into the steps, Kingsland stepped down and took the rope. Not until the skiff was secure and the oars had been stowed did the rower look towards the doctor and his daughter. But by then their attention was directed, not at him, but at the treasures the boat contained. Fronds of green, brown and yellow emerged tantalisingly from ragged bundles of sacking; bare roots, bulbs and tubers spilled from open baskets. Most intriguing of all were the lumpy sacks that did not yet reveal their contents.

The tousled black hair of the apprentice from the Chelsea garden was suddenly thrown back. Serious eyes, deep-set in a swarthy handsome face, engaged those of the doctor and his daughter.

'Good day, Sir,' Dr Pentarius said, extending a hand. 'I can't recall that we've met at Chelsea.'

'Carlos, Sir,' the apprentice replied, taking his hand. 'New from Leiden, where some of your plants have come from.'

'From Leiden? I gained my doctorate there. As a student I knew the garden well. It was where my fascination with plants really began. But should you not therefore be called Carolus?'

'My origins are more… distant, Sir.'

'Well, Florence will give you tea in the kitchen and you can discuss planting with Kingsland. There's lodging in the stable, if you would like to stay.'

'That's kindness indeed, Sir. It would ensure an early start tomorrow.'

Dr Pentarius looked again at the apprentice's olive skin and burning eyes. He was unsettled by a confidence unusual in one so young. He decided to explore it.

'Did you by chance have difficulty with the *Dendranthema*?'

'I chose for you the variety *sinensis*. In my experience it has the more vigorous growth.'

'Thank you. Margaret will assist in checking the inventory.'

Dr Pentarius left them, but he did not go far. He stood back in the depth of his study and watched the apprentice unload the skiff with muscular brown arms; then, with Kingsland's help, drag it out of the water, up the slipway and onto the grass, where they overturned it.

On the days that followed, Dr Pentarius arose ever earlier to walk the bare gravel paths that in the dawn light resembled a rough square of lace. He displaced the stones to determine if soil had been spilt; he measured with the span of his hand the distance between seedlings of the same species. To his surprise the level of water in the pond had retained its depth, attesting to the integrity of the puddling, but already he imagined there a more formal structure that would one day bear a fountain. In his mind he saw the verdant square rising ever higher like a building on its foundations. He saw it as it would appear from the river or from the road, the palms and the giant ferns elevated above the bland density of the clipped box hedge, inviting curiosity and admiration. But most of all he savoured what the garden would yield – the medicines and remedies with which he would experiment.

The next morning, while preparing tinctures in his dispensary, Dr Pentarius watched with satisfaction the three figures labouring in the garden. When Margaret excused herself from lunch he thought no more of it, then set about tidying his study to receive his patients. But even before he had finished his first examination he found himself returning to the dispensary, standing well back in the shadows to observe. It did not please him to see Kingsland working alone. 'There was a discrepancy in the inventory we needed to check,' Margaret told him at dinner. For the first time that he could recall, Margaret averted her eyes from his; then she left the room before Florence, their maid, appeared with dessert.

On the morning of the fourth day Carlos told him the planting was complete.

'Then why are there still bare patches?' he asked.

'For future needs,' the apprentice replied.

Dr Pentarius decided to spend the afternoon with Forsyth at Chelsea. He wondered about leaving Margaret alone and regretted giving Florence leave to visit her parents in Putney, then chided himself for being irrational. Nevertheless, to Forsyth's surprise at his mounting agitation, he reversed his original decision to spend the night in town.

Climbing back up the steps from the water at dusk he was reminded of Lord Somerset's son and set out to find Margaret to ask if there was news. As he crossed the lawn, he saw what he now realised was driving his thoughts – the skiff still as it had been placed there. With beating heart, he hurried his steps. He searched the house from the servants' rooms under the roof to the depths of the cellars where he stored his harvested plants. Then, returning to Margaret's room as night finally closed in, he looked across to the stables, invisible beneath the trees but for a faint reticulum of flickering candlelight that seeped between the warped and badly jointed boards of the hayloft above.

With trembling hands Dr Pentarius tried to replace his father's riding whip on the two hooks on the wall of his study. But it fell dangling, and from it red drops hit the floor and seeped between the boards. But it wasn't the blood – that much seemed deserved – but his final misplaced blow splitting the man's face that caused him anxiety. He picked up a cloth and wiped the object as clean as the plaited fibres would allow. Then he lit a fire in the grate to destroy it. He lay back in his chair, trying to sleep, but the images of the entwined bodies of his daughter and the apprentice rhythmically writhing in the loft of the stable would not go away. He made himself an infusion of *Hydrastis*, accepting that the deep, dark dreams that would inevitably follow were at least better than wakefulness. Before the drug took effect he took a candle from one of the wall sconces and went upstairs to Margaret's room, expecting to find her shaken and contrite, perhaps even receptive to an accommodation of their different passions. But her room was cavernous and empty through the gaping door. He went to the stable, where his horse regarded him with quiet nonchalance as he looked in vain for signs of human presence.

The following day the house remained silent. There was no word, no sign, from his daughter or the apprentice. When he questioned them, Florence and Kingsland just stared at him blankly, and he was too proud to probe their silence further. The upturned boat assumed the character of a beached whale that promised to remain until its carcase rotted away.

But one morning a week later, after a night of turbulent imaginings induced by a larger than usual infusion, Dr Pentarius found the boat had gone. He wandered, desolate, into the physic garden. He noticed, but without particular interest, that the bare unplanted patches were now filled with fresh green seedlings he did not recognise. He resolved to ask Kingsland about it, then forgot to do so.

As the nights grew longer, the days each seemed to pass through the same spectrum of grey. Perpetual mists hanging over the river foreshortened its vistas, transforming it into a lake traversed only by the most mundane of commercial craft. There was no longer a reason for the splendid barges and gay skiffs of early summer. Besides that, the frequent rains had made the road by the river an obstacle along which only the most intrepid of his patients chose to venture. Of his daughter and her lover there came no word.

Yet the seasons were not wholly unkind to Dr Pentarius. The autumn leaves falling across the physic garden softened its impact on his gaze and obliterated the imprint of the upturned boat on the lawn. He wondered if Kingsland understood his instruction to leave them be. Christmas passed almost unnoticed. Then snow fell, long and deep, marking both an end and a new beginning.

When spring came, Dr Pentarius busied himself in his dispensary. The bottles multiplied on the shelves, more labels now in his hand than in Margaret's. Every morning Florence would chide him about the increasing number of mortars and vessels to wash. Carried away by his obsession, Dr Pentarius began to apply the remedies to himself and assess the results more critically than he had ever done with his patients. Not infrequently Florence would find him stock still, timepiece in hand, measuring his pulse or his breathing, then, clicking the instrument shut, passing to the mirror to check his face for pallor or rubor. But he sensed she hadn't the stomach to tell him what he already knew: that the cause of the gauntness of his features must compromise his every experiment.

A year passed, then two more. The hedge around the physic garden had become tall and fine under Kingsland's deft shears. The once bare paths were now all but obliterated by bursting cushions of luxuriance. He saw there many of the plants he used – *Achillea, Cnicus, Helleborus, Symphytum, Allium, Amni, Ephedra, Hyocyamus* – and some he did not yet recognise. Like sentinels above them, there were fragrant plumes of *Yucca,* of which he stood in awe, blue-green *Eucalyptus, Datura* and *Mimosa*. And, amongst them, rising stands of a species he did not know, except as a member of the family – the *Solonaceae* – to which, besides the humble potato, the poisonous nightshades and the hallucinogenic *Brugmansia* belonged. These majestic plants, becoming higher with each season, began to bear clusters of pendulous trumpet-like flowers, sweetly smelling, in delicate shades of yellow and pink. He took a specimen for Forsyth to identify, but was no wiser: the Chelsea garden did not possess them, nor did it know of their origin. He had Kingsland set a chair for him where their tallest growths might screen him from the wind and the sun, and the distractions of the house and the river. For hours at a time he would sit with just the tinkling fountain – for Kingsland had at last secured its function – his only focus of distraction.

It was that fourth summer when the child first came to the garden. The mother had died in childbirth, Kingsland had told him. Later his wife had taken pity and taken her in. At first, the bright-eyed girl held no interest for Dr Pentarius, and when Kingsland came again to speak with him he had been occupied and brushed the man aside. The child built houses with stones on the plinth where the doctor had imagined himself immortal, and filled little cups with water from the fountain. It did not seem to him strange that she never came to him under his green canopy, even though, when he went to play with her – which became more and more often – she chatted to him with pleasure and without inhibition.

Only one aspect of Dr Pentarius' new-found existence disturbed him – his health. For some weeks his eyesight had begun to play tricks. In certain lights the letters on the page of his herbal seemed to dance to a strange rhythm that had something to do with his irregular heart beat. When he rose from his chair he became dizzy, so that for a few moments he could neither stand straight nor begin to walk. Then, one day, reacting to the child's cry of delight and invitation, he had simply fallen over, and lain there under her puzzled gaze until Kingsland chanced to find him and return him to his chair. That evening he scanned the shelves of his dispensary, wondering which of his concoctions – or combinations of them – might have caused such aberrations. He resolved to sample no more medicines, and with the passing of time his symptoms disappeared. That winter he spent long hours with Forsyth picking over his experiences, without result. Then, the following summer, his problems returned.

From the deep shade Dr Pentarius craned his neck to watch Rosa leave the garden through the arch in the box hedge. A garden of delight, Forsyth had once said; and it was indeed a casket of wonders, on a grand scale, full of botanical treasures to be experienced by all the senses. Without hardly moving his body, Dr Pentarius could grasp the fronds of *Mentha, Lavendula* and *Rosmarinus* and squeeze out their sharp perfumes, skim the seeds of *Linum* and release them, tinkling, on to the flat arm of his chair, hold up the translucent pods of *Capsicum* so that the contours within were refracted like rainbows in the sunlight. And then there was the gentle laughter of the child he was coming to love and depend upon. He saw the half-finished piles of stones and the sand and the fresh cups for water that Rosa had put there. It promised to be another day of unthreatened contentment on a scale of time stretching indefinitely into the future.

At first the child did not appear, though he could sense her presence outside the garden. Instead, Rosa returned alone, with puzzlement in her beaming smile.

'It seems Amelia has brought you a present, although I cannot get from her whom it is from.' She called to the child, 'Come Amelia, you can give it to the doctor now.'

Amelia walked slowly into view, clutching with both hands a small flat parcel wrapped in green paper and bound with silk cord of the same colour. She held it out to him.

He looked from the child's face to the parcel and back again. There was something he could not fathom, a tension that had no part in simple giving. Where there should have been only wonderment in the child's eyes he saw there apprehension also.

'Thank you, Amelia,' he said.

His trembling fingers were no match for the cord, even though it was tied in a simple bow. As he handed the package to Rosa the texture of the wrapping seemed to transform itself into shifting patterns of whorls and flourishes, more exotic, more *eastern* – that was the word that inexplicably entered his head – than could be had even in the capital itself.

Rosa unwrapped the parcel just sufficiently for him to complete the process

'A book, Amelia?' he anticipated. But as the paper fell away he was left holding not a book but a mirror in a simple wooden frame. Disappointed, he turned it over. 'What's that on the back?' he asked Rosa.

'A date,' she replied. 'Today's date. Or rather, this day six years ago. Does that mean anything?'

Dr Pentarius tried to reply, but could not gather his thoughts sufficiently, and said nothing. He held the mirror at arm's length, beside the child's face. An increasing effort of will against his faltering strength just permitted him to keep it there. The two images – his own and the child's – swam in his consciousness: his wasted, hers open and innocent, one moment so different, the next coming together as if to fuse, because of a commonality of features.

Slowly, the child turned and began to walk dejectedly away, as if her mission – whatever it might have been – had failed.

But, still holding the mirror, Dr Pentarius was engaged in a second voyage of realisation. Tentatively he sniffed the heavy scents that for many days he had inhaled without thought or caution, or even caring to identify their origin. Now he saw behind him in the mirror the contorted and vengeful inflorescences transformed by reflection from the beautiful scented flowers that he knew to be there but could no longer see.

Without thinking he expelled the air from his lungs and inhaled massively. Too late. The perfumes and vapours, inseparable carriers of pleasure and pain, filled his being. His heart pounded, the beats tripping over themselves. His breaths were taken as great convulsive gasps.

His last perception was of Amelia, his grandchild, her dark eyes wide, staring at him from across the garden.

SNOW IN WINTER

I had tried to flee, to fly back across the Atlantic to obscurity, but the girl at the desk had said no, there were no more flights because of the blizzard, and mine had been the last one in. She watched my fingers drumming on the shiny black – black, yes – counter and for a second her bright puzzled eyes engaged with mine. In my pocket Melanie's letter telling me of our mother's death nudged at my thigh. I felt a brief flicker of remorse. But it passed. As I left the terminal the snow swept in, even through the revolving door. Not surprisingly, the taxi reached Mortlake Crematorium fifteen minutes late.

They had expected stragglers. An attendant at the top of the steps waited while I kicked the slush from my shoes.

'Family, Sir?'

Why couldn't I say 'mother'?

'Eugene Harrington, her son.'

'Through there, Sir. There are still seats on the left.'

On its plinth the coffin threatened the closed red curtains like a battering ram. I looked across the score of grey female heads to the front row, where I should have been. She was there, Melanie, my sister. There was no mistaking her gold-red hair, just like her mother's. It fell to her shoulders but I'd remembered it much shorter.

I sat as the last of the amens died and the priest waited for the sea of rising faces to settle.

'Please remain seated. Berenice Harrington, as we all know, was a pianist of considerable renown. It is fitting, therefore, to end this service with a recording she made at the height of her career – of a piece that her children told me she most liked to play to them…'

What was this man saying? She'd never played for me. But I had no difficulty recognising the opening of the *Appassionata* sonata. Yes, she could certainly play. Those electrifying chords sent a sharp reminder to the nape of my neck. It felt like she was emerging from the coffin. I saw in my mind those heavily ringed white fingers pushing the cover upwards, as if it were the lid of her precious Bechstein. Did Melanie know why I remembered that piece?

The echoes came fast. *'Eugene! I've told you till I'm white to the tips of my ears never to approach the piano when I'm playing. What is it now?'*

'Melanie's cut her finger.'

And then the exasperation with me, just for being the messenger. *'Oh, then of course you had to tell me.'* There followed the familiar call into the distance, *'Melanie…'*

As the red curtains opened for the coffin I looked – frantically in my mind – for the certainty of the fire. But I was disappointed. Perhaps these days sight of it is deemed unsuitable for sensitive natures. Then, minutes later, all was done in the chapel. Those at the front began to file out.

She smiled as she passed me, my sister, with those grey-green actress eyes, ever alert, but never with guile. I followed her outside to where the flowers were laid. We stood side by side, looking down at the wreaths and posies with their dusting of snow. To my surprise she took my arm and pulled me towards her, over the flowers that from the message I could see were her own.

'Don't look down. What can you smell?'

'Tulips, chrysanthemums... jasmine. The smell of jasmine in winter! With mine, I hardly bothered about the colours even.'

'I'm not surprised.'

'Melanie, can she really have gone?'

'You wanted it that much, Eugene?'

'Didn't you?'

'Sooner or later you'll have to forgive.'

We both knew our relationships with Berenice had been different. It had always been so, but I'd never really known why. Even in death her shadow lay over us. I wanted to change the subject. Above all I wanted to know about her situation. I tried to sound casual.

'So Piers isn't with you?'

'He's... um... directing at the National. He said he might appear later, if the rehearsals finish on time. Piers is too busy for funerals.'

I wanted to ask, 'And for you?' but wasn't sure enough of my ground. I'd read in the papers they'd been an item for three years. I wanted to ask if she was happy, but feared she might answer yes, and said nothing. She took my arm as we walked away.

'How would it feel to be driven to the house by your little sister?'

'I didn't even know you drove.'

'That's why I need to spend time with you.'

She made her way cautiously, her driving at odds with her impetuous spirit.

'It's good you take care in the snow.' I said.

'Pooh. Only to let the blue-rinse brigade get ahead.

Didn't you see them all in the chapel, how determined they looked? They're doing the refreshments.'

'I wish we didn't have to go there.'

'They promised they'd leave us in peace. Honestly.'

It was seven years since I'd been in my mother's house. It was on one of the streets opposite the wall of Kew Gardens along the Richmond Road. Not much had changed in the first floor room that she'd called her *salon*. I'd heard her death had been sudden and sheets of music were piled upon the still-open piano. Open too was her great rosewood bureau, stuffed with papers. Beside it the lace curtains at the window were tied back. In spite of the falling snow I could see the pagoda in the Gardens rising high above the trees.

Many were the faces that came and went in that room. Some have become famous musicians. I've even attended their concerts, though, tainted by Berenice, I've tended to blank them out from my mind. Then there were her students. When I was small she'd get me to lead them up the stairs into her presence. Sometimes she would make me stay.

'Sit there, Eugene. Millicent will demonstrate for you how diligence can reap rewards.' There would follow a childish rendition of Für Elise, or some such piece, and then, *'That was heavenly, my dear. Now let me hear the B minor scale in thirds.'* Then her head would turn mechanically towards me. *'You know, Eugene, I think I'll see if they'll let her play the Hummel concerto at the school concert – only the slow movement of course because her fingers are still quite tiny. Little Millicent must make her mother feel so proud.'*

And so I would endure such torture, praying for Melanie to appear. But that, when it happened, only gave Berenice further opportunities.

'Melanie, I've brought you some walnut cake with coffee icing

– your favourite. Would you like it now or when you've done your homework?'

Cake? Coffee icing? But Melanie had looked at me with those apologetic eyes and while Berenice was practising we'd eaten it together in the kitchen.

A quiet voice at my elbow returned me to the world of the reception.

'Penny for your thoughts, Mr Harrington. We're leaving now.'

I'd seen her somewhere. 'Well, goodbye then, Mrs… um…'

'Prendergast… Antonia.'

'Oh, yes, I think my mother may have mentioned you.'

'She should have done. After all, I was her best friend.'

'Then thank you for all you've done, Mrs Prendergast.'

'A great musician and a great woman, Mr Harrington. We must not forget that.' She called to the kitchen. 'Bye, Melanie. We'll ring you tomorrow.'

Melanie appeared in the doorway. 'Bye, Antonia. Thanks for everything.'

The slam of the front door was of a tight lid closing upon a treasured silence.

'They've gone,' Melanie said.

'I thought they never would. Melanie, I thought I'd never see you again. It seemed as if Berenice would outlive us all.'

'Really never?'

'I didn't dare dream.'

'Look, we can talk later. First we have to look through her papers.'

'We? You're the executor. I'm nothing.'

'She's gone, Eugene. She's taken the past with her.'

'Has she? Some of it is ours too, remember.'

We made three piles – papers to be dealt with urgently, ones that could wait, and others of no apparent significance. At first we worked without speaking. I thought she was thinking what I was thinking. But I was wrong. I should have had an inkling of it when she handed me a particularly dull-looking bundle to look through, and then noticed how carefully she scrutinised her own clutch of documents from a previously unopened drawer. When I looked at her again she returned my stare with an expression of such profound resignation that I set my own papers aside. I'd be proved right in thinking she'd made a discovery. But something about her made me stay silent.

So I said, 'I think we deserve a break.'

'You do?'

'Definitely.'

'Suggestions?'

The worm that had been squirming in my brain since we started the task – probably even before we left the chapel – seemed to speak to me. It's now or never, it said. In an hour or so it will be dark. Piers will come for her and the opportunity will be lost for ever.

So, as casually as I could, I came out with it: 'Why not a walk in the Gardens?'

'Are you serious? With the snow still falling?'

'I'm sorry. It was a silly suggestion.'

She turned her head towards the window. I rejoiced that her beautiful hair no longer had to be shared with Berenice. Once, during a quarrel, she had said to me, Eugene, how can you possibly be my brother, with that black head of your's. But when I went to cry in my room, she came to find me.

The sky had lightened a little and the snow on the pagoda seemed almost sunlit. Then she turned to me and smiled.

'No… no. Perhaps we should do it.'

I took her coat from the hall stand and wrapped it around her. Even with my eyes closed I knew the exact span of her shoulders and rightly anticipated the firmness of her arms.

'Eugene, you can't be shivering. It's not that cold in here.'

She knew. I'm sure she knew.

Curiously, even in the snow there were people queuing to go into the Gardens.

'Eugene! It's eight pounds fifty to get in.'

'When we used to climb over the wall for free.'

We did. There used to be a spot just out of sight of the entrance where the branch of a tree in the pavement grew over the wall, and we were agile enough to climb it in a few seconds flat.

Once we'd paid and gone inside, without a word we made for that stretch of wall and looked up. The branch – massive now – was still there. As I looked it became attenuated in my mind until it was barely the thickness of an arm, with Melanie desperately hanging there.

'Help me Eugene. My skirt's caught.'

'Wait. I'll climb back up to you.'

Then – just like now – I was flustered and clumsy.

'You've torn it, you silly boy.'

'I couldn't help it.'

'Mother will be livid.'

I do not think the playing in the chapel had ever left my mind. And as the sound intensified it evoked an episode that was not unfamiliar. Even Beethoven would have flinched at the violence of the struck chord, and the expletives that followed.

'*Eugene, what have you done?*'

My sister was more rational. '*It wasn't his fault.*'

'*Melanie. You'll go to your room and remain there till dinner. As for you, Eugene… come here.*'

As my cries faded in my memory into a concoction of like episodes and Beethoven, the branch we had been staring at regained its uncompromised girth.

Melanie said, 'Look, I can almost reach it.'

'Shall we then?'

'Mm, not sure. But we could come back one day in old clothes.'

I wanted badly to tell her that my punishment at the hands of my mother had been no more than the blow; that being locked in the attic until the following morning had let me dwell undisturbed on the images of her body as I attempted to free her. The piece of torn cotton remains to this day between the leaves of my wallet – where it will stay. And the branch? Well, if one looks closely there is still a scar where I carved away the offending twig with my penknife. And I have that too.

I will not dwell on the years that followed. Melanie went to St Paul's Girls' School as a day pupil, and I to a far less meritorious boarding school near Taunton called Hatchett's. After delivering me there, Berenice never came again. But Melanie did whenever she'd saved up enough pocket money. When holidays came our first thoughts were always to escape to the Gardens. Hours at a time we would have together, for Berenice never varied her practise routine. We knew the Gardens like we knew each other's face: every path and shrubbery, almost every tree. And hours of dreaming of foreign lands, hidden in the lush vegetation of the greenhouses.

Our path led us between the great temperate glasshouse

and the pond that, until the previous week, had hosted a skating rink. We ignored them. Our destination was that nearby little temple of sweltering heat where even in midwinter huge water lily pads float in their tank above giant golden carp, and festoons of flowers fall to the surface from the roof. There was no doubt about our meeting of minds. The memories came flooding back.

'Look, Eugene!'

'Oh!'

I could not believe there was still a notice telling us that a single lily pad could support the weight of a child.

'Help me up. I'm smaller than you. This one, near the edge.'

'One, two, three… hup.'

'I'm on.'

'It's true!'

'Look at me, Eugene. I'm floating.'

'Get off, quick. Someone's coming.'

'It's moving away. Hold it, Eugene.'

There was tremendous splash, answered immediately by a voice from the door. 'Hey, you kids. What do you think you're doing?'

'Run!'

We ambled on, two black figures against the white snow. There was no plan, but this was no aimless wandering. Like marbles rumbling in a bowl our destination was precisely determined. So at last we found ourselves looking up at the great pagoda – that relic of pre-empire, inert and seemingly impregnable in its red and green livery, that neither of us had dared mention.

In those days the door at its base had never been open but that had not deterred us, with a builders' ladder nearby. On the third tier there was a panel that could be prized out. We went there several times, that last summer holiday, when I was back from boarding school and Berenice was on one of her tours. It happened the day she was coming back, and I suppose that might have precipitated it. I mean the knowledge that the opportunity might not come again. But we were too naïve to realise that our presence would not go unnoticed. The clattering of footsteps on the stairs below brought about a rapid semblance of decency. We recognised the red and perspiring face of one of the gardeners.

'*My God, what have you two been up to? How old are you? Right, get your coats on.*' Suddenly his eyes gleamed. '*I've seen you two before, haven't I?*'

I don't know what I would have done in his position. Nothing, I think. But he'd caught us once before picking flowers. He took us to the head gardener and a policeman escorted us home. Berenice had just returned and her bags were still unopened beside the piano. She could not recognise compassion – or did not choose to.

'*... I'm just reporting what the gardener thought he might have seen, Madam. It could, of course, have been his supposition...*'

But she would not accept the lifeline that had been offered.

'*Is it true what the gardener said, Eugene?*'

'*He didn't see anything...*'

'*See or not, is... it... true?*'

'*We only...*'

'*Only? Only? You have violated my daughter. You've contaminated her with... your filth... your father's...*' The violence dissolved into groans of distress.

Later, as I lay on my bed, Berenice thundered at the piano. That evening Melanie was taken to an aunt at Acton. I can still hear her screaming at the door. I nearly broke the window off its hinges trying to crane out, but I saw only the car departing.

I don't know why it was me that stayed in the house. Aunt Isabel would not have me, I suspect. But in the days that followed it was like I was being held under scrutiny. There were even fleeting kindnesses, as if Berenice were eliminating the possibility of some redeeming feature in my character before making a final judgement.

'Do you know how to make tea, Eugene?'

'Yes, Mother. I can make it.'

'When you bring it we can talk for a bit, before I begin on the Shostakovitch. Eugene, it's high time we talked. Perhaps if we'd done so sooner this wretched incident might never have happened.'

'I'll... make your tea, Mother.'

How sharp is the knife-edge on which fateful decisions rest. How small an action need be to have monstrous consequences. I put the teacup on the piano.

'You see, Eugene, there were... difficulties in my life to which you were... through no fault of your own... well, a party. When I have found it difficult to treat you as a son...'

It was then that she saw I had placed the cup on the polished black surface. Even I could not have anticipated the violence of the response, except that it ended, as it always did, with the instruction to get out of her sight.

A few days later Melanie and I were back at school. I wrote but nothing ever came back. From time to time I saw her at events where it was deemed appropriate for we children to be present, but always in a crowd, and mostly at opposite ends of a room. The last time was soon after she'd met Piers. Berenice had just completed her cycle of the Beethoven sonatas and the recording company had honoured her with a small reception and obviously not known better than to invite me. They were too engaged to see me approach.

I heard Melanie say, '... so Piers will be staging *Madame Butterfly*. He's wondering who to cast as Pinkerton.'

'*Yes, it's proving quite a challenge.*'

It was the first time I had seen Piers. It was difficult to account for the vehemence of Berenice's response.

'*Then I suggest the lowest the gutter can provide.*'

Melanie's eyes widened. '*Mother?*'

'*Oh, I see, Berenice,*' Piers exclaimed, giving her undeserved credence. '*Your theory is that a performance might be enhanced if the artist has experience of the events…*'

'*Take no notice of her, Piers. She's winding you up. She has this thing about… male roles…*'

It was then that they saw me. Melanie seemed pleased.

'*Eugene, what a surprise.*'

'*A surprise for me too,*' Berenice said. '*I thought you were still in the States.*'

'*An invitation went to my London address. I happened to be in town.*'

'*Then I must have a word with the office. Their administration is appalling. You know, Piers, that on my last CD they spelt my name Bernice.*'

'*That is atrocious. By the way, Berenice, is this person who I think he is? You must introduce us.*'

'*Melanie, you do it.*'

'*Piers, this is my brother Eugene.*'

'*Of course! I should have recognised him instantly.*'

Melanie looked concerned. '*Why?*'

'*The hair! The black sheep of the family. Isn't that what you called him once, Berenice?*'

'*Mother?*'

And so it went on. I made my excuses and left. There were stairs to the exit at the other end of the room. By the time I reached them Berenice had been enticed to the piano and had begun to play. As I looked down I saw Melanie detach from the group and look around. Foolishly – and wrongly – I abandoned the thought that she might actually be looking for me.

On one of my earlier visits from the States I had plucked up courage to see her. But she and Piers were holidaying in France, and no one seemed to know where. Rashly I had confronted Berenice instead.

'Mother, I've come to ask you something. Something that as your son I have a right to know.'

'Which is?'

'Why this coldness persists. As I've got older I've come to realise that the crime you accused me of doesn't justify... this alienation. If my sister can't forgive me...'

'No she can't forgive you. She'll never forgive you. You've ruined her life.'

'But when I meet her I get no sense of that.'

'You don't know half what she's told me. People don't change, Eugene. If it's in your character, it remains.'

'Mother, you're living in a bygone age.'

'Well, I don't want to talk about it. My head is simply throbbing and I've got a recital tomorrow. Just please recognise that where Melanie's concerned you're wasting your time. Perhaps time will heal it... but I doubt it. Come later in the week if you want to talk about matters of a more... domestic kind.'

So I'd continued to believe Melanie resented me for the harm I'd done to her – the reason I'd always kept apart. But as we stared up at the pagoda I saw her face, flecked with snow. There was that wry smile again and I knew to my horror that all along I'd been wrong.

'It was the third tier, wasn't it, where...' I stammered.

'It was the best, Eugene. The first and the best.'

'Then I wish I'd known.'

'Come on, it's time for some tea.'

'They won't be open in this weather.'

'It said four-thirty on the board. We can just make it.'

We paid for our teas and carried our trays to a table by the window, in the failing light brighter than the rest because of the snow on the bushes outside.

I said, 'I suppose losing a husband made Berenice what she was. Don't you think?'

'After our... father left us she had no interest in men.'

'No interest? She had a grudge against all of them. And from her perspective I suppose I'd turned into one.'

'Something like that.'

'What?'

'Look, I think we should go back.'

'You've not finished your tea.'

'I... don't want any more.'

'But we've...'

'It's maybe for the best.'

'What are you trying to say? Are you trying to tell me something?'

'I don't know. I really don't know.' Melanie put her hands to her cheeks in a gesture of wretchedness. 'I have to go. You stay. I'll leave the key under the pot by the door. You can post it through the letterbox. The blue-rinse brigade has got others to get in.'

She got up from her seat, upsetting her cup as she reached for her coat, and rushed for the door. I found her outside, crying into her handkerchief.

'Mel, you'd better tell me. It's something you found, isn't it? When you were looking through her papers.'

'Partly that.'

'Come back into the warm. Come on.'

I grasped her hand, half-dragging her back inside. She mopped at the pool of spilt tea in an effort to fend off the moment of telling me.

'Oh, this is difficult. She wrote, you see just before she died. She must have known she hadn't much time. What she said I didn't believe. I didn't want to believe it. I thought it was the vindictiveness of a malicious and lying woman.' She paused. 'She said the evidence was in the desk.'

'Is that what I saw you trying to hide?'

'Yes. I was so confident it didn't exist I even let you watch me look. But it was there.'

'So what was it you found?'

I had to strain forward to hear her reply. 'Your adoption papers,' she whispered. 'I wasn't going to tell you. I've got them here. Look, you'd… better take them. We're not brother and sister, Eugene.'

'Then what are we for Christ's sake?'

'Beyond what I've told you, I don't know.'

'And now, assuming it's true?'

'We can stay friends, can't we?'

I believed I'd lost her. The one beacon in my pointless, barren, stricken world. My longing, day after day, to be reunited with her, all come to nothing. As for Berenice, with my dream of her demise fulfilled, she'd still managed to play her trump card.

'Come on,' Melanie said, 'I'll need to drive you to the station before the snow gets too deep. And before Piers gets here.'

'You go on ahead. I'll stay here for a few minutes. I'll catch you up.'

I watched my beautiful ex-sister in her long black coat – no Hepburn or Garbo could have held a candle to her – stepping, as I imagined, out of my life. I thought of drowning myself in the lily pond, or hurling myself from the top of the pagoda. But I knew I couldn't do that to her.

Outside the Gardens I followed the pavement where it led, and found myself in Richmond. I happened upon the library and in a quiet corner looked at the papers she had given me, turning them over and over to be sure.

I arrived back at the house two hours after she'd left me in the cafeteria. I thought she'd gone already and looked for the key under the pot. It wasn't there. Then the door opened.

'I waited for you to come.'

'Why?'

'I don't know. Thoughts passing through my mind, I suppose.'

'No Piers?'

'He... rang to say he's still rehearsing. I thought I'd make some tea.'

'Tea?'

'Yes, tea. To bring you back to reality.'

While Melanie went upstairs I stayed to put my coat on the hall stand. Funny how things choose their time to happen. The tag at the collar broke and I bent to pick the coat up. There on the floor behind the stand, pretty much obscured from view, was a framed picture, face to the wall, covered in dust. I remembered it that way since my childhood, but had never given it much thought. Now I was curious and turned it round.

It was a not very good painting of a man seated at a piano, hands raised from the keyboard, as if about to receive applause. A crony of my mother, no doubt. A tear, imperfectly repaired with adhesive tape, snaked its way across the canvass. I turned it back against the wall and went upstairs. Back in the salon I tried the keys of the piano, bringing Melanie from the kitchen.

'I didn't know you played.'

'I don't, but I always wanted to learn. She would never let me even touch the keyboard, whereas you…'

'Had lessons and got nowhere. Well you can still learn. In fact you can have the piano, as it's mine now.'

'Still miserable recompense.'

'I suppose.'

They were the stalling words of someone relieved enough to tease, though I could see no change in her expression.

'While you were away I went through her papers again.'

'Why?'

'I thought there were issues we needed to resolve.'

'Like who I am, as if I care?'

'You will care. You know she kept all her correspondence. You want us to look?'

Two hours later there was still no sign of Piers and dozens of Berenice's letters lay strewn across the floor.

Suddenly Melanie said, 'I think I might have found something. Look at this. Read it.'

The letter had been typed, probably, as I later realised, to obscure any admittance of emotion. I read: *My Dear Berenice. I have written this so that it will be waiting you when you arrive in London with little Eugene. I fervently hope you will be able to read it well before your first concert as these words will not be welcome. To come to the point, I will not be honouring my agreement to follow you to London after my last recital here in Budapest. Such is the power of love over fidelity. I have done my best to shield you from my affair with Clementine, but can no longer spare you distress. I will leave the public arena for a while, and it is best that neither you nor anyone else will be able to find me. What, then, about little Eugene? Though I have tried hard to persuade her, Clementine will not countenance looking after my son and sadly I have capitulated. I will send you all his papers, and a substantial sum of money has already been paid into our account with Coutt's, which will continue in your name only. I am also shipping the Bechstein that has been in our flat here. So you see I do have a conscience. We have had good moments together, Berenice, in spite of your intransigence and temper, but they are best put behind us. Cherish my son if you can – after all, the public has come to think of him as yours – and who knows, he may have his father's musical talent. Be brave, Berenice. Affectionately, Anton Kessler.*

'So what happened to Kessler?' I asked.

'I thought everyone knew that. He died in a plane crash. In fact... there's a newspaper cutting here somewhere. Yes, here. There's even a photograph of him. Look.'

I tried hard not to believe that the eyes under the black mane were those I saw in my shaving mirror each morning. We went downstairs and I turned the painting around.

'Not a bad looking man, was he, with his dark hair?' Melanie was smiling now.

'But why would she...?'

'Out of sight, out of mind. Obviously she couldn't bring herself to hide it completely.'

'You think *she* did that... that cut?'

'Let's not go there, Eugene.'

Upstairs again, Melanie was peering intently at the newspaper article.

'It seems they never recovered the plane from the sea. It can't have been long after that that Berenice married Richard Harrington... my father... and took his name. Probably she never told him you were not her natural son. I guess she just wanted to regularise the situation by having you formally adopted. She was not to know he'd up and leave her – and us.'

'Then why didn't she tell me?'

'I suppose to block out the past. You can see why she hated men.' Distant flames flickered in her beautiful eyes.

'But it's still our secret. Ours, Eugene. Ours to do with as we please. It's… it comes down to… *what you want me to be.*'

She was right. But this was a momentous issue. Thoughts I couldn't make sense of were queuing for resolution. I needed time to think. We didn't have time.

'What will you say when Piers arrives and sees all this… waste paper… on the floor? You remember Eugene, my acquaintance of indeterminate genetic status?'

'Piers has no interest in our family.' Again I saw the teasing smile.

'You've told me nothing about him – or yourself for that matter. There's a whole decade missing.'

The smile left her face. 'You know all about me Eugene, all about me that is worth knowing. You want to know what happened after we parted? I'll tell you. I got to drama school by embroidering my credentials. I made it in the theatre through my looks and by cosying up to the tabloids. I got financial security through people like Piers, who have fat wallets and fancy having what passes as a celebrity on their arm. And where has been the satisfaction in all that? You tell me. Okay, that's me. Now you.'

'Alright,' I said, 'let's start at the beginning. That night you went to Aunt Isabel. Did Berenice tell you what happened when the police returned? The gardener's allegations? But she'd been to see him, you see, and got him to change his story. And the deal for keeping my… our… slates clean? That I got myself out of her hair and kept away from you. That's why I ended up at law school in the States, where I've managed to make living. And there was one more powerful reason for staying away.'

'What?'

I'd gone too far, but there had to be no secrets between us now. My head told me to say no more but her wide eyes prized it from me. 'She threatened to write you out of her will.'

'Me? But she loved me.'

'But she hated me more. In that instance she was a profound judge of character, Melanie. Knowing what I'd decide.'

It was dark outside and the snow was still falling. I went to the window to pull the curtains, but drew back, because the snow in the lamplight was beautiful.

'Let's make a fire,' Melanie said.

'Alright.'

'I saw some chestnuts in the cupboard. She must have got them in for Christmas. Shall we?'

'Aren't you forgetting Piers?'

'You think we should worry about Piers?'

'Well… if he's taking you for a meal…'

'I don't think that need bother us.'

'I don't follow.'

'Piers was never coming, Eugene.'

'What?'

'Piers was my security. In case you were not what I wanted you to be.'

'A reason to get me to the station on the pretext of a dinner in Richmond.'

'Something like that. Besides, Piers is not at the National. He's in Paris, with someone else. And I haven't set eyes on him for weeks.'

With those words came an immediate and profound sense of release. I let my eyes roam unhindered about the room, for the first time seeing its treasures for what they were, not strange and hostile appendages of Berenice. And all suffused by an ethereal light from the window, where Melanie was now standing.

'Have you looked outside?' I said.

'I know. My car's half-buried.'

'I could help you clear it.'

'But then the trains wouldn't be running, would they?'

'I suppose not.'

She began to stroke my hair, over the temples, as she'd done all those years ago to console me. She said, 'I always knew there was something odd about your hair.'

'I promise I won't let it worry me anymore.'

I switched off the light and stood beside her at the window. As we stared into the distance our eyes grew accustomed to the darkness. Slowly, like a photograph developing in a darkroom tray, the image of the pagoda with snow upon its countless tiers rose up, and we were transported back to where we had once been.

CHEMOSIT

Dr Rupert Murchison's dream was about to die. That much he knew and was prepared for. But of its manner of passing he was still ignorant.

He paused at the top of the stairs overlooking the Natural History Museum's great gallery. Behind him in the wall the bust of the hunter Selous, with rifle poised, presided over the stuff of trophies with an ambivalence more acute in this conserving age than at any time before. Below and before him stretched the skeleton of *Diplodocus*, the largest of the dinosaurs. He gazed along the line of its spine towards the entrance, the better to contemplate his departure.

Part of him – the realist – wanted immediate severance from a world that suddenly, with his retirement, had turned sour. The other part – the dreamer – wished to linger and for the last time commune with the incumbents of the cases in the galleries below.

He descended the stairs cautiously, into the conflicting flows of tourists and children's groups. He became for the first time part of the masses, no longer the proud, if unrecognised, Curator of Mammals with his head held high. He saw himself mistily, as if from behind, a figure walking steadily down a beach towards the troubled surf, ill-informed of the dangers beneath its surface. It was an appropriate analogy. The sea was the life of idleness that now awaited him, and the predator within it a wife for whom affection had ebbed as the dementia had taken hold. It was a new profession that he would follow, whose motto was the single word 'care.'

By the time he reached the bottom the lesser man – the dreamer – had won the day. He turned into one of the bays off the main gallery. There, in their cases, the higher mammalian orders held their court. He passed that chosen spot amongst the primates which, twenty or so years before, he had vowed to fill with a specimen so unique that the world of scientific discovery must fall at his feet. He even recalled rehearsing the lines he intended to speak – first to his colleagues, then to the press, and last of all to those members of the public privileged enough to attend.

But it hadn't happened. And Bradley Tyler – his protégé, colleague and now, today, the usurper of his position – had seized upon this of all the subjects that Rupert's productive life as a zoologist might have offered. The words had ricocheted around the bottled walls of the spirit room where they were gathered to wish him farewell. 'Most scientists,' Tyler had said, 'are remembered for their discoveries and what emanates from them; but a few are famous for leaving behind seemingly insoluble conundrums. Murchison's fragment, as it has come to be known, will assuredly outlive him.' He looked around with a thin triumphant smile, then added, 'Unless, of course, someone with sufficient insight should come along and…' He cupped his hand around his ear. 'Did I by any chance hear someone mention Piltdown?' He waited until the titters had died down. 'But we mustn't jest. Today we say farewell to a fine scientist, colleague and friend. So please raise your glasses…'

Within the pocket of his trousers Rupert's grip closed

viciously upon the small glass tube, hardly larger than his thumb, containing the famous fragment of skin that, over the years, had resisted all attempts to establish the species of origin. The unrefined microscopic techniques of the time had given way to the sophisticated tools of modern technology. But they too, despite their power, had yielded nothing more.

With Tyler's challenging words the weight of failure bore more heavily upon him than at any time before, because the doors were about to close against any remaining possibility of resolution. Now, under the stares of this dumb audience of apes, he felt the cold blade of their disdain. He turned away, resolved to look no more and complete as rapidly as possible his passage to the end game.

But such finality was denied him. Tyler had appeared at his elbow.

'Sorry to pursue you, Rupert, but an elderly gentleman has just turned up. Said he knew you. Thought he could throw some light upon your little mystery, but just what I can't imagine. Didn't seem too nimble on his feet, though, so I said I'd follow you with his card.' He handed the card to Rupert. 'Ah, a man of the cloth I see.'

'Thank you,' Rupert said, glancing at the card, then putting it into his pocket.

'You won't see him?'

'I've had enough socialising for today, Bradley. His number's here. I'll give him a call.'

'Right, I'll tell him. Well, goodbye then, Rupert. Take care.'

'You too, Bradley.'

Angry with himself for his cowardice, Rupert made his way along the railings towards the subway to South Kensington station. Suddenly weary, he slumped onto the bench at the top of the steps, then closed his eyes. In moments he was on that train from Nairobi to Lake Victoria, all those years before.

The train had climbed out of the Rift Valley and over the Mau Escarpment. The carriage swayed in a manner at odds with the more regular clatter of the wheels. As daylight waned the ochre hues at the window turned leaden-grey with the beginnings of a tropical rainstorm. Soon the fusillade against the glass began to dominate the train's more drum-like beat. Under their influence Rupert could hardly tell whether he was dreaming or awake. He recognised only that his eyes were closed and his mind was numb, vaguely aware that the future – or what he could read of it – held nothing that warranted any adjustment of this state of melancholy.

The uncomfortable truth was that he had stayed in Kenya too long. The magnet that had drawn him here had captured others in its field, and the fruits of their collective labours had to be shared. The time had come to return to the museum and his laboratory high above the Cromwell Road, and reconstruct his career around what his colleagues would see as rich pickings. He knew that he would be less easily satisfied.

A sudden crash of the door to the forward carriage forced his eyes open. He shut them hastily, sensing involvement, but too late to avoid eye contact. The African poised to enter had been on the platform at Nakuru, the starched white collar identifying his trade, the proffered bible searching out those around him as if it were a device to find souls ripe for harvest. But the remarkable thing – that which Rupert remembered most vividly – was that the man's hair was red. Or rather it was not so much the colour of the hair itself – which is not unknown amongst members of the Bantu race – but that it was matched by the colour of the book to a degree that could not have been coincidental.

Whether through intent or because the carriage happened to lurch violently at that moment, the man fell heavily into the seat opposite. Rupert was immediately resentful. There were other seats he could have taken.

'Please sit down,' Rupert said facetiously.

The priest smiled, without embarrassment, seeming not to notice the intended slight. 'Thank you. I am grateful.'

In spite of the polite and cultured response, Rupert was not reconciled. 'Forgive me for asking, but is it accident or design that dictates your choice of seat?'

The priest placed his bible squarely in front of him, as if deliberately lining it up with Rupert's chest. 'Choice is something that must always be qualified.'

'Of course,' Rupert replied. 'A man of God must act in circumscribed ways.'

'That is true. But occasionally we are allowed to act outside the definable boundaries.'

Rupert's eyes closed wearily, but then snapped open. An issue had been raised. Suddenly his companion was interesting.

'Where are you going?' he asked, in better humour. 'And I am not accepting truth as a destination.'

'I am going home.'

Rupert scrutinised his companion's features as if he were a zoological specimen. 'You are...'

'Nandi. Of the Nandi tribe. And my name is Jackson. As you will appreciate, my home – Muhoroni – is a long way from Peterhouse.'

'Ah, Cambridge. I had wondered.'

'Yes. After four years things have changed.' He paused to spread his hands in mock resignation. 'Or, taking the long-term view, nothing has changed.'

'How so?'

'My people are afflicted. Some say it is of the mind. Others try to explain it in… I was about to say human, but let us say… well… physical terms. It's a phenomenon found in many cultures.'

It was getting dark now. The rain continued to beat against the window. The feeble lights of the carriage seemed incapable of dispelling the gloom.

'Does it have a name, this affliction?' Rupert asked.

'My people call it *chemosit*. A malignant spirit that can assume visible form, wreaking havoc. Men die of it.'

'But here men die from many causes.'

'Indeed. And for all those causes there are as many cures. I offer but one.'

'You are an exorcist?'

The priest smiled. 'I choose to think that I am… something more than that.'

Rupert felt he needed a cigarette. There was something about the man's self-assurance – like the hands motionless on his bible and the stillness of his expression – that disturbed him. He rose to pull down his jacket from the rack above.

'Please sit down, Dr Murchison.'

The authority and urgency of the instruction were replaced by the thought that Rupert had not revealed his name. Against wilting indignation, he sat down. 'So what else do you know about me?'

'That you are ready to go home.'

'Oh?'

'You are tired. Africa has not been what you hoped. The rewards not quite what you anticipated. I see it in your eyes. Am I right?'

'I sail next week.'

'Ah, so soon. That I did not know.'

Suddenly the carriage jerked tentatively, once, twice, three times. Then the brakes shrieked and the train stopped. The bible on the table flew into Rupert's chest, winding him. The lights went out.

The rain was now clawing at the window. In the grey light the runnels might have been blood from torn fingernails. Perhaps, Rupert thought, it was Jackson's chemosit trying desperately to engage him.

Within seconds the corridor filled with agitated figures trying to flee the carriage, seemingly preferring the hostile conditions outside to the confinement and darkness within. There were shouts and the sound of feet running through puddles. Cries from the front of the train carried back the message of a tree across the line, a monster so large that it would take a whole village to shift it, and then only in daylight.

Jackson made no effort to retrieve his bible from Rupert's lap. 'We must go now, Dr Murchison. Come, bring your bag.' Seeing Rupert's reluctance, he said, 'There are those still on the train who would take… well, let us say… advantage of the darkness. In any case,' he added brightly, 'we are almost at Muhoroni.'

'How close?'

'Oh, two, three miles only.'

Rupert marvelled at Jackson's assurance in a situation that seemed potentially dire – water everywhere, the light failing, the uncertain antics of an unbalanced crowd. He sensed in Jackson not just a player, but an agency. There was no other explanation for how he found the obscure gap in the forest edge that led to the path they took. Or how, in near darkness, he could pick his way through the detritus on the ground with such certainty. The residual grey oval of light closed behind them, like a snuffed candle. Then there was silence, total and oppressive. To Rupert the forest felt like a squeezed sponge refilled with still, dank air, as if all the processes of nature had been suspended.

At first Rupert could only follow the purposeful sway of his companion's shoulders, but gradually his eyes became accustomed to the gloom. It seemed that the rain was unable to penetrate the canopy above, but as his ears became more attuned he began to hear its passage. The blackness above slowly became speckled with points of light, until they were sufficient to reveal the silvery lattice that clothed the branches of the trees. Then came the tinkling and plopping of water against the leaves of the lower strata, the only sounds to break the absolute silence.

For many minutes they walked without speaking. Then Jackson stopped and turned. 'You see,' he said, pointing upwards to the pale light of an emerging moon, 'how prayers can be answered. Now, I think it is your turn to lead. And besides, I need to pray alone for a moment or so. Our predicaments are not the same, Dr Murchison. Be assured that mine is the more unenviable.'

Rupert realised that he was still carrying Jackson's bible, which he held out to his companion. 'No, no,' Jackson said, refusing it. 'You must guard it for me. I have no immediate need.'

This reversal of roles was no chance thing. Rupert had been given a part to play, an opportunity, almost, but to what purpose he could not determine. Outwardly it was the sort of challenge that faced military recruits on orientation exercises when, alone, they had to extricate themselves from demanding situations. He set off in the direction that Jackson had pointed, along another path identical to the first. He looked back to see the dark figure immobile in the clearing, with head bowed. An imperious gesture of the hand waved him on. Given no conceivable option he obeyed.

He moved forward, guided only by the faint ribbon of light above the path. He began to feel free of Jackson's presence, and with that came the realisation that the forest was no longer a dumb lifeless thing but full of myriad sounds from the whole spectrum of sylvan fauna. Cicadas rasped and amphibians roared their repertoires against the distant crashing of larger forms.

But gradually the previous silence again prevailed, as if a dampening blanket had been drawn over the entire forest. Then, after what might have been half a minute or ten, Rupert made the inevitable association. Icy fingers of fear explored his body and he began to sweat profusely. He found that, by increasing his stride, it was possible – for just a few moments – to re-summon, in the minutest measure, the living manifestations of the forest. But with their demise came the certain knowledge that his companion was closing upon him. He looked back but saw nothing. He wanted to run, but Africa had taught him that the consequences of flight were seldom advantageous. So he stood still, as a condemned man might wait, unspeakably fearful. The footsteps behind were measured and purposeful. They stopped, but still Rupert did not turn.

What surprised him most was the strain in Jackson's voice, as if he had reached a decision of awesome magnitude that had drained his body. 'You are fortunate, Dr Murchison,' he said.

'To have survived this far?' Rupert replied, with a levity so inappropriate that it elicited no response. But he knew that the crisis – whatever it was – had passed.

After a few seconds Jackson said simply, 'If you continue along this path you will reach the township. There will be people to help you.'

Rupert did not look back and did not see Jackson again. Ahead was a pinpoint of light in the far distance. A minute later he emerged from the forest.

The miscellany of low buildings – some brick with tin roofs but mostly of mud and thatch – had the same exaggerated incongruity as any remote colonial outpost from the early days. Even in the dim lamplight, Rupert could see frangipani, oleander and bougainvillea in profusion. He remembered that Muhoroni – if indeed this was the place – was still a district centre. However undeservedly, it still possessed a district officer.

It was not difficult to find the house, perched on a ridge, encircled by lawns and trees, all enclosed by a neatly trimmed hedge at odds with everything outside it. It was the ultimate distillation of British colonial style. Lighted oil lamps at intervals along the veranda each cherished its own microcosm of swarming insects, illuminating the palms in their pots below.

At the door the sullen eyes of the houseboy expressed anxiety rather than the usual resentment. 'Bwana is not home. He has important business.'

'I need somewhere to stay,' Rupert said.

'It is not possible here.'

'Then perhaps the memsahib…'

'Bwana said…'

A woman's voice, clear and melodious, called out, 'It's all right, Mwangi. Dr Murchison is welcome. You can leave us.' It came from the past, with the same sweet bite that he'd tried so hard to forget. As she emerged onto the veranda her slender figure seemed little changed.

Being independent of the process, Rupert had never concerned himself with the cruel lottery that was the posting of government officers. And when it happened he was indifferent to the squeals of delight or despair. It shouldn't have surprised him to find Catherine in this forsaken place, but it did because her bonding with Nairobi society had seemed unbreakable. Even now – whatever his feelings for her might be – it seemed, if nothing else, unfair. What despot sweating behind his desk would have taken pleasure in transplanting such a flower? But therein, he thought later, lay the probable explanation.

That she seemed pleased he was there contrasted sharply with his memory of their last, bitter, encounter. She came to stand close to him.

'Let me just say I'm sorry, Rupert. I did not set out to hurt you.'

'You succeeded with a vengeance.'

'A married woman – even in Nairobi – is like a caged beast, always under scrutiny. It could not have continued.'

'It didn't seem to bother you with others.'

'Times were changing. Please, may we put it behind us?'

Rupert smiled ruefully. 'I suppose I must, if I want shelter. By the way, where is Richard?'

'Out. Away. I'll tell you about it. But first, where on earth have you been? People from the train were here hours ago. They're all up at the guesthouse.'

Rupert was incredulous. 'You know about the train?'

'It was almost at the station. I had a look myself.'

'Then I have a mystery on my hands.'

'Well, I hope it's nothing to do with Richard's wild goose chase.'

He followed her inside, into that strange mixture of cultures that typifies the dwellings of colonial government servants: a print of a Constable on the wall next to a fading zebra skin, drawings of orchids – for she was a gifted artist – alongside west African masks. Rupert recognised them all. She set a lamp on the table in the dining room and they sat facing one another, sparring in the way – or so Rupert imagined – of all ex-lovers brought together by chance, reliving the dregs of their first attraction.

'Richard told me you are leaving us soon.'

'After I've collected my things from the Lake. I sail from Mombasa on Monday.'

'Only four days!'

'You're safe, then.'

Catherine's eyes widened with anger augmented by fear. The bitterness against the perceived injustice of the transfer erupted in a torrent. 'Safety is the last bloody thing I'm after in this hell-hole,' She was immediately ashamed. 'I'm sorry, Rupert. That wasn't the cool hostess you once knew, was it?'

'It's a strange feeling to think I've touched base – something solid at last. That never happened before. With you, I mean.' He leaned back in his chair, the better to scrutinise her face.

'It came close at times,' she whispered.

'Then you might have shown it.'

There were shadows beneath the hazel eyes that were not just tricks of the light. Rupert had seen before the hall-marks of loneliness in those forced to forego social advantage for the greater good. And Catherine was the most inflexible of subjects. He knew, too, that Richard could not fill the void. He could feel his own heartbeat and saw his fingers tremble as he reached for the glass she pushed towards him. He hoped she hadn't noticed. He began to recognise within himself a developing conflict in which sympathy and the settling of scores were joined by a third contender – a reawakening of the same passion he had felt all those years ago. Then – could it have been by chance? – her foot brushed his.

'In case you're still wondering,' she said, 'Richard's gone to sort out some panic with the Nandi. There's been a return of their favourite form of persecution, where things come out of the forest and leave them in a bit of a mess.'

'The chemosit?'

'You know? Ah, but you would, wouldn't you, as a zoologist. Everyone thought it had stopped a few years ago, but it seems it hasn't.'

'Actually, someone told me on the train.'

'Anyone interesting?' She said it dreamily, distantly, as if not expecting an answer.

'A Jackson somebody.'

'Oh... yes. I know him. He's the minister here.'

Rupert felt the warmth of her bare foot on his own. It was, he remembered, how it had started, at their house at the foot of the Ngong Hills just after he had arrived in Kenya ten years before. Living in a tent nearby, he must have seemed eccentric enough to warrant an invitation from Richard Hedley. The rapid path he had trodden then, even with hindsight, was no less inviting now. He could not prevent himself saying, 'Your boy – when does he leave?'

'As soon as he's cleared the kitchen.'

They waited in silence, fingers touching tentatively across the table, until the door slammed and the footsteps were absorbed into the night. Rupert wanted to tell her about Jackson, but the risk of diverting her attention held him back.

Together they checked the muslin net above the bed. As it fell into place he saw through it an image of the woman as she had been and could be again for one last time.

He rounded the foot of the bed, expecting to encounter a pair of soft expectant eyes, but there was a noise outside and her expression turned fearful. The room was suddenly suffused by the pale light of a lamp from somewhere in front of the house.

'Richard?' he suggested.

'Oh dear God, it must be. Don't move. I'll be back.'

There were animated voices from below. A minute later she reappeared.

'I think you'd better come,' she said. 'This could interest you. Don't worry, it's not Richard.'

There were three Africans in the room below. Rupert could tell from their agitation that something of great moment had happened. He assumed it had to do with the train, but it did not, at least directly. He recognised the houseboy among them.

'Mwangi,' Catherine said, 'you had better tell Bwana Murchison what the men say.'

'They say that they have caught it, Memsahib. In the railway shed.'

'Caught what, Mwangi?'

'The chemosit, Memsahib.'

Catherine seemed puzzled. 'What is it, Mwangi?'

'They do not know.'

'Surely they must know,' she said impatiently. 'Is it a leopard – or a hyaena?'

Mwangi addressed the men, translating.

'These men say it is not a leopard or a hyaena.'

'How big is it?'

'Bigger than three men, Memsahib.'

Catherine moved to the window and stared out. When she turned back to them the strain of the decision told upon her face. 'Tell the men Bwana Hedley will come when he gets back in the morning.'

'Then Bwana Murchison must come.'

'Bwana Murchison is very tired. Can the creature escape?'

'The shed is locked.'

'Then Bwana Murchison will come later.'

From the shadows Rupert watched the men file dejectedly from the room and out into the rain. He had listened without interest, experience telling him that in Africa truth gets embellished in the telling. But now they were gone he was curious.

'I ought to follow,' he said.

'Nonsense. They've caught a hyena or a baboon perhaps.'

'But Catherine, these men know what those animals look like.'

'They've been drinking.'

'I didn't notice.'

'Well, they have.'

'I think I ought to go.'

Catherine's anger suddenly surfaced. 'Then you can tell me about it at breakfast.'

'You won't wait for me?'

'You never would grasp opportunities, would you? Your one great failing. You fool!' She was at the window, sobbing into the curtains that were clutched between her hands. He guessed that these were tears dammed up since she came, released because he, Rupert, had turned the key.

They returned to the bedroom, Rupert's mind calmed by the drumming of rain on the roof, Catherine's by a skirmish fought and won.

'You've lost weight, Rupert. I can feel your heart beating. For a moment you took me away from this place. You can't imagine how that felt.'

'You didn't make things easy for yourself.'

'Lovers into enemies, is that what you mean?' She paused. 'Are you my enemy, Rupert?'

'Just now I'm a friend.'

'Not more? After what we've just done. What I let you do.' She rolled over to face him. 'You could stay. Just for a few days. Cancel the boat. There's always someone wanting a berth.'

'And how would I explain that?'

'Tell them in London you've got the fever.'

'No, I meant to Richard.'

'I don't know. Help him sort out these killings. Something like that.'

'That's for the police, surely.'

'Police? I can tell you it's not a matter for the police.'

'The Church, then?'

There was a sudden clattering noise from somewhere beneath the window. Rupert said, 'What the hell was that?'

'Just an animal. Richard probably left some rubbish out. It always attracts them. I'll take a look.'

'You won't see much. It's pitch black out there – no moon at all.'

She moved to the window and parted the curtains. 'One of the veranda lights is still on. There's nothing there now.' Slowly she drew the curtains together and returned to the bed.

'Catherine, you're shivering.'

'It's got colder.'

'I wouldn't have said so.'

'You're not always bloody right.' She grasped his arm tightly. 'I'm sorry.'

'It's okay. Anyway, it's quiet now.'

'Yes, quiet. It's either the rain beating down or…'

Images from the early evening crept into Rupert's thoughts. 'Like in the forest.'

'Oh?' She squeezed his arm more tightly. 'Sometimes I think I'm losing my senses. Last week... I went there to get some orchids to paint. Climbing up, into the dripping branches – and then... silence.'

'That frightened you?'

'At first. While I thought I was alone.'

'And then?'

The pain in Rupert's arm was becoming unbearable.

'Because nothing is what you expect. And if you expect nothing, what appears is...' An animal-like snarl from below the window caused her to release her grip on his arm. 'Oh, Christ!'

'I'll put on the light.'

'Don't touch it! Be silent.' There was a long pause, then she whispered, 'What can you hear?'

'Nothing. Nothing at all.'

'Listen harder.'

'Really nothing. Not even the cicadas.'

'That's right. Not even them.' She stroked his arm gently. 'Go to your own bed now, Rupert. There's nothing more for you here.'

'Catherine, you're still shivering.'

'Dread and intoxication, all at the same moment. Strange bedfellows, don't you think?'

'I don't know what...'

'One day you'll thank me.' The push into his back was as violent as her next utterance. 'Now go!'

Rupert picked up his clothes and left the room. For what seemed like hours he lay staring through the window at the black and troubled sky. He imagined he heard voices, but whether in reality or in a dream he did not know. He remembered waking to see a sliver of light appearing in the clouds, and hearing the buzz of a mosquito, reminding him that he had not lowered his net.

Richard swept up in his jeep while they were having breakfast on the veranda. He seemed pleased to see Rupert, who was at first relieved that his erstwhile affair with Catherine seemed to have remained undiscovered.

'So has Catherine been looking after you?'

'Very well.'

'As only she can.' He poured himself a coffee, as if giving Rupert time to dwell on what he had said. 'These attacks – it's a bloody puzzle. Till now there's been no pattern. I mean, all the victims were mutilated, sure, but there was no common motive. The first could have been theft, the next sexual, but last night's...'

'Last night's?'

'Next village. Just come from there, actually. Hut entered, youth disfigured, for no reason. A sighting of sorts, but in that downpour no-one was sure what they saw. Anyway, let's take a look at the railway shed. You coming, Catherine?'

'What do you think?' she replied facetiously.

The railway shed turned out to be a substantial brick building beside a single length of track. Richard explained that it had once been a store, which accounted for the bars at each of the windows. The doors could be closed by a stout pole between the handles. It was this simple device that had allowed the villagers to imprison whatever they had believed to be inside. But it had proved insufficient, as the small knot of disgruntled figures standing outside the now open doors testified.

Inside the shed one of the men Rupert had seen the

night before pointed to a skylight high above, its broken glass jagged and sparkling in the bright morning sunlight. There were drops of blood, still fresh, on the pile of boxes and abandoned furniture that seemed to have had aided the creature's ascent. Richard was relieved. 'That can only be a baboon,' he said. 'We'll have to look elsewhere for our assailant.'

On the pretext of retrieving his hat Rupert re-entered the shed and studied the route of escape. The more he looked the more convinced he became that the items in the pile had been placed deliberately to aid the creature's flight. No baboon could have managed that. Nor for that matter, could a chimpanzee, even if there had been any around. That left only one other possibility. He climbed up the first few feet. Then he saw it, a tiny fragment like a piece of sackcloth adhering to a wooden beam. But, coming closer, he saw it was a mass of dense hair matted with congealed blood. Carefully he prised it from the protruding nail. Jumping down, he wrapped it in his handkerchief and put it in his pocket.

And with the raw blow of the sun against his eyes he was gripped by a feeling of desperation. Ask them again, he implored Richard, what they saw. No, Bwana, it was not an animal they had seen before. Then was it a man? But this was a superfluous question, because Rupert the zoologist knew that no ordinary man could have accomplished such an ascent.

As they bumped back along the track to the house Rupert said nothing, realising the magnitude of the lost opportunity.

'Could it really be,' he asked Catherine when Richard had left the room, 'that there is a creature out there in the forest still unknown to science?' Then he grew angry. 'Why did you make me stay?'

'Your choice,' she said, 'not mine.'
'But why?'
'It gave me satisfaction. That's why.'
'I can't believe what I'm hearing.'
'Frankly, Rupert, I do not care.'

They were the words that had dismissed him all those years before.

Richard drove him to the station where the liberated train stood waiting. He looked around for Jackson, but he was not there.

'On the train… someone lent me a bible,' Rupert said. 'I have it here,'

'Hair the colour of the book?'

'Jackson, yes.'

'Our local boy made good. Give it here, I'll return it to him.' He paused. 'On second thoughts I'll give it to Catherine. She's something of an admirer of his. He's often at the house, you know.'

'She said she knew him.'

'Yes.'

As far as he could recall it was the first time Rupert felt pity for Catherine's long suffering husband.

Two days later, under a cloudless sky, the same little train steamed back from the lake. As it sped through the township Rupert recognised the railway shed and the platform, now deserted, and the piles of logs from the tree that had blocked the line. He looked for the gap in the forest edge where Jackson had taken him but saw only an impenetrable green wall. He checked in his bag for the fragment of skin in its bottle of fixative, thought once about Catherine and in a terrible mood of despondency searched for a pen with which to finish the report to his sponsors in London.

The squeal of car brakes on Cromwell Road jolted him back to the present. He rose from the bench and looked for one last time at the building that had been his temple, trying in vain to fight off whatever it was forcing him not to go back. In a dream he wandered towards the subway leading to the underground.

A party of Japanese tourists – probably ones he had passed on the stairs of the museum – looked down upon him from the pavement above. He could feel their eyes following him down the steps into the tunnel which once, with the naivety of youth, he'd likened to a sewer carrying human effluent. Yet, over the years, he'd come to relish its shrill echoes because the unintelligible snatches of human voice reminded him of the forlorn cries of the animals that were the subject of his trade.

It is curious how the memory plays tricks, drawing upon past experiences and playing them back in distorted but recognisable forms. As he walked through the tunnel those piercing utterances diminished until all that remained were barely audible threads of sound, then… nothing. He stopped still, fearful of the silence. He looked down, half expecting to see at his feet the decaying vegetation of the forest floor. And with that came the recollection that told him what he must do.

He continued to walk slowly to the point where the tunnel turned abruptly towards the station. Then, supposing himself out of sight, he broke into a run. When he paused again, breathless, the hubbub within the concourse of the station was as it had always been. 'You are getting old, ex-curator Rupert,' he said to himself between gasps, 'to believe such nonsense.'

Yet he had not escaped. He stood on the platform where the carriage doors would open, knowing that their closing would mark both the end and a new beginning. But until that moment came the platform edge was as finite as the bars of a cage. His fingers closed over the vial in his pocket.

The voice at his elbow was not unexpected, nor even unwelcome.

'Dr Murchison, I believe you have something that belongs to me.'

The hair was white now, but the face was little changed. The benevolence was still there, the quiet assurance as forceful. Against his will Rupert was withdrawing his closed fist, knowing what the loss would mean.

'Reverend Jackson.'

'Indeed. How could you forget? Dr Murchison, I once thought you a fortunate man, but you did not grasp the opportunity that was offered. As a result I was – how shall I put it? – condemned, for my cross – if you will forgive the euphemism – I have continued to bear. But that is my problem, not yours. Before we finally part I want to show you this. It should at least lay some doubts to rest.'

In one swift decisive movement he pulled up his sleeve almost to the elbow, and Rupert saw there on his forearm the pallor against the blackness of the skin that was the scar.

SHEP STONE

No-one knows what induced Graham Onslow to return to the Shepton Circle. Some of his colleagues in the History Department even claim to have heard him say that he never would. Whatever the reason, it must have had something to do with the anniversary – the tenth – of Rebecca's death. Otherwise it would have been too much of a coincidence.

That mid-summer day had started fine, so perhaps it was on an impulse that Graham had decided to join the Department's outing to the iron-age settlement at Shepton Magna. His secretary recalled him smiling as he gave her last minute instructions before boarding the bus. On the other hand Jim Meredith, sitting next to him, thought he was subdued; but then they were rivals in the field of early English mythology and never got on. Still, it is difficult to explain why, when the bus departed from the site at the end of the day, no one realised – or chose to notice – that he was not on board.

The earthworks at Shepton are for the most part the stuff of dry papers in the county archaeological archives. They lie in a green and fertile valley between high heather-clad hills where wheeling buzzards and kestrels seem permanently to pepper the sky. The public passing through on its way to Manchester would remain oblivious were it not for the splendid stone circle – and the equally enticing picnic spot some two hundred yards away at the foot of the eastern escarpment.

Had any of the party thought to look back as the bus left the car park they might just have seen, half way up the cliff and illuminated by the sunlight that was fast becoming denied to the valley floor, Graham's ant-like figure on its way to the top.

Graham, for his part, had been well aware of the bus's departure. In fact, he had stayed with the group until the very last minute before sidling away just as the remaining stragglers were boarding. At first he had climbed quickly, remembering the route he had taken before. But ten years – and early corpulence – had slowed him down. When he paused to watch the bus go he was already breathless and perspiring.

As he turned back to face the rock wall he remembered that it was at this precise spot that Rebecca had overtaken him. He had watched her lithe body making light of the difficulties of the climb, stretching high for each new handhold and exploring the rock intimately with her thin brown legs. In passing him she had exposed details of her body that were still unfamiliar – in spite of their previous intimacies.

There had, of course, been constraints. As a university teacher he had responsibilities towards his research students and for the most part he observed them. But with Rebecca things had been different. It was a relationship that could not have continued unresolved.

Not that he had brought her here deliberately. Quite the reverse. One day she had knocked on his study door and he had opened it to find her flushed and eager. 'I have a theory,' she had told him, 'about the Shepton Circle.' 'And what is that?' he had replied, amused but sceptical. But she had refused to answer. 'I'll have to show you,' was all she would say. And that was the reason they had ascended the cliff on which Graham now found himself.

He remembered his surprise when, reaching the summit, he had found her standing erect and expectant, nostrils slightly flared, her proud grey eyes engaging his in anticipation of a final judgement on her intellectual journey. Then he saw that she was standing before a pink-white slab of rock, square, and creased gently and vertically along its centre like an open book. The sun was low over the hills on the other side of the valley, so that the valley itself appeared to be in darkness; but here, high up, the light was still bright, forcing her shadow hard into the stone. Around them white daisies studded the tufted grass. In the soft air Graham thought he could detect the fragrance of wild strawberries. 'Feel the stone,' she whispered. To his surprise he found it warm against the back of his hand.

She took that hand and led him beyond the rock, turning him around so that they were looking together down the length of the depression in its surface, and beyond into the valley below. 'Look!' was all she said, and it was enough. Graham could see that the line of vision led precisely to the centre of the circle. And at the centre was another slab of rock, deliberately placed to be in alignment with this, their stone.

So powerful were the forces reaching across the ages that, without thinking, he led her back to the foot of the stone. As if according to some arcane rite in which they were passive players, she lay back upon it, her body fitting snugly within its folds. For Graham there were no moral obstacles to overcome: it was the practical testing of his student's hypothesis, and when their passion was over he thanked her solemnly for the honour of sharing her contribution to the advancement of archaeological knowledge.

They idled away the time lying in the long grass, making daisy chains, which he threaded into her long black hair. Then Graham noticed the shadow creeping up the base of the stone.

'There's a village up here somewhere,' he said. 'We'd better make for that. Get a drink before the light goes completely, then think about a taxi back.' 'Just a few minutes longer,' she said, and Graham wandered away to hunt for the wild strawberries that he would collect and give to her.

When he returned to the stone he was alone. He searched in the long grass for yards around. For a brief moment it had to be a student prank, but his relief was short-lived. He tried to climb back down the cliff but it was too dark and he almost fell. Then he ran, hard, to the nearby hamlet, to the inn called the *Shepton Stones* where they called the police for him. But it was only in the light of dawn that they found her body, broken by the fall, at the bottom of the cliff.

All his had happened exactly ten years before, to the day, to the hour.

Graham had paid his respects to her memory before scaling the cliff and was in control. But on reaching the top he was drawn to the slab of rock, pink and warm in the dying sun, just as it had been before. He knelt down, then lay prone upon it, squeezing into its fold as if the crevices and fissures might exude their memory of Rebecca's form. And perhaps they did, for there surfaced in his mind the worm of doubt that had lingered all these years. So again he examined the edge of the cliff at the point where she must have slipped. There was no clue, no hint, no prospect of resolution. But in the act of seeking there was a finality that lightened his spirits as he set out for the nearby hamlet. He could return home with a troublesome ghost laid to rest.

A narrow ribbon of trodden brown earth almost lost to encroaching stands of nettle and bracken led down towards the small cluster of buildings a few hundred yards away. The distance seemed longer than he remembered from his crazed sprint of ten years before. Away, now, from the escarpment and the highway it concealed, the moor was silent and still. Midges danced in the warm evening air. Once a partridge rose up on clattering wings. As Graham approached the hamlet he sniffed the scents of honeysuckle and jasmine, then saw the climbers themselves clothing the walls of the inn.

He had no reason to reflect on what sustained this remote community on the moor, nor why it should need an inn at all. But he had cause to do so later.

Outwardly the *Shepton Stones* had not changed, but it was odd that the beer garden was almost deserted on such a fine summer evening. A figure dressed in black motor cycle leathers lounged within the frame of the doorway. He scrutinised Graham carefully as he approached.

'Where you from?' he asked.

'Sheffield,' Graham replied blandly.

This seemed to suffice and the man moved grudgingly aside.

To Graham's surprise the interior was crowded, but there was little of the noise he had anticipated. A score or so of mainly well dressed, middle-aged men were clustered around the bar. Their talk was animated, but the voices seemed held unnaturally low. In contrast, the floor of the room was bright with tables that appeared to have been set for an occasion. There were flowers in profusion, and lit candles in spite of the residual daylight. At each table sat a man and a woman whom Graham judged to be in their late twenties or not much older. Although the women were in summer dresses and the men were casually dressed, all had taken particular care with their appearance. They had obviously dined well.

Graham felt himself an intruder. There was a need to be careful, to take stock. The bar was inaccessible without making his presence obvious, so he made his way to the only vacant place he could see, on a high-backed settle near the chimney piece. Its only occupant, a small spare man in his fifties, shuffled aside to make room for him, then extended a hand.

'George, by the way. They give you trouble at the road block?'

'Graham. No... no trouble at all.'

'Must have recognised you then, Graham. Come to think of it you do look familiar. About half an hour ago a bus full of strangers came up. Took a while to persuade them they weren't welcome.'

'That couldn't have been easy.'

'Did it gently, mind. Won't suspect anything. By the way what's your chapter?'

Graham was now out of his depth. He checked that the line to the door was at least clear.

'Sheffield.'

'Thought it had gone quiet up there. But with so many members now it's impossible to keep track.'

'It's not exactly the most active,' Graham said apologetically.

The activity at the bar suddenly increased. From behind it a figure rose up above the level of the heads. The hair was black and the eyes dark and deep-set, the demeanour magisterial. Every head in the room turned towards him. Those close to him were smiling, but the couples at the tables looked apprehensive. It was clear to Graham that this was no party game. The man spoke with an authority in keeping with his bearing. He was no barman.

'This year the competition has been – how shall I put it – as fierce as any we have seen in recent times. You will appreciate that coming to a decision has not been easy, but we trust you will agree that your committee has made the correct choice. As has often been the case, the need to balance presentation against individual circumstances has caused particular difficulties. For all their good looks some here have harrowing tales to tell. It's just a pity there can be only one winner. But let's not prolong the suspense: this year it is… the couple at table number six.'

At the burst of applause the couple rose to their feet and embraced one another across their soiled plates. A knife on the man's side fell to the floor, but no-one seemed to notice. Many of the men from the bar crowded round. Graham noted with amusement that their only purpose seemed to be to steal a kiss from the lucky lady. She relished the attention, not minding that her carefully coiffured hair was now awry. Her companion looked on with pride and – curiously, Graham thought – with deep relief.

'In a way that's a pity,' Graham's companion exclaimed.

'Why's that?'

'She's pretty – such a bloody waste.' He leant across to whisper in Graham's ear. 'It'll be a good one though. I can promise you that.'

'You had a hand in the decision?'

'Deciding vote.'

Graham smelt the alcohol on the man's breath and wondered if he was giving too much away.

'Think of it,' George continued. 'Every year, infertile couples competing to have their way with each other on that stone. Every year for thousands of years. And all kept secret.'

'Do you think it works?'

'Whether it works or not is irrelevant. It's the deeper meaning that counts.'

'I suppose that's right.'

'And then, every tenth year… to satisfy the greater powers…' His voice became hushed. 'Well, no need to tell *you* what happens.'

The couple were at the centre of a cluster of bodies that was quickly becoming an entourage. The man who had spoken from the bar now had a chain around his neck and a multi-coloured staff in his hand. The group moved towards the door, which Graham noticed had to be unlocked to let them out. They left to the sound of gently tinkling bells and the braying of an unseen and not particularly melodious horn.

'You need to keep your eyes peeled to appreciate the subtleties,' George said, getting up and walking towards the tables. He stopped at the one vacated by the successful couple, picked up the card bearing their names and read it. As if by accident a napkin fell to the floor. He bent down, fumbling to retrieve it, and replaced it carefully on the table. Graham thought he put something into his pocket, but could not see what it was. Then George followed the others out into the night.

Through the window Graham watched the party melt into the darkness of the moor. With the last faint call of the horn he turned to survey the room. The tables were being cleared and there were fewer people at the bar. Graham wandered to the table where the winning couple had sat. Brian and Fenella Browning, the card said. He tried to imagine what had led to the couple's participation. A waiter came to collect the plates. With his arm loaded the man paused for a moment, as if looking for something, then shrugged and walked away.

For the first time Graham felt relaxed. He joined the others at the bar and ordered a beer. He was about to ask for the phone to order a taxi home but, remembering George's story about the bus, decided to wait. It seemed odd that all the couples had gone, and more so that there was now not a single woman in the place. He began to survey the prints and paintings on the walls, at first casually, then more intently. There were several of the stone circle. Some had the stones steeped in sunlight, while in another they were in darkness with just an orange glow in the position of the central stone. Disappointingly, there was none of Rebecca's stone. Then he noticed something quite bizarre. Along the far wall – and previously invisible from where he was sitting – was a series of women's heads. Or, rather, blank ovals of wood, the size of faces, topped with carefully arranged hair in a variety of styles and colours. He rose and walked over to them.

The waiter appeared at his shoulder. 'Interesting, aren't they,' he said, pointing to one of the more extravagant examples.

Graham stood on tip-toe to see the small brass label on its base. '1876,' he read.

'Yes, that's one of the oldest we have,' the waiter said. 'It's a complete series, you know. The others are in the cellar. I could get the key if you're interested.'

Before Graham could answer the door to the moor flew open. A dishevelled figure whom Graham recognised as the successful Brian held itself momentarily in the frame before lurching towards the bar. He was breathing heavily and there was blood on his hands. Graham forgot about the hair-style collection.

'My friend,' the waiter said to Brian, 'you seem to have a problem.'

'There's someone dying on the path from the stone... bleeding badly. Please... please call an ambulance.'

'Where's your companion?' the waiter said, unperturbed.

'She's with him. She's a nurse, but she can't cope alone. Please get help, quickly.'

'Was your union... consummated?' the waiter asked.

'Yes... yes it was, but that's irrelevant, for God's sake!'

'Irrelevant? I hardly think so,' the waiter said quietly, 'but we'll do as you suggest.' He turned to one of the barmen. 'Frank, can you call the... er, 999?

'They'll be a while coming,' Frank replied. 'So we'd better go and look ourselves. I suggest you come with me, Eric, and the rest of you remain here.'

When the two men had gone Graham approached the stricken Brian, now abandoned on a bar stool. 'Look,' he said, 'you need to wash the blood off. I'll come with you to the gents.'

On the way to the toilets they passed more of the hair-pieces. The last was a twirled construction in black hair that resembled the top of an ice-cream cone.

'Bloody creepy, if you ask me,' Brian said.

'No time to look now,' Graham said, whilst glancing quickly himself. He ushered Brian through the toilet door.

They looked at each other in the mirror above the sink.

'However did you get involved in this?' Graham asked.

'An advert in *Aphrodite* magazine,' Brian replied. 'An unusual but effective treatment for infertile couples, it said – and a pleasant weekend in the country. Looked marvellous. We all met up at a hotel in Derby. Then, to our surprise, they bussed us here.'

'Had you heard of... this place... before?'

'Well, yes, it's quite well known in our... circle.'

'What happened to the others?'

'They were bussed back. It was over for them. Didn't you see them go?'

As the two men emerged into the bar a car crunched onto the gravel outside. A flashing light through the window sent streaks of blue chasing shadows around the walls of the room. There were raised voices outside which Graham did not recognise. A policeman in uniform entered the room, but the other voices were heard receding into the distance.

'Everyone remain inside please,' the policeman said.

Brian went up to him. 'Where's my wife, where's Fenella. I need to go with them.'

'Please wait here, Sir. It's all in hand. It's dark on the moor and you could easily get lost. My colleagues will be back just as soon as they've assessed the situation.'

A few minutes later Frank, Eric and another policeman returned from the moor. The second policeman approached Brian.

'We found your wife, Sir, and are arresting you for her murder. We'd be grateful if you'd come with us. No trouble, now, Sir.'

Brian suddenly made a run for the door, but was stopped by Frank with a vicious punch to the stomach. With a policeman on each arm, he was dragged from the room, protesting violently.

Graham felt sick and bewildered. He needed to think, to be alone, to puzzle out what had happened. Nothing seemed to make sense. He made for the toilets, passing the last of the hair-pieces, which again caught his attention. Once inside he locked himself in the furthest cubicle. Lowering the seat, he sat heavily upon it.

He was not alone in seeking seclusion. A few moments later he heard the door open. Through the gap between the cubicle door and its frame he could see Frank, the barman, talking to his former companion on the settle.

'You were great, George. Hope you didn't have to lie still too long. Better tidy yourself up, though, and get the grass out of your hair – and get rid of that shirt. I take it that's sheep blood and not yours. That was a brilliant ploy to get rid of the husband.'

'I always did have a penchant for theatrical solutions,' George replied. 'Much more satisfying than the last one, eh Frank? Never did get much credit for pushing that biddy over the edge. Some of the membership still think she just slipped. Only one small problem this time, though. Your steak knives are getting a bit blunt – or the cow had a neck like leather.'

'Which reminds me,' Frank said, taking a plastic bag from his pocket and opening it. 'Here's a fresh handkerchief – with the woman's blood on it this time. Better fish his one out of the bin – we wouldn't want to confuse the real police when they come looking tomorrow, now would we?'

The walls of Graham's cubicle seemed to shrink before his eyes, expanding the gap between the panels and the floor and the band of light where the door just failed to close. He imagined himself growing moment by moment like a metamorphosed pupa within its cracking case, ready to burst into a hostile and hungry world. For the first time he noticed the drops of water falling from the cistern above his head and the rivulet beside his feet that was advancing towards the shrinking door. On top of that he was fighting an urge to sneeze.

But worse was to come. Into Graham's mind came the image of the brass plate below the last of the female busts, and the year: 1996 – ten years before. His stomach churned. He spun around to be sick into the pan. But not so quickly that he did not hear the final snatch of conversation outside the cubicle.

'Just one thing, though,' he heard George say.

'What's that?' Frank replied.

'That bloke from the Sheffield chapter. Must have left with the others. Can we trust him?'

'Sheffield chapter? There isn't a Sheffield chapter.'

JOHNNY'S RIDE TO TOWN

I like riding on buses 'cause then I can think properly. So I was angry when Chloe poked me in the side and I caught her grinning with her hand in her armpit. She was in one of her taunting moods, sitting behind, like when I hate her most. Ma just watched, as usual.

'He doesn't remember where we have to get off,' Chloe said. 'He really doesn't remember!' She could be a real pain when she wanted.

Actually I did remember, but it was no use telling them. I remembered the black gates and the big red letter for hospital. And the word, though I was no great reader. 'Hos-pi-tal,' I said.

'Cor…ect.' Chloe said. I saw her sniggering.

After we'd piled off – just to show I remembered – I ran up the path, darting in and out of the crowd. But Ma thought I was trying to lose them and came storming after. When she caught me she was breathing hard and her face was red. Her fat body wobbled like a jelly on two legs, 'specially when each foot came down. I could see her raise her arm to cuff me, but a look came into her eyes and she peeked around, like she does in the supermarket sometimes when I know she's nicked something. Maybe she thought she'd look stupid, hitting a boy as big as her, 'cause I'm fifteen now, but that never stops her at home. She doesn't do it to Chloe, though she's just as bad, even when Chloe's on my side. But Chloe's a bit younger and perhaps that's why.

We walked up to the building with Ma in the middle, holding our hands. I wondered if she was squeezing Chloe's like she was squeezing mine. But she couldn't be, because she would have squealed. As for me, I'd learnt not to.

There were lots of people on the path. Each side there were miles and miles of grass and trees, but no-one there, well not many. I wanted badly to go there and run about, like you couldn't do at school 'cause the playground is all concrete, or at home 'cause the back yard – the garden Ma calls it – is all bricks and broken bottles. You'd only fall and cut your knees, Ma said, and Chloe said why don't you clear them up and Ma gave her one of her looks and that shut her up.

We reached the hospital steps and I remembered the crowded entrance where we'd come before and I'd run off 'cause the people pressed in on me and I got scared. It took them ages to find me and in the end Chloe did, in the blanket room. It was warm and safe in there, and smelt a bit like Chloe when she was a baby and had just been washed. I was glad it was Chloe what found me. Play scared, she said, then they won't be so angry. But the nurse – the one with the yellow hair – wasn't angry at all, nor was the doctor. I liked them for that and was quite good when he examined me, though I got a bit fidgety towards the end.

Anyway, we were walking up the steps. At the top there were two ladies in front of the big doors who weren't there last time. They were rattling cans and you could see they wanted to shake them in front of people's noses, but couldn't because their feet seemed stuck to the ground.

Funny that. I couldn't read what was on the tins, but Chloe could.

'Tsunami appeal,' she said

I knew what that was, 'cause I'd seen the waves coming in on television. Chloe cried when she first saw it, but I liked the way the cars floated along like boats and got bashed. Then she said about the people and I cried too. Actually I cried until I went to bed then dreamt about how it was for the dogs and cats though I hadn't actually seen any. I suppose the water got them first 'cause they're not so high.

'We should put some money in the tin,' Chloe said. Ma said we didn't have enough money to put any in and pulled on our hands. Then Chloe whispered to me she'd given me a pound for an ice-cream and I could put that in. And I said no way would I give up my ice-cream and for once Ma was on my side and tugged Chloe's hand harder than mine. Then Chloe was angry.

'You never help anybody,' Chloe said. 'You just think about yourself, all the time. Doesn't he, Mum?'

'He can be a right selfish little bugger sometimes.'

And I thought about that.

When Ma got us to where the chairs were I started to think Chloe might be right, 'cause Miss Mabbs my teacher sometimes says the same thing. I never could see why I should help anybody, but maybe the Tsunami thing changed that. I felt bad about not putting my pound in the tin.

When Ma'd finished doing something at the desk we seemed to walk miles along the corridor. At the end there were magazines and toys scattered around and Chloe said they were the same ones as before. Ma said, 'You do remember why we're here, don't you Johnny?' and I said I did, and that pleased her. So she took superman out of her bag and gave him me. Then she watched me playing with him and got angry 'cause I made superman noises a bit loud and when people told me off she shouted at them.

It was Chloe who spotted the nurse coming towards us like before and I liked her yellow hair even more. I didn't remember her name, but Chloe could. 'Hello Miss Willetts,' she said.

'Mrs Tranter, Johnny... and Chloe. You see, I remember too,' she said.

This remembering thing was making me uncomfortable.

'Sorry to have kept you waiting,' she said. 'Dr Scundrel will see you now.' It was the first time I'd heard doctors called by bad names.

'Put superman in my bag, Johnny,' Ma said. 'You won't be needing him.'

'I want to keep him out,' I said, and Carol said I could give him to her, but Ma wouldn't let up.

'Johnny, you're not going to see the man clutching that toy, so put it in here.'

'It's alright, Mrs Tranter,' the nurse said. The doctor won't mind in the least. There's a whole shelf of toys in there.'

But Ma wouldn't stop. 'Johnny, I won't tell you again,' she said.

So I did what she said. I don't even like superman. I only brought him to annoy her. I like soft toys, like Chloe's bunny, but Ma caught me nicking him before we left. Chloe wouldn't have minded, though. She was kind to me today. 'This is your big day,' she said. 'They'll help you.' 'Why will they?' I said, looking into her eyes. But she wouldn't look at me straight, just turned away. When I ran round to look at her face she was crying.

The doctor didn't seem quite as big as before. That nice nurse followed us in and I liked that because she smiled at me. Then she went out and closed the door and the room felt all cold.

'Take a seat, Mrs Tranter. Johnny, you sit here by me,' the doctor said. So I did, and he smelt a bit like the flowers in the shop we'd just passed. Better than Ma's smell though, when she has her hot flushes. She's always talking about a change, so maybe she should. 'Now, Mrs Tranter,' he said. 'How have we got on? Did the tablets help Johnny?'

Ma said it was difficult to know as sometimes it seemed they did and other times I was as bloody-minded as ever. He stopped her there, which was a pity for her 'cause she was on the right track.

'How about you, Johnny? Have they helped, do you think?'

'Tell the man what you think, Johnny,' Ma said.

'Dunno really,' I said.

Dunno really. Useful that. Use it a lot in class. That Miss Mabbs, likes asking questions – you know, for info, like. Dates, places and that. When she first started on me you could see she was embarrassed 'cause her cheeks went pink, though I was sorry when she gave up too soon. But we weren't at school, and I'd promised Chloe to give it a go. So I told him they worked sometimes, and he looked at me real hard. I think he knew how horrible they were and that half the time I kept them under my tongue and spat 'em out when Ma wasn't looking.

I don't remember too much else, 'cause I was thinking again, except that the doctor said the new tablets would taste a bit better. I wanted to try one but the doctor said he didn't have any on him.

Then he said, 'Right, Johnny, there's just one more thing you can do for me, then we're through. Look out of the window and tell me what you can see.'

'Look out of the window, Johnny,' Ma said.

'Two cows and a lot of people,' I said.

'I beg your pardon?' he said. 'I can see the two cows – just. And lots of grass and trees. But people?'

'That's how he is, doctor,' Ma said.

'Where are the people, Johnny?' he said.

'A bus just went by,' I said, clever like.

'Ah, I see. And we missed it. But that was far away – how do you know there were lots of people on it?'

'Sick people like coming to hospitals,' I said.

That seemed to set him thinking, and he began to get up, and he looked at Ma.

'Well, fortunately they do. Mrs Tranter – a quiet word with you outside. Johnny, we'll be back in just a moment. Here's something to keep you busy.'

He pushed a comic into my hands. But I was still looking outside, and through a door window to the outside. Then I saw there was a key in the lock. Sod the comic, I thought, let's see if it turns.

It was a cinch. As I opened it the sound of the birds came at me and the wind blew my hair. I remembered to close the door. Somehow getting out had made me think better.

Out on the grass everything seemed... well... clearer. People coming out and going in, not on top of me anymore, and that was nice 'cause I could choose what to do. Then I saw that nurse, with a coat on, but I knew it was her from the legs and the wiggling bum. So I got in behind her on the path with all the people going to the gate, keeping just behind, but she never turned, even with me thinking about her hard. I liked the yellow hair touching her shoulders and how she moved, not fat or anything, you know, straight and nice.

When we got to the bus stop that feeling came again, with people pressing in, like when I go into class. I saw her join the queue, and I stayed near but still she didn't turn, maybe 'cause there were people between.

Buses come at you like elephants, except that they don't have ears that flap and the people stay put. This one was a number five, the one we'd come on from the town, so I knew where we were going and that made me feel better. When it stopped I just climbed in with the rest.

The driver was not very nice. He said, 'You waiting for Christmas, son? Do you want a ticket or not?'

I thought, hell, no money! Then I remembered the pound in my pocket Chloe'd given me for an ice-cream.

'There!' I said, banging it down.

'Good,' he said. 'Ten pence change. Careful how you spend it.'

I said I would be.

She was sitting by the window. Didn't see me, didn't look up when I passed. She looked sad, like Chloe says I look when no-one's around to annoy me, and I'm thinking about things. I thought first I'd sit next to her, but that could have ended it, 'cause I'm no great talker, so I went two seats behind, and after I'd sat down we got to the next stop and more people got on.

I knew when he got on where he'd sit, even though other seats were free. His hair was black, not brown like mine, and he had to bend his head. 'Is this seat taken?' he said.

I thought, silly bugger! Anyone could see that!

'Of course,' she said. 'I'll move my bag.'

Soon he was telling her he could see from her clothes she was a nurse. Then he asked her which hospital and she said Weatherden Hospital and he said he knew it. So she asked him why and he said his wife was treated there and then died of cancer.

'I'm so sorry.' she said, really kind like.

But he told her there was no need to be because that was two years ago and they'd done all they could. He said the staff there were just wonderful and that pleased her.

'They're a good bunch,' she said.

'But still overworked, I guess,' he said. I liked the way he said the right things all the time.

I could have sworn he shifted nearer to her, moved his head closer to hers. Then someone rang the bell and people got off, but not them, and I was glad 'cause I was getting worried about where I was going. Then they started talking again.

'After your wife died... it must have been difficult for you,' she said.

He told her he'd become a bit of a recluse – which I guess is someone very unhappy – and drowned himself in his work. Though it couldn't have killed him as he said he'd come out of it now. Then he told her he was a fashion photographer and that she was far too young to have tasted life's problems. Funny how I can remember them talking like it was just now.

'Well, actually, no.' she said. 'You see, I lost my sister, about the same time as your wife, it must have been.'

'Can I ask what happened?' he said.

'Knocked off her bicycle – and she hardly ever rode it. I can still see the ambulance coming up the drive. Somehow I knew even before they brought her in. We did everything together – parties, discos, holidays in Spain. We were twins, you see.'

'It does explain something,' he said.

'What?' she said.

'Something about you – when you first spoke. Something in your voice. Compassion, understanding, I don't know. You have a beautiful voice.'

She seemed to think that was a funny thing to say. 'Have I?' she said.

'Yes, strange we should have so much in common.'

'I suppose it is.'

I'd watched their heads getting closer and closer. All along I'd felt sorry – about the deaths, I mean. But there was something else that made me listen, made me think about couples in the park, going about holding hands, making me feel… well… empty inside. I could never understand that, like I could understand what they do indoors, like in Chloe's magazines that she hides from Ma.

Then, hey, we were coming into town. There was the Odeon, and it was Lord of the Rings and Chloe had promised to take me. Then, shite, they were all getting out, and these two, but it wasn't my stop yet.

I watched them get up, keeping together like they would never separate, and he said to her, 'By the way. I'm David,' and held out his hand. Then people coming down the stairs pushed between them and I don't think he heard her say her name was Amanda, though I just could.

There were so many people on the pavement, some fighting to get on, others just milling about. From my window, high up, I could see they'd lost each other. I saw their heads looking round, worried like, as if they didn't know what to do. Then David tried to push back into the crowd. He almost reached her but didn't go far enough. Once they almost touched, but there was this big bloke between. Then they began to walk away.

Something Chloe said comes into my head. She said, 'Johnny, you're only ever thinking of yourself, you never do anything for anybody.' It was like Chloe was sitting next to me talking into my ear, telling me to do something. And I suddenly saw it wasn't too late. The last bloke in the queue was arguing with the driver, so I still had time. I had to push though.

'What the hell do you think you're doing?' the man said. 'That was this lady's toe!'

I told him I had to get off to help someone, and he said I couldn't push people around like that and then I jumped off before he could grab me.

I dunno where she went, but I could still see him, being so tall and that, way down near the cinema. It was him I had to follow.

I thought I'd lost him. Always a loser, Chloe says, before she feels sorry and cuddles me. So I ran up and down a bit, but no good. I thought I'd go into Macdonald's, but even I knew 10p wasn't enough. Then there he was at the crossing, making to run for it before the light went red. Silly bugger, I thought, to do so dangerous. Perhaps he was still thinking about her, to be so stupid. So I ran up behind him.

'Mr David, Mr David,' I shouted.

He was halfway across when he heard. Maybe he was expecting to hear, 'cause I was close then. Anyway he stopped and turned to look.

That was when the car hit him. A big black one with windows you couldn't see through. People came running and then I couldn't see him. When I pushed through there he was, with blood running from his head into the gutter. I felt bad that I wouldn't be able to help him much now. Getting them together, I mean. By now a lot of people were crowding round and jabbering. The driver said, 'He came right across me, I had no chance.'

'Has anyone called an ambulance?' someone said. And another man said he could hear it coming. And people quietened down a bit.

I could see he was breathing, but his face was white. There was grey hair over his ears. Perhaps he wasn't so young after all, and too old for her. But maybe that didn't matter too much. A bit later the ambulance came, then the police. They were quick taking him away.

'You with him, son?' someone said.

'No,' I said. But someone next to him said, 'I heard you call out to him. David, you said – I heard you call it.'

'Whatever,' the first man said. 'If you want we can follow them to the hospital – my van's just around the corner.'

'What about the police?' the other man said. I could see he wasn't happy.

'Best avoided, mate, in my experience,' the first man said.

It was a little blue van, with a ladder on top and full of paint cans. It smelt horrible inside, a bit like the man's leather jacket. I could still see the blue light flashing in the distance. The man asked me my name, and I told him Johnny. I could see a reflection of the light in the Macdonald's window. A man inside seemed to be biting at it, which made me laugh. Then I saw the driver looking at me a bit queer like. There was a queue at the cinema, so maybe it wasn't a good time to go.

'I want to see that film,' I said.

'Haven't you got other things on your mind, sonny?' he said.

I didn't answer. I don't think he was interested in films. There was something going in my head that made sense. What had happened to David and where we were going somehow seemed right.

I don't think the driver liked me very much, from the way he looked at me when he wasn't driving fast and just missing people.

So I said, 'This is fun.'

He seemed to think so too, although you wouldn't have known it from his face. He said, 'You just go on thinking that, kiddo. Make the most of it – enjoy it while you can.'

Then we turned a corner and I spotted the big red letter and the black gates of the hospital. There was a queue at the bus stop and for a second I looked for her there. But of course she wasn't because she'd have to have flown back to beat us and wouldn't have been going anywhere anyway.

'Am-an-da,' I said.

'What did you say?' the driver said.

'David's friend,' I told him. 'She's a nurse in this hospital.'

I could see the ambulance at the entrance. I jumped out when the van stopped behind it and then they were all too busy getting David off to notice me. I'd done enough and wanted to go home now. So I crept round the building to the door I'd come out of. It was locked, but the next one wasn't and then I found myself in the corridor where Ma'd had bad thoughts about superman. I wondered if she still had him. I wanted to hold him again, so I sat down and waited and then they found me.

Ma wasn't too pleased. 'You little devil,' she said. 'Where the hell have you been?'

'Helping someone, like Chloe told me to,' I said.

She said they'd all been worried sick and emptied the blanket room.

We went into another corridor, past where the ambulances came, but I couldn't let on I knew that. Another one was coming in. I stayed back a bit to see where the body went so I'd know where they'd taken David. Where I knew Amanda would find him.

Outside the sun came out and that seemed right. I knew I would see her there, coming up the path from the gate. And there she was, holding an armful of clothes that Chloe said were from the cleaners, which is why she went to town in the first place, I suppose. She saw us and stopped. I liked her smile.

'Johnny Tranter, isn't it?' she said.

'I did what you would have wanted,' I said.

'Did you? Well that's good. Well done you.'

I liked it that she hadn't even noticed Chloe.

Then Ma spoilt it and said, 'Johnny, what nonsense are you talking? Take no notice, nurse.'

She walked away. Then something funny happened. Like someone took hold of my head and was trying to turn it round, and I had to move my feet to stop falling over. She'd got to the top of the steps, Amanda, and was standing there, not moving. Then she put the clothes on the wall and looked back at us. Didn't wave or anything, just looked. There was a man in black clothes behind the glass door, waiting for her. I saw her pick up the clothes and go inside and they started talking. Then Ma grabbed my hand and yanked me away as if I'd done something wrong.

Ma didn't understand. I don't think she'll ever understand. But this time I didn't get cross or try to annoy her. So I looked up at her, sweetly, like Chloe does when she thinks she's being clever.

'You know something, Ma,' I said. 'I think I'm good at helping people.'

Then Chloe's grinning face popped out from behind a tree, and suddenly I felt hungry and thought about watching telly and how it was getting a bit cold.

And at the gate another bus was coming in.

THE TWO NUNS

The regional paper – the *Eastern Aegean Weekly* – made much of the story and, by appearing to endorse the popular interpretation, had given it credence. Sister Anna had disappeared on the Thursday, the name day of Saint Annabel but, more tellingly, Ascension Day in the Christian calendar. The combined power of these associations had not only filled the island's churches on the following Sunday, but had led to an invasion of Mount Vathos by the curious and the blindly faithful during the days that followed. The ancient monastery of Moni Agiou Ioanni – two thirds of the way to the summit and previously visited by only the most intrepid of travellers – was destined to become both a site of pilgrimage and a perennial tourist attraction.

I am not a native of this, one of the most easterly of the Greek islands. In fact I am an American, a graduate in aviation science at Washington State University. I came here when the Department of Conservation needed someone to pilot its newly acquired helicopter for forestry surveillance. But the little machine quickly found other uses and before long various remote communities on the island began to construct landing pads for use in emergencies. The monastery on Mount Vathos, at the limit of the forest and, at 965 metres, the highest habitation on the island, was arguably the most deserving of them all, until then being approachable only by a narrow path for the most part cut into the rock face. As an ambitious walker and climber during my time off from flying it was by this route, and not by air, that I made my first acquaintance with the monastery. That happened several months before Sister Anna disappeared.

For a long while I have speculated on why a site at such high altitude had been chosen, and by whom. Legend has it that a hermit lived here, but the splendour of the surroundings and the panoramic view of the Turkish coast, only a few kilometres away, somehow seem at odds with an ascetic life style. But as a means of survival the site was well chosen, occupying as it does a wide and fertile terrace indenting the mountain, unique on the island at that altitude. After negotiating the last few precipitous steps, travellers are surprised to find themselves in a green and luxuriant garden with roses and chrysanthemums, raspberries and currants, and vegetables of many kinds thriving in the shelter of fig, peach and pear trees. Having taken this in, their eyes follow the wide gravel pathway meandering through the garden to the buildings. Originally whitewashed but now grey with grime, they are of indeterminate shape and rather featureless, yet somehow still splendid in their setting. It would be difficult for a traveller coming upon them unexpectedly to guess their purpose, were it not for the high and brilliantly coloured glass windows of the chapel projecting out towards the sea on the eastern side.

My intention that day had been to skirt the buildings to gain access to the track leading up to the summit of the mountain and contemplate my next step from a point of vantage. I did not get that far. To my surprise a figure in the habit of a nun rose up from behind a clump of raspberry canes.

'Good morning, brother,' she called. 'I am Sister Maria. It is customary for us to offer travellers hospitality. You are welcome to take bread with us. If you are interested you can also see our fine chapel.' My Greek was just sufficient to make out what she said.

The spectacles perched upon the beaked nose above the blackness of her habit engendered in me mixed feelings of respect and revulsion. Crude though the analogy is I was sure that the arachnid qualities of Sister Maria cannot have been lost on other travellers passing this way. I sensed, too, that she herself was not only aware of the comparison but chose to cultivate it. She led me to the buildings and set me on a terrace facing the sea. A platter of dry crusts of bread was already waiting, along with a dozen or so cats attracted by my arrival. Having witnessed the swallowing of the first crust to her satisfaction, she left me to enter the building. Soon I heard her talking to someone deep within: muffled voices, speaking with urgency. Then she returned and led me to the chapel along a dank corridor sparsely lit with candles, with closed doors on either side and between each pair of doors a fresco so dark with age that its subject was barely discernible.

I remember how surprised I was at the chapel's paucity of interest. The stained glass windows, close up, were disappointingly modern. The candles illuminated bare flaking walls that must once have been brightly painted. But its interest for me then, as will become clear, was of a different order. As I left, my way was barred by a collection plate held by another nun seated just within the door, so small in stature that I had not seen her when I entered. The remarkable thing about the plate was the large denominations of the notes it already contained. Startled by the tiny haggard face and too weak not to conform I put in my 2000 drachma note. It seemed a reasonable investment, however tenuous the outcome looked then.

Outside the chapel I took the first tentative step towards our goal. I tried to be casual. 'They tell me you have a library here?' I said. 'Can it be visited?'

'Who told you that?' Sister Maria's response was guarded.

'Just someone in the town.'

'What did they tell you?'

'Oh, nothing specific… I just wondered…'

I suppose that strict honesty is an inviolable requirement of the moral code these ladies observed. After a moment of thought she said, 'It is rumoured that there were once caves below these buildings. Books might have been stored there. I have never seen them.'

'Rumoured?'

'They were already sealed up when I came. That was forty years ago.'

My exit seemed hasty, probably because Sister Maria had sensed another traveller on the garden path. With no further word she hustled me to the terrace and left me to resume my ascent of the mountain.

Returning from the summit three hours later the garden was in shadow, the sheltered trees and bushes curiously still against an evening sky still in motion. In this quiet place a remark of Sister Maria came back to me. 'There are always two of us,' she had said. That thought stayed with me during my flight down the path, and lingered during the weeks that followed.

Summer had long passed when I saw the monastery again. The second nun, Sister Helena – the one holding the plate in the chapel – had become critically ill and Father Kalvos, the priest at the seminary on the coast, had asked me to fly her to the hospital. 'She will never return to the mountain,' he said. 'But you cannot leave the other alone,' I ventured. 'Indeed not,' he replied, 'and that is why I have a second request. When you go you will take her replacement, Sister Anna? Sister Anna is new to the island and has not visited the mountain. She is twenty-eight years old, from an obscure convent in Czechoslovakia, about which I know almost nothing. We were very lucky to find her – or should I say she found us. It's remarkable that someone so young and attractive should seek seclusion, but there we are. Oh, and like you she is an American.'

Father Kalvos dropped Sister Anna at the Department's complex at the foot of the mountain. We three sat in the coffee room over steaming cups, surrounded by posters depicting the island's fauna and flora and dire notices warning travellers against too close a familiarity with them. I congratulated myself that my Greek was now good enough to hear that Sister Anna was not yet a fluent speaker. She seemed nervous, and that was out of character. Her sparing smile appeared to result more from inner musings than the events around her. She reminded me of a philosophical prisoner being introduced to her cell. I thought of making a joke about it until it struck me that that was precisely what she was about to become. Never had my self-restraint been so tested as on that occasion.

Father Kalvos said, 'Sister Anna tells me she is used to being alone, but I have told her she must signal to us if ever…' He paused, choosing his next words carefully, '… it becomes difficult to cope. After all, Sister Maria and Sister Helena have been alone together for many years and the parting will be difficult for both of them. Hard as I tried, it was impossible to persuade Sister Maria to come down from the mountain.' Then he whispered so that only I should hear, 'There is no longer a *need* for a religious house up there.'

Sister Anna looked at me and said, 'Father Kalvos has lectured to me on horticulture and, look, even given me some seeds to plant.' As she spoke I saw wrinkles at her eyes: tiny crow's feet from stress and sleepless nights that I had never seen before.

My unstifled expression of surprise must have worried her. She looked anxiously towards Father Kalvos to see if he had noticed. But he was studying the mountain through the window and concern for his charges was all I could see written on his face.

We walked together to the helicopter. Father Kalvos and Sister Anna said little to one another but perhaps they had already made their farewells. I stowed her suitcase and noted its lightness relative to its size. Then I saw she was watching me, and again there was that transient nervous smile. Throughout the flight Sister Anna looked out, across the sea, to the storm clouds that were gathering over the Turkish coast.

From a long way off we could see Sister Maria on the landing pad and, beside her, Sister Helena in her wheelchair. Closer, we saw that they were clasping each other's hands. They continued to do so until the moment when Father Kalvos and I lifted Sister Helena into the helicopter.

Sister Maria would not let me accompany them to the building. 'Your responsibility is to Sister Helena,' she said. If she recognised me she gave no sign of it.

As they were walking away Sister Anna turned. 'How often will you come?' she asked.

'As often as I'm needed,' I replied.

They were the only words she spoke to me. Our second parting had been no easier than our first.

In the weeks that followed I had no further contact with the monastery. On the rare occasions I flew nearby nothing moved. I had no excuse to visit, and there was no invitation to do so, though I held myself in readiness. Easter passed. The bright sunshine – others might have supposed – led me to the path up the mountain. High up the season started later and the garden was still forlorn. I walked slowly, the better to scrutinise the buildings. The few windows that were not shuttered were dirty and lifeless. I continued on, past the helicopter landing pad and up the path to the summit of the mountain. It was a risky strategy but one for which I saw no alternative.

From the summit the other islands were black shark fins in an infested and darkening sea. When the sunlight finally left the tip of the mountain like an extinguished flame I set off back down the track, knowing that no other walker would have ventured to remain here so late. If all else failed I could lay out my sleeping bag in the wood-store, or even in one of the sheds that housed the garden implements. A lost traveller – especially one as foolish as me – would be believable.

I was in luck. The door from the terrace was not locked – but then what need was there for security? My overshoes were quite silent on the flagstones of the corridor as I made for the chapel. I listened at each of the doors as I passed, watched by the suspicious eyes of erstwhile saints in the faint candlelight. The door to the chapel was ajar, just as we had agreed it should be.

In the light of a single candle, even from the side, her drawn features were plain to see. When she turned the relief we saw in each other's face nearly made us cry. We realised the fulfilment of our dream was almost within our grasp.

'It's all right,' she whispered, 'she sleeps till four and is very deaf – so often have I put that to the test.'

'Have you found it?' I asked.

'Yes,' she replied, 'but I've left it hidden in one of the caves.'

'So can we agree a day?'

'Yes, yes, please,' she replied, with tears trickling down her cheeks.

I had no qualms about violating the sanctity of the chapel. It was not until much later that I pressed the small vial of sedative into her hand.

I waited until two, then crept out of the building to the wood-store, where I sat contemplating the grey mass of the mountain rising almost sheer above me. When the first rays of the sun illuminated the summit, so that within minutes it became a great pyramid of golden light, I began my descent of the path.

No-one could quite remember the sequence of events the following Thursday. Some said that Sister Maria had signalled with the torch that was trained on the police station four miles away on the coast. Others, who had been walking on the mountain, claimed that they alone carried the information Sister Maria had given them. Whichever it was, it was clear by the evening that Sister Anna had disappeared.

The following day, and the days after, rescue teams fanned out across the mountain but found no trace of her. Except that, on the Friday, a climber came upon her light cotton shawl on a stunted bush near the summit of the mountain. Those that saw no relevance in this were outnumbered. Sister Anna had scaled the mountain. And when those who were so inclined saw the date – Ascension Day – the explanation became clear. She had been 'taken up'.

It was probably a rash thing to do, but the following Tuesday I, along with a dozen others, climbed the path to the monastery. I left them there with Sister Maria holding court behind a vast tray of dry crusts. I skirted the end of the chapel and made for the landing pad. It was curious the police had not thought to look there when they first arrived; or, if they had, then not carefully enough. There was not much to see after both our helicopters had been there but if you counted the impressions there was still enough to incriminate. Putting on my overshoes – for which I had no further use – I trampled the ground until no signs remained. No one, it seemed, had heard us, or seen the lamp that had guided me in as darkness fell on the Wednesday evening.

The *Codex Kusadasiensis* – as the earliest extant copy of the Bible is now known – first emerged a year later in the premises of a dealer in antiquities in the little town of Kusadasi, on the Turkish coast. It was part of a miscellany of documents that an intermediary, acting in secret on our behalf, had randomly assembled so that no particular origin could be ascribed to it. At the auction in Paris the bidding was intense, but in the end it went to the Metropolitan Museum of New York for a formidable sum, in spite of its uncertain provenance.

From time to time my wife – whose real name, incidentally, is not Anna but Lianne – and I spend long weekends in that city. We often stay at the Ritz or the Astoria, but we always go to see the codex. Alongside it in the display case is a photograph of the dealer's house where it first came to light. If you look carefully you can see, in the distance across the channel, the mass of Mount Vathos and its shining white peak. With a magnifying glass – and we really did try this once – you can make out the green and white spot towards the summit that is Moni Agiou Ioanni. Of course, the geography doesn't wholly explain why we searched for it there but, sipping coffee in

Lianne's Washington study, which we do from time to time under her treatises on biblical archaeology, we congratulate ourselves on having chosen it as the place to start. Hanging on Anna's wall beside her nun's habit is an interesting framed composition that our guests invariably assume, erroneously, to be by one of our less comprehensible contemporary graphical artists. We still have to decide when it will be safe to explain that it represents the system of caves and chambers under the chapel of the monastery.

As for the shawl, we had seen it rise into the air as the rotor blades began whirling. Too late to do anything about it, and impossible to predict the fickleness of human nature.

Lianne has never been back to the island. Increasingly I get up to find her having been writing since dawn to complete her account of how, as a research student, she had come across an obscure and still unknown medieval manuscript that led us to the island, and of her imposture as a nun. She says it is better to consolidate her career as a biblical scholar – she has just been made an assistant professor – before our story of the deception breaks. Such is avarice.

From time to time I return to the island, but only to take tourists up the mountain, or occasionally fly them to the monastery in my own helicopter. I aim to arrive about twelve, giving them ample time to tour the chapel and the shrine and for the more intrepid to venture to the summit, where an enormous cross now stands. But if they do the climb the chances are they will have to forego the pleasures of Sister Maria's crusts. We need to be gone by two; too much exposure of the place could still be risky.

Whenever I am on the island I make a point of visiting Father Kalvos. Sometimes, at quiet moments, I catch him gazing anxiously up at the mountain, for Sister Anna was never replaced.

DAWN LIGHT

Bentley gave one last desperate tug, and he was free, leaving only wisps of his coat sleeve to the teeth of the closing door. Alex, Sargon's son, was not so lucky. For a moment Bentley contemplated the anguish through the stocking covered head as it moved behind the plate glass. He was reminded of a fish in an aquarium, desperate for food, except that Alex's gaze was not on him, but searching wildly for escape. Then Bentley saw him produce the gun, which he shouldn't have brought, because they had agreed it. It was difficult to tell whether the single sudden crack was of breaking glass or gun-shot. Whichever, the clear glass in an instant fractured like a car windscreen does to a stone and Alex, still trapped, was lost from sight – although not to Bentley's consciousness. Then another alarm began to sound. Bentley's grip on his case tightened as he turned to confront the options that were as terrible as they were unplanned.

No time to consider that Alex was the one who had hung behind, had minced back across the marble floor and peered over the counter to where the second assistant – the one they had not at first seen – had pressed the alarm button. And, extending his arm and pointing the gun downwards, had not even seen his target as the trigger was pulled. But the scream had told him to run and Bentley, at the door, had waited as long as he dared. Yet, he was Sargon's son, and Bentley, as number two in the gang, had been responsible.

With his back to the door the choices were stark. To his right the car, black and funereal at the end of the dark alley, had already begun to move, just as they had agreed. Slowly, no fuss, uncompromisingly, it drew forward. Twenty seconds worth of time maybe. To the left, equidistant, figures moving in the high street, beneath street lamps radiating yellow through the dank night air. The jewels bulging heavily in his case weighed against the fate of Sargon's son – possible gain against abject failure and worse. So Bentley ran, his coat flapping over his coal-black suit. Towards people, and into a mire from which he might, if he was lucky, pull himself free. The human filter that absorbed him clogged the car's progress, muffling the crazed horn and the single, wild shot. They had risked much with that, and it quantified his plight.

The street was still unsafe. Along its length the pimps, the three-trick fraudsters, the beggars, were half of them Sargon's men, with their mobiles *communicado*, just as capable of swarming – when the order came – as dissolving into the night. Bentley, with his hat pulled down and coat collar up, tripped his way through them as nimbly as his bulky frame allowed.

His car, known only to him – as, heaven be praised, he had just stolen it – was parked too far away to be reached safely. Most of the shops were now closed, and those that weren't were unlikely to give refuge to a criminal they knew only as an extortioner. And dead-end alleys, in his experience, tended to be just that, in fact as well as metaphorically. Then, suddenly, he was confronted by a back he knew well, moulding itself to the pillar of a traffic light, mobile scrunched between shoulder and jaw, the body seething with alertness despite its sack-like frame. Bentley dared not pass, nor attempt to cross the road. He looked to his side, hesitantly, then again into the depths of a building – a church – that he had never before entered and did not know.

The girl at the door smiled in a way that Bentley barely recognised – benignly, without intent. She handed him a piece of paper as he passed and he took it with head down, but missing nothing. At first he sat in the rearmost pew, but that was too exposed. Further forward now, the pews filled up around him. Thus trapped, he thought again of Sargon's son. A priest ascended the pulpit. Bentley scanned his companions, identifying one that matched his own appearance whose movements he determined he would follow exactly. For the first time he glanced at the piece of paper he still held – a service in memory of Philip Ironside, he read. The girl next to him, pretty in black but with the hollow eyes of grief, smiled sweetly and asked him how he knew the boy. 'Only distantly,' Bentley replied, 'but he was a fine young fellow. And you?' 'He was my cousin,' she replied, and he watched a tear course down her cheek. Once, while he was kneeling, the door behind banged. There were footsteps, aggressively into the body of the church, but they receded and the door slammed shut. When the service ended the girl smiled again. 'Thank you for coming,' she said. 'I think I'll stay a while longer,' Bentley replied, sinking to his knees and bowing his head, and touching the case beside him, just to be sure. 'Well, Philip Ironside, you've gained a friend by dying, that's for sure,' he muttered. 'That's a first in my experience.'

Then he thought of Sargon in his office overlooking the boxing-ring. They would all be there now, at their wits end – Cowley, Quintex, Elias the Greek – heads bowed, desperate to account for the double failure. They would try to call on Bentley's mother, and his sister Beth. He was glad that he'd moved them to safety, though for him that was a usual precaution before a job. Then, with no other leads, they would wait in his own room next to the Spread Eagle and when he didn't appear, trash it. Sargon would contact tougher men better trained to seek out and kill. And it would take a hard man to get Bentley.

His mother was hard like himself, and responsible for creating him in her own image. But Beth, his sister, was guileless, a teacher by vocation who never quite believed the mountain of circumstantial evidence that spoke – or rather screamed – of her brother's fifteen years of crime. He was Uncle Ben to her fatherless child and the nearest thing either of them had to a family.

Within the church the mourners had gone, but a new set immediately invaded the space behind him. An older crowd this time, milling around a sharp voice that lectured them on city churches. As a body they marched into one of the side chapels, leaving Bentley to contemplate the piles of clothing draped over the last pew. He took off his overcoat and exchanged it for one that was colourful and loud, with a bobble hat to match. Then he found a scarf for which he had nothing to offer in exchange. More confident now, he set off to look for his car, hoping that the police had not yet traced it. Once he looked back, and in his mind saw his own name, Philip Bentley – for Philip was his name also – on a similar order of service. But the church was black and desolate and he knew of no-one, besides his sister, who would remotely wish to hand out anything that had to do with him.

An hour later he was still driving aimlessly. Then he realised that the petrol in his tank was a precious commodity that could not be wasted. Distance equated with motorway access, so he sped north, hitting the M11. Someone had once told him that he would never like East Anglia because the sort of cities he frequented did not exist there. So when the choice of the Midlands or Norwich presented itself he chose the latter. For mile after mile he saw only trees, and black spaces that were fields. Apprehensively, he was confronting the unknown. He stopped once for petrol, but the lights around him were just an oasis in a desert of darkness. Driving on, there were stars above, brighter than he had ever noticed before. Quietly, insidiously, tiredness gripped his body and stilled his mind. Sargon's son behind the glass became no more than the soft movement of a shadow, the case lying on the seat beside him almost an irrelevance. His light-headedness encouraged him to drive on, around the outpost of the city that was Norwich, beyond the airport, eventually into deeper blackness. He negotiated tiny villages, faintly pocked with light and, linking them, narrow lanes across which bats and night owls flew. He came to a sign marked 'to the beach' and followed it into a car park in which stood an abandoned caravan and a cart bearing a load of waste under a tarpaulin. He drove to its furthest boundary, marked by a row of white posts, drawing up to them as far as he could go. He switched off the engine. Then he slumped over the wheel and slept.

Sargon sat behind an antique rosewood desk with his legs stretched out between the pillars. On the desk was an open and empty briefcase. The lamp that he had set up to examine its contents, of which there were just a few meagre banknotes, he now trained on Cranford's face. Looking from behind, across the boy's shoulder, Bentley observed Sargon's impatiently mincing feet which, given their surroundings, resembled the maw of a predatory crab. Bentley, who had been amused by this often enough, wondered if Cranford had made the same association. But perhaps he had other thoughts on his mind right now. Bentley knew what those movements of the feet presaged; but Cranford was too new for that, and had not calculated the odds.

With a sudden thrust of his arm, Sargon swept the case forward. It crashed against Cranford's knees and fell gaping to the floor. Bentley leaned forward and tapped the boy's shoulder. His voice was neutral. 'Pick it up, son, and put it back – open – on the desk.' As Cranford obeyed Sargon rose from his seat, rounded the desk and stood beside him, placing his hand on the trembling boy's shoulder. 'Fill it,' he said. Cranford squinted up at him, at first mystified, then slowly began to feel in his pockets. Into the bag he put his comb, his keys and his wallet. 'That doesn't fill it,' Sargon said, at the same time delivering a vicious thrust to the side of Cranford's head with his fist. Bentley leaned forward again. 'He means everything – everything you possess – son,' he said. As the case began to fill, Sargon returned to his seat behind the desk.

When Cranford had placed the last item – his underpants – in the case, Sargon withdrew from the desk a small package bound with pink ribbon, and handed it to him. He spoke over the boy's head. 'A fair exchange, wouldn't you say, Philip?' 'Open it,' Bentley said to Cranford, poking his shoulder.

Two minutes later Cranford stood before them, shivering, in a pair of blood red boxing shorts.

Sargon rose and looked out of the window at the ring below. 'Heh,' he said, 'Connors must have read our thoughts. He's already down there waiting for you.' 'You'll find socks and boots in the ring,' Bentley said. Sargon turned to Bentley.

'Can we afford one more this year?' he asked. Bentley shrugged. 'It's what we agreed with the fuzz,' he replied.

Sargon looked searchingly into Cranford's face. For several seconds the room and the people in it seemed frozen in time. Then, just for a moment, the chiselled features seemed to relax, transforming themselves into something that might have passed – at another time and in another place – for fatherly concern.

'There's a lock-up in Islington, green door, behind Brent's place. I'm sorry, Mr Sargon, really sorry.'

'Take him down, Philip,' Sargon said, 'but this time, use your judgement.'

When the noise had ceased Sargon looked at the clock. Twenty minutes had passed. The room, like the building, was now cold and silent. He sorted the papers on his desk and placed his pen on top of the pile. Then he went to the window. What he saw did not at first seem to please him, then he smiled to himself. 'Philip, Philip,' he muttered reprovingly under his breath.

With the dawn light the four white posts of the boxing-ring turned into the painted fence in front of Bentley's car, the agitated figures outside it into the twisted trunks of young Norfolk pines planted between the car park and the sea. But something more significant, at that moment, had caught his eye and made him reach for the gun that he had hidden under the folded coat beside him. Parked alongside was a black Mondeo, just like Sargon's. He opened his door and crept round the bonnet, close to the ground, covering the other car with his gun. But the car was empty. Moreover, it was not Sargon's.

With lighter heart Bentley moved forward into the belt of trees, stepping carefully – as he had trained himself to do – to avoid leaving footprints on the ground. The sky was pink now, the beach beyond a cloth of gold edged with white lace. He stared and sniffed the salt air, and stood puzzled because the unfamiliar experience had made his thoughts wander too far.

He was not alone on the beach. Further along there was a figure near the water's edge laying out a structure – surely an enormous kite – whose coloured and segmented surface rippled in the wind. He crept closer, safe behind the grassy dunes that fringed the sands. Slowly, confidently, the kite-surfer negotiated himself into the water. Bentley shivered at the thought of it and with his hand brushed back the wisps of his hair caught by a fresh gust of wind. Then, quite suddenly, the kite rose up, dragging the figure across the surface of the water, the feet describing a perfect and sparkling arc that reminded Bentley of the necklace that, with seconds ticking away, he had decided to retrieve from the last of the cabinets. He shivered again, but this time for a different reason. Then, as the wind dropped, the kite came down, as quickly and silently as it had risen.

When the kite went up for the second time, Bentley's coat began flapping against his legs in a violent gust that drove the kite both upwards and towards him. The suspended figure was snatched high into the air, then fell back awkwardly onto the sand amid the spent folds of material. From behind the dune Bentley contemplated the crumpled form, clinically, dispassionately. Then he walked towards it.

It was not the first time Bentley had witnessed the contusing violence of death. But on such occasions, in his own world, there were seldom decisions to be made. Others, not he, would do what had to be done – to clear, to tidy, to hide, then to deny. He looked into the clear morning air, at the sky and the sea, and along the beach. There was no movement, except for the swell of the surf.

It was not enough. The residues of a lifetime of crime and bitterness could not be expunged this easily. There were no mechanisms for imparting sympathy or explanation to others, and it was too late to learn. He saw no other course, no means of grasping the line that was offered, or even of telling whether it was a lifeline or a snare.

Turning away, he began to retrace his path. Then he picked up a piece of driftwood from near the water's edge. As he made his way back to the car he dragged it behind him, obliterating his footsteps in the sand. Looking back, he was pleased that the tide seemed to be coming in. He reached the car with quickening steps. Establishing that he was alone, he hurled the stick into the trees and scrambled into the car.

A plan was hatching in his mind. A slow smile began to contort his thin, pursed lips.

He was going back.

TREXLER'S ORCHID

Dusk was approaching and still Bloomfield had not arrived. From the table in his study Martin Trexler peered through the open doors and the grey-green gloom of the conservatory to the orchid house in the garden, where the last rays of the sun were painting the glass with golden brush strokes. He stroked his beard, half expecting to see his rival skulking there in his usual aggressively inquisitive manner. But he knew the man was too subtle for that.

Perhaps the visit had something to do with the vacant position of Keeper of the Herbarium at Kew and Bloomfield, who already worked there, wanted his support. But even if Trexler did not know the reason for this unexplained wish to see him – and Bloomfield had given nothing away when the telephone suddenly went dead – he was sure that his adversary had no inkling of the revelation that he, Trexler, was about to deliver. On this day of all days, there were more important things to think about than Dr Ray Bloomfield and his ambitions.

Trexler's study was the product of a bygone age. Visitors usually needed a moment or so to convince themselves they were still in suburban London and not a faraway museum dedicated to the relics of colonial rule. Around the walls, Victorian stalwarts in antique frames posed trenchantly against impenetrable jungle backdrops reflecting expeditions of unspeakable hardship. They looked down upon a miscellany of hideous masks, barbarous weapons and wood carvings littering the room that were the spoils of Trexler's own wanderings. High above the central table, drapes of threadbare linen cloth drooped tent-like from the ceiling rose to the upper walls. On the table's carpeted surface an assortment of academic botanical volumes were stacked as if for no other purpose than to gather dust. For Trexler, this room had the cosiness of a womb.

He swivelled in his seat and looked up at the most impressive of the figures, his grandfather, his idol. He was reassured by the approbation that he chose to see in the piercing eyes. Gerhardt Trexler, the doyen of collectors, the chief of Sander's team, the leader of men praised in that heyday towards the end of the last century as vigorously as they were now reviled by those who understood the despoliation of the jungles of the world.

Of course Trexler understood all that, but it was not how he saw his grandfather. From early childhood Gerhardt's exploits had fired a rampant imagination and fuelled an unquenchable urge. Of these deeds one had held a special place in orchid lore, ever since a tantalisingly cryptic note in *Curtis' Orchid Magazine* had referred to a species of *Cyprepedium* quite unrivalled in its distinctiveness and beauty that no-one besides Gerhardt himself was destined ever to see. Until today.

With Bloomfield quite forgotten, Trexler rose from his chair and entered the conservatory. He re-emerged carrying a small grass-like plant with curiously spotted leaves and bearing a single slipper-like bloom that, with unbearable slowness, had developed from the ripe bud of the previous day. He set the pot beside Gerhardt's notes that lay open on the table. As he had done repeatedly throughout the day, he again compared the features. There was no longer a need to convince himself. The two flowers were undeniably the same.

The paper he had written on this assumption lay pristine and complete on the table beside an envelope addressed to the editor of the *Orchid Review*. For the moment it was all that was needed to establish his claim to the species, which he had named *Paphiopedilum trexleri*.

While he was absorbed with the plant a young Asian woman, twenty years Trexler's junior and with straight black hair to her slim waist, had entered noiselessly through the open door. She stood behind him, waiting patiently until he should notice her. She spoke only when he acknowledged her with a slight turn of his head.

'Is it ready?' she said.

'If you must know, it is ready.'

'I can post it for you?'

'Thank you, but I'd prefer to do it myself.'

'Of course,' she said, leaving the room.

He had been distracted by his wife's entrance. But his spirits quickly returned. Perhaps he had been harsh. After all, without her, more or less, there would have been no cause for celebration. And there was always a way… But no, he would not sully his success with black intentions that could safely lie dormant. Besides, did not the manner of his discovery have the makings of a legend just as potent as the scientific one he had just made? No, caution must prevail and he must bide his time. He began to speak, addressing an imaginary audience: 'Ladies and gentleman, when my grandfather left Siam for the last time, his fever having subsided, no one could have guessed…'

He was interrupted by a loud knock at the front door. He heard his wife's footsteps, and then Bloomfield's loud voice in the hall. Stealthily he returned the plant to the conservatory and stood with his back to the fireplace, hands clasped behind him, waiting for his visitor to appear.

After a few minutes Bloomfield knocked lightly on the door and entered. His first words concerned Trexler's uncanny resemblance to the figure on the wall above him.

At the beginning, it seemed that providence must have had a hand in it: that it had fallen to Trexler, after desperately craving a new species – any new species – to be handed the very one he had sought both in his dreams and in reality. The years of tramping the forests of the orient with this his primary – if unadmitted – objective had come to an abrupt and delicious end. And all in the privacy and convenience of his own greenhouse.

The consignment had come from one of his newer shippers – Anova Orchids in Bangkok. At first he had not been sure. There had been just a single plant. It had no flower as such – that had withered in transit – but the tessellated leaves were as familiar to him as the backs of this own hands. This sole example in a batch of otherwise mundane specimens was surely the most bizarre of accidents. He spent the afternoon in the Herbarium at Kew, just to make sure, and on the following morning booked his flight to Bangkok.

Trexler was widely known and regarded in orchid circles, so his first decision – whether to arrive incognito – was agonising. But, as far as he was aware, to Anova Orchids he was still just a name. As the time to leave approached he shaved his beard, trimmed the residual moustache, practised speaking with a Welsh accent and referred to himself as Jones, the name that appeared in his second – and nefariously obtained – passport that had lain in his drawer in readiness for such an eventuality for a number of years.

At Don Muang International Airport he hired a car and made for the small hotel on Rachadapisek Road that on previous journeys had passed the test of obscurity. Later, having installed himself on the veranda with a glass of beer, he was content to let himself melt into the lengthening shadows and subject himself to the noises of the night. It fell to a selenid moth, alighting on his grandfather's journal on the table beside his nodding head, to bless his endeavours.

The next morning he searched the orchid stalls at the flower markets of Pak Klong Talat, Bangrak and Phahonyothin, as he had done many times before. But where previously the exercise would have been a cause for delight, now it was a mechanical race against time. In his haste he handled the plants roughly, and was chided for it. Then, empty-handed, he drove to Sukhumvit Road to put in his first appearance at Anova Orchids.

He was flattered by the attention given to him by the pretty Thai girl in the office. He noted particularly the smile with which she received his visiting card, carefully improvised at the airport.

'My name is Maia. You will follow me please?'

She led him down a corridor lined with specimen plants in full flower. He held back a little, pretending to scrutinise them, the better to observe Maia's slender and perfect figure. She stopped at a closed door and called out, then opened it, standing aside to let him enter.

'Mr Rama is manager here, Mr Jones,' she whispered as he passed. 'He is also my father.'

The office was more grand than Trexler considered appropriate for a plant nursery. Mr Rama rose and extended a hand bearing several rings, at least one of which, in gold, bore an orchid motif. Maia did not leave them, but withdrew to a nearby desk and sat upon it cross-legged while her father presented Trexler with his card.

'You are new to this business, Mr Jones? Your name is not familiar to me.'

'Not at all. I've grown orchids for many years. But only as a hobby, you understand. The commercial side is a recent interest.'

'May I ask what led to that interest?'

'I own a small supermarket chain. Orchids are back in fashion. But the Germans and the Dutch have got too expensive and the English – well, frankly, they aren't very good at it.'

'Then I hope we can do business together. First my daughter will show you around, then we will have some tea and talk.'

Within the polythene dome the diffuse sunlight passing through the high cooling fans fell like yellow petals onto the carpet of colour below. Here were species familiar to him from his early days as a collector and hybrids in profusion. The same shifting light turned Maia's long black hair momentarily red and caused the gentle contours of her white blouse to glow. She extended her arms above her head to capture a raceme for him to examine, then released it with a smile.

'You mentioned slipper orchids in your letter, Mr Jones. But as you see, they are not well represented here.'

'My friends tell me that you supply them regularly.'

'They are from our nursery at Attuthya, about two hours from here.'

'Could I see them?'

'It would be my pleasure to take you.'

They continued to walk amongst the profusion of flowers. There opened up a vista leading to an area of intense human activity. As they walked towards it the air became heavy with the dank smell of the composts that about a dozen young women were scooping frantically into black pots. Seeing the visitor, one of them put down her implements and came up to them. Trexler noticed that she did not approach him directly but held her face away. Only when he deliberately shifted his position did he see that her left eye was sightless.

'This is my sister Sirita,' Maia said. 'She is responsible for all the production here, while I am merely… a secretary.'

Trexler looked for a response to Maia's self-abasement – a smile, a grimace, perhaps. But none came. Something akin to pity – for she was otherwise as beautiful as her sister – made him fall behind the departing Maia. Then for twenty minutes he and Sirita talked seriously about orchids.

Compared with those of the previous night, the moths around the naked light bulb above Trexler's bed seemed to dance in tune with his quickening expectation. Sleep was beyond his grasp. He read – as he had on many occasions in this very room – the paper by his grandfather, Gerhardt. There was no need. The features of the orchid were imprinted indelibly in his memory. It was now a matter of riding out the night while waiting for dawn to break. Only once did he think of Maia, asking himself in genuine puzzlement why he had not paid her more attention.

Trexler's offer to drive her to Attuthaya had been rejected politely but firmly. By eight she was waiting for him in reception, black hair shining against her fresh white blouse. By ten they were walking up a winding track between clumps of oleander towards a clearing in the scrub.

'This is not a… well… a conventional nursery, Mr Jones, as you will see', she said. 'I know we can count on your discretion.'

'Of course.'

They followed a barbed wire fence clothed in creeper, broken at one point by a rusting metal gate opening just sufficiently to let them squeeze through. Going ahead of her he tried to open it further, but managed only a few centimetres against the reluctant grass at its foot. He felt the warmth of her body against his straining arm as she passed. His embarrassment was stilled by the innocence of her smile.

Trexler found himself at a dimly remembered threshold experienced years before in this same country when anticipation of finding the treasures he sought sent waves of pleasure surging through his body with an intensity that was almost sexual. Maia, apparently sensing this now, seemed to be searching his face, as if trying to separate the truth from the deceit, although that could not possibly be. 'I hope we can find something to interest you,' she said. 'I suggest we go on a bit, down this path.'

They entered a clearing bounded by dense festoons of purple and red bougainvillea. Rows and rows of slipper orchids, many in bloom, were laid out on low trestle tables in the shade of mimosa and frangipani trees. The entire genus *Paphiopedilum* seemed to be represented here. Established species mingled with hybrids that in quality matched any in Trexler's own collection. And then he saw it, next to where the girl was looking innocently up into the tree above, where birds were twittering. It was as if all of them had been waiting for him to find it.

Trexler approached the plant circumspectly, fearfully almost. Though there was no flower, the pattern of blotches on the leaves left him in no doubt. So rapt was he that he hardly noticed Maia had put her hand in his.

'Is this one for sale?' he asked huskily, trying to sound calm.

'Everything has its price,' she replied, laughing.

For a moment Trexler was silent. Then he asked, 'Are there others?'

'A few. They came from one place only, in the north. As far as we know all were taken and we have them all. We searched very hard.'

'And you have seen the flower?'

'The collector did. But since then none of them has flowered. So I cannot help you.'

'I would like to buy... all of them.'

'Then you must talk to my father.'

They drove back to Bangkok in silence, embarrassed by the awareness that each was withholding information from the other. At his hotel she left him almost no excuse not to walk away, but then called after him.

'You couldn't let a girl go hungry,' she teased.

Over dinner she told him that her father was away on business until the following afternoon, but would be back in time to watch the races at the Royal Turf Club. They danced, they looked at the moon with their arms around each other. Then, under the single light bulb with the moths now revelling in ecstasy, they made love. When he woke in the morning she was gone, but on her pillow lay a leaf of the orchid to which he had vowed to give his name.

At breakfast, the waiter set a phone beside his plate, and he received instructions for the meeting with Maia's father.

The Mercedes that took him into the city he remembered seeing parked at the Anova Nursery. The black curtains at the window remained undrawn. He knew where he was only when the driver set him down somewhere near Chulalongkorn University.

From the street and on its lower levels the apartment building was unremarkable, and remained so until they reached the third floor. 'Mr Rama uses a separate entrance,' the driver whispered, as if apologising. 'You will be met on the top floor.' He stood to attention at the lift entrance and remained there until the doors had closed. Trexler felt himself whisked upwards.

The penthouse flat overlooked the racecourse. Trexler saw below him the gathering of horses that heralded the start of a race, but Mr Rama drew his attention instead to a bank of computer screens through the open door of an adjacent room.

'See, Mr Jones, how we marry tradition and technology. I like to see how my investments perform. Perhaps I can tempt you to a small wager before the race begins. There are a few minutes left.'

'I'm afraid I have only a few thousand baht,' Trexler replied nervously.

The response was an icy stare that caught him unawares. 'If you have no money, Mr Jones, what are we doing talking about orchids?'

'That is a different matter, Sir.'

'Indeed it is.' He turned to the window to contemplate the final preparations for the race. 'I understand you got on well with my daughter, Mr Jones.'

'Very much so.'

'And found her attractive?'

'What man wouldn't?'

'That's good, very good. Because it might make the orchid affordable for you.'

'I beg your pardon?'

'Ten thousand sterling for the orchid and the hand of my daughter in marriage. You see, Mr Jones, I want a life for her in your country so that she can be allowed – if you'll forgive the euphemism – to blossom.' He turned again to the window. 'Ah, the race begins.'

That night Trexler slept fitfully. The moths around the bulb were conspicuously absent, as if aware that there was just too much excitement to share. However much Trexler tried to bring logic to bear there was always the spectre of his grandfather to over-ride it: in the mirror above where he filled his glass, in the pattern of flowers in the curtain, even when he looked down at the matting on the floor. You owe me this, the cold, demanding eyes seemed to say.

In the morning he telephoned Mr Rama's office to convey his decision, but both father and daughter were away. With ice in his heart he left a message: tell Mr Rama that my answer is yes. 'Mr Rama will be very pleased,' said the receptionist. 'What do you mean?' Trexler replied, alarmed that his secret might be out. 'Why, to receive such an important order,' the voice replied.

In the days that followed, Trexler's attempts to see Maia seemed thwarted at every turn. First her grandmother had summoned her to Chiang Mai to give guidance on the marital state. Then, by telephone, she told him that she had visited the site of origin of his orchids, where he should join her the following day. But when he reached the rendezvous at the beginning of a forest track she was not there, and he was taken to see only patches of recently disturbed earth. On telephoning the Bangkok office he was told that her father had taken ill and required her immediate attention. Trexler asked himself if it mattered that much, and returned to his Bangkok hotel having, for the moment, written her out of the equation. The marriage and its foreseeable aftermath was a diversion, albeit a pleasant one, that was best looked upon as an embellishment of his great deed. There would be plenty of time to come to terms with it and enjoy the pleasures of the flesh.

It was in this frame of mind that he accompanied his wife to be, his prospective father-in-law and diverse family members unknown to him to a registry office somewhere across the Chao Phraya River. She made no attempt to lift her veil, whispering to him that she did not know what the impact of a kiss might make on her family. In fact they had hardly spoken since the now familiar black Mercedes had collected him from his hotel. Something was amiss, but he could not put his finger on it. It therefore came as no surprise when Mr Rama touched his arm and led him aside.

'There are small problems with the paperwork for your plants – CITES permits and the like. I may have been a little less generous with the information than was expected. If I take your wife with me to sort it out she can meet you at the airport with the plants. Best to give me her ticket in case you get separated.' Then he added, 'It's a good thing the documents are in her family name.'

It was not until Trexler reached the departure hall that he felt he had played with and lost ten thousand pounds, besides having no plants and no wife. On the screen the line for his flight crept steadily upwards like the water level in some medieval aquatic torture, but still there was no sign of her. When it indicated the boarding gate he accepted defeat, cursed himself for being a fool and made his way sadly to the check-in area, vowing never to return.

But he was wrong, at least in part.

'Ah, Mr Jones,' the girl at the check-in desk said, 'your companion could not find you and has already gone through.'

'Was she carrying a… package,' he enquired tentatively.

'We argued about it,' the girl said casually, 'but it just made it as hand luggage. But Mr Jones, you must hurry. The gate will be closing.'

At the gate the last few passengers were showing their boarding cards as Trexler joined them.

In the plane he thought he saw her long black hair, encasing her head like a shroud, halfway down the plane. Then, to his joy, there in the open luggage rack above her was the box, clearly marked with the Anova logo and the legend 'plants – this was up.' Never had the English language seemed so sweet. He sat heavily in the vacant seat beside her. 'Thank you!' he said softly. And slowly she turned her head to acknowledge him.

Trexler's wife answered the knock at the door.

'My husband is expecting you, Dr Bloomfield.'

'Ray, please.'

'Of course. How silly. I still haven't got used to having you as a brother-in-law.'

'Maia managed to keep it from you all that time?'

Sirita blushed. 'Well, no, of course not. We are too close for that. Actually I've known since you brought those plants to us from Chiang Mai.' She brushed an imaginary speck of dust from his lapel. 'I can't think how one of them happened to find its way here, though.'

'Oh, these things happen. We can't all be perfect, can we?' Suddenly Bloomfield looked embarrassed. 'Oh, I'm sorry,' he said, 'that was tactless of me. Please forgive me.'

'No need to be, really. They say the cataract can be removed and that there's sight behind it. I go in next month – it should be fine.'

'I'm really glad,' Bloomfield said. 'Oh, before I see Martin – if you don't mind me asking – is everything all right... between you, I mean?'

Sirita smiled ruefully. 'No, but when it happens I think the separation will be... well... cordial.'

'Do you think he'll accept me... as a member of the family, so to speak?

'It will be a great shock for him.'

'Yes, true. But not half as much as this.' Bloomfield withdrew from his coat pocket a large brown envelope and laid it on the hall table. 'I sent it off two days ago. This copy is for Martin.'

'What did you decide to call it?'

'*Paphiopedilum bloomfieldii.*'

'It will hurt him.'

'I know,' Bloomfield said, making for Trexler's door.

DUST TO DUST

The Reverend Lucas Parsons smiled to himself as he replaced the *Church Times* in the rack beside his chair. Curious how the recent spate of thefts had occurred around his own minster town of Bixworth. First it had been lead from the roofs, a crime he had forestalled in his own church by installing CCTV. But that hadn't prevented the theft of the church plate from the chest in the vestry and candlesticks from the altar, even though the church door was kept permanently shut. He rose from the chair, called to Mrs Webley, his housekeeper, to say that he was going out and ambled across the lane to the graveyard where mourners were already gathering for the interment. Drops of rain struck his starched white cuff, narrowly missing the half-concealed book of common prayer under his arm.

The hearse was already drawn up outside the porch. He could make out in its sombre interior only a single wreath of white carnations on the teak coffin. As he approached, the incongruent simplicity of it made him slow his pace. Here had been a man whose ostentation in life had marked him out as a likely villain, a petty criminal of humble origins with a taste for cars, women and fast living. And that was how Lucas had portrayed him in that last fateful sermon; not naming him, of course, but indirectly denouncing the evils that had descended upon the village that everyone believed had only one origin. Looking back, might he have been a bit hasty in assuming that Harvey Crib's lifestyle had been funded by crime? Hinting, even, that the theft of the church plate – upon no evidence whatsoever, as one parishioner had pointed out – could be laid at this man's door? It came as a not unpleasant surprise to be told that, with Harvey's suicide, the police files had been effectively closed.

But Lucas was not one to dwell on such matters. Whatever the weather he enjoyed these outdoor services: the mown grass between graves in the shadow of the great yew, the dashes of colour that flecked the graveyard after recent inhumations. Especially, he savoured the rich loam walls of freshly dug graves – and an order of service more in harmony with these outside elements than with the sullen interior of his somewhat dilapidated church.

Besides the bearers there were precisely seven people, stiff and erect, peering into the void. They included the deceased's nephew, Tony Crib, and his wife Samantha, whom he knew as neighbours. The rest he assumed were relatives; it seemed unlikely that the surly Harvey had had any real friends, and his business acquaintances would have thought it in their best interests to stay away. But one never could tell.

Lucas was soon in full flight, revelling in the drama of the words. 'Man that is born of woman hath but a short time to live, and is full of misery. He cometh up, and is cut down, like a flower; he fleeth as it were a shadow, and never continueth in one stay…'

Accustomed to fixing his gaze on the church tower at such times it took several seconds before he realised the gathering had been joined by a young man shabbily dressed in black who looked about him nervously before bowing his head. Unaccustomed to being interrupted Lucas ignored him and continued, '...in the midst of life we are in death: of whom may we seek for succour, but of thee, O Lord, who for our sins art justly displeased...' He could see the mourners' sidelong glances, but the flow could not be interrupted, not now. '...yet, O Lord God most holy, O Lord most mighty, O holy and most merciful Saviour, deliver us not into the bitter pains of eternal...'

'Reverend,' the intruder whispered.

'... eternal death. Thou knowest, Lord, the secrets of our hearts; shut not thy merciful...'

'Reverend!'

'... merciful ears to our prayers; but spare us...' Suddenly his resolve was broken. 'What?'

'I need to speak with you.'

'Can't you see I'm burying someone?'

'That's just it, Reverend.'

'Just what?'

'You're not.'

Lucas beamed at the mourners and soldiered on. '... spare us, Lord most holy, O God most mighty...' Then he gave up. 'Friends, I think my colleague has a special message of condolence that must precede the casting of the earth. Pray bear with us for just one moment.'

'Who are you?' he hissed. 'What do you want?'

'Palin, Sir, from the undertakers. There's been a... em... mix-up.'

'I beg your pardon.'

'He's not in there.'

Sensing something was amiss Tony Crib shuffled up to them. 'Something up, Reverend?'

'A small technicality, Anthony. Sorted in a moment.'

Palin was now becoming agitated. 'Didn't you hear what I said? I said that's not him in there.'

'Where is he then – soaring over the treetops?'

'Boring his way downwards, more like,' Tony said.

Tony Crib grasped Palin's lapels. 'Look, you. My uncle's waited a lifetime for this – but not half as much as we have – and you're not going to spoil it.' A look of enlightenment crossed his face. 'Hey! Penny's just dropped. Local uni. It's rag day, isn't it?' To Palin he said, 'You're a bloody student aren't you?'

'Do I look…'

'Admit you've been rumbled. Good try but now you can just bugger off. Empty handed.'

'Alright,' Palin said. 'I tried to tell you but you wouldn't listen. On your own heads be it. I'm off.'

'Well spotted Anthony,' Lucas said. He turned to one of the bearers. 'You know that man?'

'Seen him about. Trainee I think.'

Samantha, who had been listening intently, came across to them. 'Well, we're not burying anything until we're sure it's Uncle Harvey.'

'Here, Sammy,' Tony said. 'You got your mobile? Telephone the undertakers, there's a good girl.'

'So resourceful, your husband. Try 801349. Always remember it – year of the black death.'

But she was beaten by the phone ringing.

'Who's that?… Who?… Aunt Ada's in Australia… Well, fancy that, I'd never have believed it. She grinned at Lucas. 'It's Harvey's sister – she's on her way. Now we'll have to wait.'

'Where is she?'

'At the station.'

Lucas lost no time in addressing the bearers. 'Look, we

have to wait for the deceased's sister. Can you chaps come back in an hour?'

'Well, I dunno, it's a bit irregular. Is the pub still open?'

'Assuredly, assuredly. They'll make you most welcome.'

When the bearers had left the churchyard Lucas said, 'Now, we must think. How can we be absolutely certain that…'

'Try lifting the coffin. He didn't weigh much.'

'Think you can tell?'

'If we rock it a bit, he'd roll wouldn't he. He, he, geddit… rock and roll…'

'Good one, Tony,' Sam said. 'Hey, look, it's beginning to rain again.'

They lifted the coffin. 'Bloody heavy,' Tony said.

Sam was becoming agitated. 'Now it's pouring. We can't leave him here, but I'm going home. I suggest you take him inside.'

Lucas and Tony grabbed the handles and manoeuvred the coffin into the porch. Lucas grappled with the door, which failed to budge. 'Does this when it's wet,' he said. They tried again. The door gave way and they were in. They placed the coffin on the floor.

'Thirsty work,' Crib said.

'There's some red in the cupboard. If the ringers haven't beaten us to it.'

Cribb returned with a bottle. 'No goblets, Vicar?'

'Sorry. They went when the silver got… er… taken away. But, changing the subject, what are we going to do…'

'What would your good lord have us do?'

'You mean…?'

'Use your nous. Darkness to light. Enlightenment. Open the bugger. Take a look, then we'd know, wouldn't we?'

'I can't… I see where you're coming from. With what, though?'

'The church doesn't have a tool kit?'

'Good gracious, no! Things spiritual, not temporal.'

Cribb looked at the screws of the coffin. 'Bloody Philips screws anyway.' He paused. 'We could always… um… try another way.'

'How, Tony?'

There was a tinkling sound from outside the church door. 'That's Agatha's bicycle,' Lucas said. 'If she's here the other flower ladies can't be far behind. If they should see us… Shouldn't we just take him back before the bearers return?'

'And live in doubt for the rest of our lives? Vicar?'

'Quickly, then. Into the vestry with it.'

They manhandled the coffin into the vestry and pulled the curtains.

'Look,' Tony said.' In my car I've got a drill. Only needs a little hole.'

'I can't permit…'

'Body there, put it back. Something else, well…'

Using the vestry's side door, Crib fetched his electric drill and made a small hole just below the lid of the coffin. Then he inserted the serpentine length of fibre-optic cable attached to a small screen. 'Bloody hell!'

'What do you see?'

'Wonderful things! Cups, plates… candlesticks…'

'Chalices?'

'Come again? Yeah, them too.'

'Let me see.' Lucas peered at the screen. 'This is something for the police, I think.'

'Well, don't let's be hasty about that, Vicar.'

'Those pieces look familiar. Remember the theft at the Minster? Are there gold chalices, by any chance?'

'Could be. Look for yourself.'

'My God, there are.' Lucas was becoming distraught. 'What are we to do?'

'For sure we can't bury them.'

'Assuredly not.'

'So here's how I see it. We take them out. You got space in your chest, Vicar?'

'Well, yes, as it happens, since…'

'Then we weight the coffin with something heavy, seal it up, get the bearers in and away we go. Bob's your uncle.' Crib suddenly became serious. 'After all, no-one's going to enquire into stolen goods, are they? At least not yet. Then you sleep on it, and tomorrow you'll come up with a solution.'

As they transferred the silver to the chest Tony examined the two golden chalices. Ignorant of such matters he failed to notice that each was of an unusual design and featured a glass bottom.

Their work done, they manhandled the now slightly lighter coffin back into the nave, just in time before the bearers came looking for it.

That night, back in the vicarage, sleep was even harder for Lucas to achieve than deciding on a course of action. He couldn't get out of his head that the coffin – which he believed was now six feet under the earth – contained half an oak beam from the belfry, a coil of rope and two bags of bat droppings strategically placed to limit possible movement inside when they carried it back. Then there was Aunt Ada's barely concealed satisfaction as the earth closed over the coffin. And he had never seen Tony Crib looking so… well… innocent as when he tossed in the last handful of earth.

The key from the chest seemed to grow under his pillow. Yet wasn't there some kind of logic here, some ordering of events that smacked of a controlling hand besides his own, or even that of the felons – whoever they were – who had used the undertakers for their nefarious work, if indeed it had not been the undertakers themselves. When he'd… well… found a home for the plate from his own church, was this not so that repairs to the roof – so necessary to keep out the dripping water that week by week had reduced his congregation – could be effected? No worse, surely, than selling indulgences in medieval times. And the resignations of the two churchwardens just before it happened, so that no-one thought to compile the annual inventory – was that not more than just fortuitous? And now here was his chest replenished, as it were. Ignoring for a moment the one or two clearly identifiable pieces, the contents of the collection looked much the same as they had done before. In short, no-one would be the wiser. Only then, with that resolved, did he think to wonder what might have happened to poor Harvey Crib's body. Hopefully it had found its way to the crematorium – but that was someone else's concern.

After breakfast Lucas thought he would take a stroll in the churchyard, if only to stifle a little niggle that all might not be as he remembered it. He headed for the grave, now a raised mound of earth, still waiting to be set off by the headstone that he knew would never come. But he failed to notice that the flowers from yesterday were not quite in their original positions, nor the little spoils of earth trampled by heavy feet around the mound's edge when yesterday the grass had been raked clean. It was then that he saw Tony watching him from the other side of the graveyard hedge. Lucas walked over to him.

'A very good morning to you, Anthony. The golden sun shines upon us, I believe.'

'You could say that, Vicar. And so quiet here this fine morning – after yesterday. One might almost say that silence is golden, if you take my meaning.'

'I'm not quite with you, Anthony.'

'Only that discretion sometimes merits reward.'

'Ah. I see. By golden you mean…'

Tony beamed. 'Got there in one.'

They walked together to the church door. Lucas took out his keys and turned the lock. All was as it had been; enhanced, even, by the flowers that the good ladies had placed there the previous afternoon. He glanced up at the figure of Christ, half-expecting a turn of the head and a reproving look; but none came. Tony was already in the vestry, contemplating the chest, fidgeting in anticipation. When the great doors swung open, there was the silver plate, exactly as it had been. Tony reached in, removed the two golden chalices and clutched them to his chest. 'Episode closed?' Lucas said.

'Indeed. But has it not occurred to you, Vicar, to wonder where Harvey actually is?'

'The undertakers must surely have…'

'Found alternative accommodation? Maybe. But I should tell you, Vicar, that I believe what we buried yesterday was replaced during the night. I watched from the other side of the hedge. Very discreet they were about it.'

'Palin there?'

'I believe I saw him, yes. With two others.'

'So you think he's under there after all, your uncle Harvey?'

'I think so.'

'Then doesn't that deserve a prayer, Anthony, by the graveside?'

'A short one then, Vicar. And this evening perhaps a little refreshment at the vicarage?' He patted his pockets where the two golden chalices were concealed.

'You'll be most welcome.'

Lucas felt that a burden had been lifter from his shoulders. He spent the rest of the day in the vicarage garden, tending the roses. In the afternoon, in an unprecedented act of cordiality, he invited Mrs Webley to take tea with him. They mused upon many things: the incompetence of the new churchwardens, the cost of flowers to beautify the church – and then the unexplained thefts from the minster church, at which point he sent her home. As evening approached he fetched two bottles of his finest claret from the extensive cellars under the building and in the dying light opened them to allow the wine to breathe. Tony appeared just as he was setting glasses upon the table on the veranda.

'I think we can dispense with those, don't you, Vicar?' Tony said, producing from his pockets the two golden chalices.

Lucas poured wine into each chalice. The light was fading now and he switched on the veranda lamp that, coincidently, was across from where he was sitting. They toasted each other's good fortune. But as Lucas raised the near-drained chalice to his lips the translucent disc at its bottom caught the light. And there, etched in the glass, was an image of Harvey's grinning face.

INTERCITY TRAINS

Every morning the clatter of the postman's bicycle as it sped up the drive to Partridge Farm was Gabriel Broadacre's cue to stand behind the ancient oak door and wait for the letters to fall. But today he was disappointed: there were no new subsidy payments for land left fallow, no fat cheques from the sugar beet factory; instead, just a simple envelope in the palest shade of mauve, addressed to his daughter Claire. Without even having to stoop he was able to make out the florid imprint that read *Dreamtime Model Agency* and knew what that portended. He picked up the envelope and flapped it noisily against the fingers of his other hand while he watched the ducks on the pond outside and sensed a threat to a way of life that had been sustained for generations. For one brief moment he grasped the envelope roughly in his two hands as if to tear it apart, then relented in the realisation that this might just be the first in a flood which he would be powerless to stem. Hearing a sound in the hall, he turned to see Claire standing behind him, her eyes sparkling within a pale oval face framed by long golden hair. Meekly he handed her the letter. 'I think it's what you've been waiting for, love,' he said, and turned away so that she could not see his apprehension.

Claire was not to blame, of course, just as she had not

been to blame for the nights on the tiles, the wild parties in her parents' absence and, earlier in the summer, certain wilful extravagances in Ibiza. They were all the influences of others. And if that boyfriend of hers, Scott Richards, had not sent off those photographs – he shuddered at the memory of seeing certain details of her scantily clad body for the first time – she might still be what he had always intended for her, the future wife of a local beet farmer.

'My appointment's on Tuesday,' she said. 'At ten in the morning, in Colchester.'

'Then I suppose I'll have to take you,' Gabriel replied. 'That's no place for a seventeen-year-old to be on her own.'

'Daddy, Daddy, that will give us the whole weekend to go out and buy new clothes.'

And that's why, on the Tuesday morning, the pair found themselves on the 'up' platform of the local station waiting for the 7.49 intercity train to Liverpool Street, via Colchester, toeing the yellow line like the hordes of London commuters around them.

Gabriel, in spite of the black suit that he kept for funerals and the spotted blue tie he had stolen from the wardrobe of his son Tom, felt himself as conspicuous as a lighthouse in a storm. Nor was this feeling lessened by Claire's presence beside him. He had the distinct impression that several of his fellow travellers were marching up and down the platform for the sole purpose of ogling her. He reflected upon the milk churns that had once stood waiting on this same platform and wondered how it was possible that these foreigners could so comprehensively have invaded the county of Norfolk. After the train pulled in they all stood aside to let Claire step into the carriage, but then closed around her before he could follow. A hatred for this modern world into which he had been thrust welled up inside him.

The carriage was not quite full, even after their companions had jostled amongst themselves to be seated. There were only two unoccupied seats together and on one of these lay a large dark blue travelling bag, apparently belonging to a young man of Middle Eastern appearance sitting across the table. Gabriel fixed him with an expressionless stare designed to offer an opportunity to remove the offending article. He took in the dark blue suit – for which the bag seemed a deliberate match – the creamy silk shirt and the spotted tie that outclassed his own. He noted the trimmed and parted black hair, and the neatly sculpted black fur between the mouth and the chin that was a mockery of a beard. There was a laptop computer on the table in front of him and his thoughts seemed remote from the world that Gabriel and his daughter inhabited.

'My daughter and I would like to sit here, if you please,' Gabriel said, in a voice that was neither his own, not that of the culture he was trying to imitate.

Suddenly the man seemed to realise he was being addressed. 'I beg your pardon?' he said, without changing his expression, or looking up.

'Please remove your bag, Sir, so that we can sit down.'

'Oh, of course, of course. Not a problem.' The man was with them now, and apologetic.

He began to rise but Gabriel motioned him to remain seated. 'Let me do it for you,' he said, grasping the handles of the bag and swinging it up upwards onto the luggage rack. There was a look of acute alarm on the man's face as he rose to a half-standing position with his mouth open. 'Please be very…,' he began and then stopped as Gabriel punched the bag twice with his fist to force it into the limited space.

'There,' Gabriel said, 'that wasn't too difficult, now was it?'

'Thank you,' the man replied, sitting down gingerly. 'I am grateful.'

The tapping into the laptop resumed with a nonchalance that Gabriel found offensive. Remembering that he had brought a newspaper with him, he removed it from his pocket. With as much noise as he could manage, he unfolded it and placed it on the table beside the laptop, part of which became obscured by the rustling sheets. After a few seconds he judged that enough time had elapsed for the point to be made. 'I do beg your pardon,' he said, flapping the paper over with much gusto before folding it flat on the table.

'It's not a problem,' their companion replied, in a manner that seemed to negate Gabriel's easily-won advantage.

The train entered a tunnel. When they emerged into the bright sunlight Gabriel became aware that something had changed. The man was no longer concerned with his laptop, but was looking directly at Claire. A small, sly smile moved across his lips. Gabriel looked at his daughter and was horrified to see the same conniving expression replicated on her own fair face. Instinctively he moved his head sideways and downwards to see below the table, but the geometry was wrong. He felt powerless and breathed heavily. Then, to his horror, the man had the impudence to ask Claire where she was going.

'I'm going to be a model,' she said.

'That doesn't surprise me,' the man replied.

'What do you do?' Claire asked.

'I? I am a consultant, with a special interest in railways. I advise colleagues on the logistics of rail movements – timings, capacities, that sort of thing.'

'Is that what you're doing on your laptop?' Claire asked.

He turned the computer through ninety degrees, but away from Gabriel. 'This is the route we are on,' he said.

'I can tell you where we will be at any moment, almost to the second. And here – you see these rectangles? – these are other trains on this line. Did you know that each of the trains at this time of day can carry up to one thousand people? When you get two trains running side by side – like they will be here – you get the highest density of human bodies on earth.'

'That's really interesting,' Claire said. Gabriel thought that she meant it. She turned to him and smiled. 'Isn't it, Dad?'

The man told her that he worked in London and had travelled to Norwich to discuss railway matters with colleagues there. 'We go there sometimes,' Claire said, 'but I've only been to London once.'

'Then we'll have to do something about that, won't we?' the man replied.

'That would be *great*,' Claire said dreamily.

Gabriel's wordless attempts to attract the attention of these young people proved fruitless. He snorted noisily to himself, picked up his paper and rustled it. 'Best get yourself ready,' he said to Claire. 'it's Colchester coming up.'

They had to battle against another influx of commuters. When Gabriel looked back into the carriage he could no longer see the young man and suddenly felt relieved.

The time was still only 8.45, so they found a table in the cafeteria and Gabriel brought coffees and a cake for Claire. She took a sip from the cup, then excused herself and made for the toilet carrying her make-up bag. Gabriel leaned back in his chair to watch *Sky News* on a screen opposite. It held little interest. The goings-on at Westminster were a world away. He hankered after his radio and *Farming Today*. Then, on the screen, were images of police on the streets and around stations. A voice-over warned the public to be especially vigilant, it being the anniversary of some atrocity or other. He was glad that these days he never went to the city.

Then, there she was coming back towards him, his bright spruced-up smiling daughter, about to embark on a career that even he had to admit might suit her. There was a lightness in her step and an elegance about her that heralded the onset of womanhood. In his own youth it had been an experience of a most transitory kind, before his young and promising new wife had been caught in the clutches of the beet industry. He saw the first glimmer of light in the release that this turn of the wheel seemed to be offering, a chink in the armour of his determined resistance to change. He thought that when Claire was occupied with her photo-shoot he would see what suits Marks and Spencer might have, perhaps even saunter further down the High Street to look at what else was on offer. Then there was the matter of a present for his wife, which he always brought back when he travelled this far afield. Life was perhaps not as bad as he had thought.

Then his heart sank. There, behind Claire, his dark head half obscured by hers, was the young man from the train. How could that be possible? Perhaps he had been foolish to assume that the man had been destined for the capital. Maybe, after all, there were railway matters of great importance to be considered at Colchester. The couple approached the table. Gabriel saw that the man was clutching his laptop computer.

'It's alright if Ahmed joins us, isn't it, Father?'

'It's a free country,' Gabriel replied, trying to appear disinterested but inwardly seething. 'Remember that we need to be going in a moment.'

Ahmed sat between Claire and her father and placed his

laptop on the table. Almost immediately there was the jingle of a mobile phone from his pocket. As he answered it he looked closely at his watch. There was a brief exchange in a language Gabriel did not recognise. A smile of immense satisfaction spread across Ahmed's face. He looked at his watch again, but this time more intently and appearing to follow the movement of the second hand. Then, to Gabriel's surprise, he handed the older man the mobile. 'Stupidly I left my reading glasses on the train,' he said. 'Would you be so kind as to dial that number for me?' He pointed to a number typed on a tiny piece of paper stuck to the casing with tape.

Caught unawares, Gabriel took the phone and sat clutching it sheepishly, not knowing what do, or how to give it back without loss of face.

'Go on Dad, ring it,' Claire said.

'Funny number that,' Gabriel said, perplexed.

'It's a mobile number,' Clare explained, 'you should know that!'

'Well, okay then.' With clumsy fingers Gabriel entered the number and held the mobile to his ear. 'It doesn't seem to be ringing,' he said.

'That's not entirely unexpected,' Ahmed replied.

With a movement of his body indicative of supreme satisfaction Ahmed leaned back in his chair. Without looking at Gabriel he held out his hand for the mobile. There was a finality in this gesture which suggested that something of great moment had been accomplished. He turned to look at Gabriel. 'You have done me – us – a great service,' he said. But it was not gratitude that Gabriel saw in the man's expression, more like revenge. Ahmed looked at his watch again, and to Claire said, 'It has been the greatest of pleasures meeting you. I feel sure we shall meet again.'

To Gabriel he said nothing. Then he rose, grasped his laptop and left them. 'I've another train to catch,' he mumbled.

'Well, what was all that about?' Gabriel exclaimed.

'He was nice,' Claire said.

'Anyway, he's gone and we've got to get to where you're going. Come on, young lady.'

They walked out slowly beneath the television screen. As they did so the news item seemed to change. The presenters – a man and a woman – looked concerned in a way that was momentarily personal and somehow unprofessional. A red band appeared with a message that said *breaking news*. 'News is coming in,' the male presenter said, 'of a major rail accident outside London.' The camera swung onto his female companion. 'We are hearing that at about 8.57 a commuter train bound for Liverpool Street...'

'My God,' Gabriel said. 'Another one. What is this country coming to.'

'We'll have to find out later, Dad,' Claire said, pulling at his hand. 'Otherwise I'll be late.'

They walked out of the station into the sunlight. Gabriel thought again about the suits he would see in the High Street. It suddenly occurred to him that the father of a model might have responsibilities that were not necessarily negative. He called a taxi and, hearing himself critically for the first time, thought that he might do worse than to take the edge off his Norfolk accent. This new life might have possibilities after all.

'No luggage, Sir?' the taxi driver asked casually.

Luggage? The dim remembrance of the impact of his fist upon a blue travelling bag on a luggage rack entered his mind. Well, that might have been coincidence. The man might have put it in left luggage. But then he remembered Ahmed's anxious glancing at his watch and the sly grin as he handed Gabriel the mobile phone. He saw in his mind the hands of the clock on the cafeteria wall as they left, and calculated backwards through the five minutes to the time just before the young man had left them.

Gabriel felt a sharp burning pain in the tip of his index finger – the finger that had touched the last of the digits. He remembered particularly straining to hear the ring tone that did not come.

He felt his body swaying and clutched wildly at the top of the open taxi door.

The radio in the cab was playing.

'They've really done it his time, the bastards,' the cabby said. 'Two trains at once, passing each other apparently.'

MUNTJAC

Christopher's morning had not been kind. First it was Alice from the almoner's office, stepping uninvited into the notional space around the table that was barred to all but himself when an autopsy was in progress. Then there was Bertie, his assistant, clattering about on the second table, saw and chisel in hand, as if he were in a calypso band. Fortunately there were no police today. Time, then, for one more body before lunch with Alice.

Though the instruments were already laid out for him, he rearranged them – unnecessarily, as he always did – in accordance with that tiny manifestation of autism known only to his family. He called for Bertie to help him pull out the drawer and together they manoeuvred the ice-cold cadaver onto the stainless steel table. Then he remembered it was the one with the curious history.

It was clear the man had died through asphyxiation caused by vomit blocking the airways. What had caused that was not immediately apparent. It was a while after he started probing the stomach contents that he found it, the object that would transform his day: a tiny glistening ball hardly larger than a pea that dropped from his forceps and tinkled across the steel surface before coming to rest on what he saw was one of its many faceted surfaces. It first crossed his mind that the object was a perfectly cut diamond, so brightly did it refract the light from the lamp above, but on closer inspection there was no doubt it was metallic. He looked up once to see Alice gesticulating at the partition window, then waved her away and put it from his mind that they had agreed to lunch together.

Under his magnifying lens the object was not just a simple sphere. The colour of each of the many facets was distinctly unique and beneath the surface of each he believed he could see – although sense was probably a better word – tiny oscillations in the refracted light. A cloud began to form before his eyes, followed by a throbbing at each temple. But that was just the beginning.

No-one saw – not even Alice – that when they lifted him from the floor the metal sphere rolled as if propelled by its own energy along the gully and into the drain, from which – although of course no-one looked for it – it was never recovered.

Exactly a week later Christopher – or rather his cadaver – suffered the indignity of being autopsied on the very same table. And then Bertie took Alice for lunch.

The Robinsons had moved to Suffolk in anticipation of their joint retirements. For George it was a logical progression from the chic, but rather dismal, town house in Hackney to a listed farmhouse with three acres where he could bed himself in for retirement. Alma accompanied him reluctantly, not realising that the bane of her life, the urban fox – one of which had threatened their grandson Tommy in his pram – had country cousins with a taste for guinea fowl and chickens. That was minor, though, compared with a new arrival some two years into their *translatio in paradisum*. There had been odd sightings of the hound-like creature –

hardly a deer at all – in the village, but it was only when, one morning, George found his rose-heads decimated and the agapanthus leaves truncated – with characteristic teeth marks – that they knew there was a problem. At first seldom seen, the sand-coloured beasts quickly became less timid. In full view of the house they cropped the lower strata of the laurel bushes, so that the animals lurking in the undergrowth became more visible below the browsing line. And so with the vegetables. The one obvious solution – to fence the garden – failed at the first hurdle when George paced out the quarter-mile perimeter and Alma resolutely refused to forego their holiday in Ibiza to meet the cost. So they fell back on simple solutions: devices which emitted frequencies that allegedly only deer could hear; talking boxes that only excited curiosity; and, as a last resort, an imitation fox that jumped out of a box to flashing lights when triggered by movement (usually George's). By the end of the summer the muntjacs – which had now multiplied alarmingly – showed only disdain, while the bird population, to Alma's dismay, had upped and left. In a last desperate measure George fenced the flower and vegetable beds with wire netting, but admitted defeat when one of the creatures, having jumped the fence, had caught its leg in the netting when chased by George and had to be cut free, to the sound of loud bellows from both parties.

So ended the first skirmishes in the war of attrition. George and Alma spent the winter thinking laterally and seeking help on-line. Following the advice of the Royal Horticultural Society to plant species that muntjacs don't like (prefer would be a better term), following radical replanting in the spring the garden took on a more homogenous look with the proliferation of thorn-bearing and dull-leaved shrubs. The result was that the browsing line of the specimens that had survived had become higher. 'They can stand on their back feet,' Alma exclaimed, realising that the heavily-blossomed branches of the potentially fruit-laden trees would sooner or later come within reach.

'It's your mind-set that needs to change,' Ferdinand, their neighbour, told them. Think of them as an asset, a decorative addition to your estate, to be cherished.' George thought he saw Ferdinand try to stifle a guffaw of laughter as he turned to walk away, but Alma had grasped the message. 'They are rather cute, aren't they George? And have you seen the little ones – they're *so* sweet.'

But George had one last ace up his sleeve. 'They can't abide male pheromones,' a guest at one of their dinner parties had told them. 'They see you as territorial – perhaps even sexual – competitors.' So while it was still light, and foregoing their desserts (although imbibing an extra glass of beer each), the males, young and old, tramped into the garden, stationed themselves strategically along the flower and vegetable beds, and freely urinated. The following morning George pulled the bedroom curtains apart to reveal two stags locked in combat on the lawn. It was then that he realised outside help was needed.

It came in the form of a master's degree student from the department of animal behaviour at Avonbridge Polytechnic. Wayne Parfitt was looking for a project for his second year dissertation. 'One of our brightest stars,' his tutor had assured George, adding, 'Something of an oddball, though.' Against Alma's better judgement, George invited him to stay. That first morning, over coffee in the kitchen, Wayne expounded his theory of niche adaptation, for which the muntjac deer afforded an unparalleled example. This was partly because the whole population – now expanding rapidly across southern England – was derived from a single escapee from a herd imported from China, known to Wayne and his companions as Fleance. 'When you eliminate genetic variability,' Wayne said, 'the data is so much more robust.' George could just about see that. Alma was more impressed by Wayne's apparent affinity with Shakespeare, which to George was at odds with the dreadlocks, rings in the ears and bangles at the wrist. But in spite of that they gave him the room vacated by the couple's teenage son Tommy, who was at boarding school. Wayne kept himself to himself, at least at the beginning.

Each morning George would watch Wayne from his study in the turret of the west wing, from which the expanse of the encircling lawn was fully visible. He saw Wayne pace a full circuit around the house, following the tracks in the grass made by the muntjacs – bare streaks of exposed earth that had long eluded an explanation. 'Creatures of habit,' Wayne said. 'Same pattern every day.' 'And at the same time?' George asked, not really caring. Before long a map had appeared taped to the refrigerator door alongside a note to the family requesting the addition of the times of sightings. Unlike George, who saw no practical outcome to this exercise, Alma was becoming enthused, which may have had more to do with an infatuation – in a very minor way of course – with Wayne. Daily and religiously she entered her data, and on the fourth day stood back astonished. The entries for the point of vantage of the morning room were identical to within minutes. But what was more surprising, those were the only times when she had been present in the room, to rest her feet and peruse the scandal pages of the daily paper. She, like the muntjacs, was a creature of habit. She offered Wayne a coffee and was slightly put out that he for once gave more attention to his results than to her.

The following day Alma made a small detour to pass by

George's study on her way to the morning room. There he was, head down over his accounts, dead to the rest of the world. She could see beyond him into the garden and held her breath. And sure enough the same creature as before, as if on cue, emerged from the undergrowth and sidled across the lawn. It stopped momentarily, as if an intoxicating perfume had wafted for an instant across its nostrils, and then continued on. Alma moved to the morning room. 'It showed no interest in your husband?' Wayne asked. 'No,' Alma said.

Outside the morning room window the deer was idly nibbling the grass. As Alma gazed out it raised its head and engaged her in a fixed stare. Alma experienced a moment of elation, as if something of great significance had passed between them.

Then the link was broken as Fleance – for that's what they now called him – resumed cropping the grass.

'They do that – just stand and stare,' Wayne said. Then he thought for a moment. 'What I'd like to do,' he continued, 'is measure the stare time. Would give me data for another table, and you can't have too many of those.' He gave Alma a stop-watch and over the next five days she recorded the stare times meticulously. On the sixth day Wayne plotted them on a graph. It showed a consistent, if miniscule, increment one day upon the next. 'Curiouser and curiouser,' he said.

The following week George was summoned to the Department of Extra-terrestrial Exploration, where he had been retained as a consultant – and where he and Alma had met while in their thirties. Alma, to some the more gifted of the two, had declined a similar appointment, but in bed every evening they would discuss the affairs of the department. George's speciality – and what made him an asset – was an overt scepticism to anything that contravened conventional wisdom. So when, years back now, public awareness had been inflamed by reports of alleged extra-terrestrial phenomena – including a few ridiculous accounts of alien landings – George, in his letters to *The Times*, had scathingly extinguished the issue. But it seemed not quite, and it was surmised that there had been a rash of recent sightings. In all this Alma, the more open-minded of the two, had remained neutral. But, fancying a couple of days in London, she decided to accompany George.

When she returned home ahead of her husband Wayne was waiting at the door. 'Funny thing,' he said, 'when you were gone Fleance showed no interest outside the morning room. He just nibbled the grass a bit and continued on. It will be interesting to see what he does now you are back.' At this suggestion Alma felt a sudden delicious spurt of anticipation. 'I'm looking forward to it,' she said, then chided herself inwardly for being irrational. But, stopwatch in hand, she resumed her former relationship with Fleance. Strangely, the stare times had increased and after each communication – for that was the word that sprang to mind – she'd felt increasingly queasy and had to lie down.

'I've... er... been asking around,' Wayne said at dinner. 'Seems you're not alone in... well... getting their attention. I've had some mates do some recordings. There's a village in Berkshire, same thing, same results, and another in Sussex. Here's a list. I'm waiting for others to come in.' Alma's ears pricked up. 'Those names ring a bell. Don't they with you, George? Aren't they villages that had... well... sightings?' 'Just coincidence,' George said. 'Nothing more. Get it out of your heads, both of you.'

But Wayne couldn't get it out of his head, nor could he sleep. So tempting was the hypothesis that was forming in his brain that he'd managed to persuade his supervisor to allow him to convert his master's to a PhD. 'What you've got there,' his supervisor said, 'is a population ever expanding into the community and increasing their exposure to human behaviour by exploiting conducive habitats and territorial riches.' And Wayne saw that the very places the muntjacs chose to colonise were precisely those where human intellect – and therefore position in society – was of the highest calibre: big houses in big gardens in affluent areas. Why?

Wayne applied his mind to the problem. He realised there were two contributors to this relationship he was observing. So he took to watching Alma's response to Fleance's presence. As the animal appeared in the frame of the window Alma's eyes glazed over, as if in a trance. Wayne looked from one to the other with increasing rapidity. Something had passed between the two, of that he was sure. And more significant still there was a time-lag – in milliseconds, it is true, but there all the same – between Fleance's averting his gaze and Alma's countenance returning to normal. It could mean only one thing: Fleance was in control.

That night, with George still away, Wayne bedded Alma. Her outpourings of affection were peppered with nuggets of pure gold minted from George's revelations about recent supposed extra-terrestrial happenings. Before even Alma awoke Wayne was at his desk superimposing that map upon another showing the spread of the muntjac population. Surely there was a correlation. He saw in his mind the beaming face of the vice-chancellor as he received his doctorate – and the customers in W H Smith as they flicked through copies of *Nature* in search of his paper. These were thoughts he had to share; rashly, he shared them with Alma.

George returned to an atmosphere pregnant with expectation. Quietly entering the morning room he observed his wife staring through the window. Wayne was beside her, with an arm around her waist and a stop-watch in his hand. George withdrew silently to his study, removed his shotgun from the wall safe, then had a strong coffee to steady his nerves as he laid his plans.

For many weeks the following Saturday evening had been earmarked for a barbeque in the garden. George's recent trip to London explained the invitation of a number of professional colleagues not on the original list. 'Leave the arrangements to me,' he told a mildly surprised Alma that morning, 'but you could help by getting a few more things from the supermarket.' Reluctantly Alma agreed, accepting that for once her relationship with Fleance could withstand a missing session. 'Take Wayne,' George said. 'Strong lad, he can carry the drinks.'

While Alma and Wayne were away, George shot Fleance.

The evening promised to be a great success. The weather had held and all in the garden glowed with that enchanting pale yellow-pink light unique to an Indian summer. Heavily spiced steaks and burgers sizzled over greying charcoal. Lightly browned chicken legs and sausages were tastefully arranged on the hot plate. And there were other treats besides. George's speciality had always been to surprise his guests with the unexpected, and tonight he produced an old favourite of Alma's: brains deep fried in brown butter with herbs and capers, thick succulent slices of which nestled temptingly amongst the other meats and delicacies. The guests approached in single file, and George filled their plates before dispatching them to the chips and salads.

No-one enjoyed a joke more than George, but in his experience such things were never to be rushed. When all his guests had loaded their plates he made sure Alma and Wayne were served generously. With an amused smile he savoured the appreciative grunts of pleasure. Now, surely, was the time to tell. He clapped his hands for attention, lifted his plate, chose the juiciest morsel from it and began to chew with an exaggerated expression of delight. 'I invite you all to guess…' he began. But no-one could because at that moment the plate fell from his hands. He began to choke, and then cough violently. His face turned purple, his eyes rotated heavenwards. He fell to the ground…

In the commotion that followed few noticed the several pairs of eyes fixed upon them, deep within the recesses of the laurel bushes. As Wayne remarked later, they were probably choosing Fleance's successor.

THE CHAPEL OF ANTONIS STAVROS

The Pelion Peninsula points like a fingerless appendage towards the islands of the western Aegean Sea. At its shoulder the town of Volos and, to its east, the bare mass of Mount Pelion guard its forested spine and fringing beaches against all but the more adventurous of travellers. For the previous two summers the Maxwells had holidayed there, benefiting from the seclusion and tranquillity. For Hugh Maxwell it had seemed a salve for an incident that had blighted the twilight of his career as a High Court judge, when he had, against his better judgement, presided over the conviction and hanging of an innocent man. But over the course of an otherwise successful career he had built up a resistance to the personal consequences of occasional errors and could live with it. Not so his young wife Emma, who knew more of the background to the case than she could comfortably bear. Nevertheless they stayed together. Their decision to purchase and renovate an old farmhouse had been shared, up to a point, though Emma had puzzled over Hugh's choice of a remote location at the peninsula's southern tip.

In those days – in the early seventies – there were few neighbours, and none close. The farmhouse looked down a deep green valley of mixed deciduous and pine forest leading to the sea a kilometre away. From the tiny harbour a rough and indistinct track led back through an ancient olive grove, then upwards through the trees, passing close to the Maxwell's veranda before continuing more steeply to reach the old monastery of Agia Triada perched precariously high above the house. Referring to the cliff, Emma had once jokingly compared it to a barrier against the traumas of their former life; but Hugh had turned away, unamused.

These days the track saw only the occasional rambler, and it was a while before they learnt from the locals that it was part of a network of pack animal trails, once extensively used, connecting settlements throughout the peninsula. Knowing this, they one day scuffed away the soil and detritus with their feet and were surprised to find a paved – and surprisingly intact and serviceable – surface. But excursions into local history could wait, and they resumed planting the garden with oleanders and frangipani, and trailing bougainvilleas over the veranda trellis. Each evening they would sit with their glasses of rough local wine and thank providence for allowing them a few years yet to enjoy their new-found existence. But the bland deliciousness of it all had its downside in that, for the novel Hugh had promised himself he would write, the moving finger had perceptibly slowed, if not stopped altogether. The hand that should have held the pen more often than not was clutching a wineglass.

From the veranda they would watch the fishing boats in the distance: tiny specks on the deep blue waters beyond the village and its harbour. In the evenings the lights would twinkle dimly, but one evening they were joined by another, bluish and brighter than the rest, that seemed to come from a boat moored a little way out to sea. Emma remembered that moment particularly because it coincided with the first appearance of a person on the track passing the house. The indistinct grey figure had emerged momentarily from the deep shadows beneath the overhanging branches of the chestnut trees.

'Look, Hugh,' she whispered.

The urgency in her voice made him turn. 'What have you seen?'

'A figure, just for an instant, on the old track.'

Hugh peered into the gloom. 'I can't see anything. No-one comes here when it's getting dark. It's just the breeze moving the branches.'

'It stood quite still, watching us. I'm sure of it.'

'I'll get a torch, take a look.'

'No, stay with me. You're not to leave me alone.'

The following morning Hugh and Emma climbed the track to the monastery. Most of the building was hidden behind a formidable rough stone wall. Hugh pulled on a cord beside the studded oak door that somewhere within caused a bell to be struck. A minute later the door swung open to reveal the surprised face of young monk who seemed at first reluctant to admit them. They entered a courtyard neatly laid out with beds of carefully tended vegetables, at odds with the rampant reds and purples of the bougainvilleas clothing the surrounding walls. The monk led them through a door into a dark hallway where another monk, elderly with greying hair and a shrivelled face, introduced himself as Father Petros. 'From my cell I could see you coming up the track,' he said. 'Few people come that way nowadays. It's much easier to reach us from the road higher up the mountain.'

'We did see one person on the track last night,' Emma said cautiously.

'Really, that surprises me. The locals are far too superstitious to use it at night.'

'Perhaps one of your monks…'

'Tucked up in their cells by six. Not possible, I assure you. Sometimes our eyes play tricks on us.'

'Exactly what I told her,' Hugh said.

'I know what I saw.'

'A foolhardy tourist, then,' Father Petros said with a smile, ending the discussion. Now, after some tea I'm sure you would like to see something of our humble community.'

They climbed a flight of steep stone steps leading from the hallway. 'As you see,' Father Petros said, 'much of the building is carved out of the solid rock. We'll begin with the library at the top. My old legs find it easier to do the hard bit first. Once it was the scriptorium – that was when we had fifty monks here and not the present six.'

'But this is a remarkable collection,' Hugh said, running his eye over the many shelves of dusty volumes. 'May I look?'

'Of course, But let me draw your attention to these few volumes,' he said, pointing to half a dozen bound codices on an upper shelf. 'These are why we keep this door locked. They date back to the time of the inquisition.'

'The Spanish Inquisition?' Emma's eyes widened.

'Hardly here,' Father Petros said. 'Inquisitions were common throughout the medieval period, in all sorts of places.' He reached for one of the codices; as he opened it a sheet of parchment fell to the floor. 'This is a summary of the questioning of one of the monks of this monastery. The charges were without foundation but unfortunately that was realised only after it was too late to save him.'

'Was he… tortured?' Emma asked.

'I'll come to that,' Father Petros said, 'when we go downstairs.'

They entered a stone-vaulted room with windows looking out over the valley and the sea. The sole item of furniture, besides a couple of chairs, was a massive wooden table in the centre of the room, placed parallel to the windows. 'We believe this is the actual table used by the inquisitors,' Father Petros said. 'But the brothers fear to come here, so this room is rather wasted.'

'I can imagine the inquisitors sitting with their backs to the sunlight,' Emma said, 'so that their victims couldn't see their faces.' She drew up one of the chairs, in the supposed position of an accused, and looked across to where her husband was observing her from the other side of the table, his face in shadow. 'Uggh!'

'Beneath this room,' Father Petros said, 'is a cellar where we believe… But I'm sure you don't wan't to go there.'

'But I…' Hugh began.

'I think we've already taken too much of the good Father's time,' Emma said. 'I'm sure there will be other occasions.' She looked at Father Petros for acquiescence but was surprised to see no sign of it in his expression.

Father Petros said, 'Should you think of coming again, you would be most welcome to attend when the monks meet for singing liturgical chant. The few visitors that do attend write to us to say what an uplifting experience it has been. I suppose it's our way of communicating with the outside world. The door is left open at such times – you can come straight in.' As he opened the door for them he said, 'Now, as you go back down the track be sure to note the remains of a chapel on your left. It's dedicated to Antonis Stavros, the unfortunate novice we spoke about.' He lowered his voice. 'It's rather grim and partly why the locals choose not to come this way. You hear all sorts of stories, but I'm inclined not to believe any of them. I'd advise you to do the same.'

The chapel turned out to be little more than a pile of rubble and Emma passed it by without further interest.

She was surprised, on looking back, to see Hugh stiffly contemplating the displaced stones, deep in thought.

That night Hugh slept badly. A dream that on previous nights had been a chaotic jumble of indeterminate shapes and colours took more tangible form. Faces dimly familiar but never quite remembered mingled with images of forested mountains and precipitous descents into black and turbulent seas. In the morning Emma told him of his nocturnal sweats and incoherent ramblings. It became the pattern for subsequent nights, except that animate objects in his dreams began to assume more recognisable form. Then one morning he awoke with an after-image of himself sitting at a vast table that remained with him throughout that day. So occupied with it was he that when Emma said she was leaving for her weekly traditional dancing class in a nearby village he was startled by his forgetfulness. Then he realised what he had suppressed during the past few days: an urge to revisit the monastery. Was it just fortuitous, then, that this was the evening when the chanting of the monks would be shared with the public? No, he told himself, and as soon as Emma had gone he locked up the house and set off up the track.

No longer was there the bright sunshine of the week before. The freshening wind was already disturbing the boughs of the chestnut trees and the tips of the pines were bending perceptibly. And was the light really beginning to fade this early? He drew level with the ruined chapel, keeping well to the opposite side of the track. He looked around for the figure that he only half-believed Emma had seen.

As soon as he pushed open the door in the wall of the monastery he could hear the chanting from the chapel. But he had no intention of going there and tiptoed past into the hallway where Father Petros had first greeted them.

He was surprised to find the door of the inquisition room unlocked. Funny how just looking at that massive table could conjure up images from his past, as if its surface had been impregnated with some invisible substance that had 'legal persecution' written on its jar. He thought of Tony Savage, one of the last men in England to have been hanged, and it came back to him how he had allowed the man's arrogance in the dock to sway his summing up to the jury. And how, before the verdict was given, he had read innocence in the man's eyes – and seen disbelief and hatred in the eyes of the family in the gallery above. He drew up a chair to sit at the centre of the table with the light behind him and wondered if the inquisitor who had faced Antonis Stavros had entertained similar doubts. He withdrew from his pocket the fragment of parchment that he had taken from the codex in the scriptorium, and had perused in secret during the days since. He spread it flat on the table. So powerful were the words of incrimination it contained that he looked up sharply, as if to see the novice monk's face crease up in terror while his own expression was concealed by shadow. Involuntarily he pointed a finger and felt, as much as heard, himself say the words 'take him down for torture.' His gaze drifted across the room to where a small door gave access to the cellar below. He rose, walked to it and pulled at the handle; but like the door to the inquisition room it was unlocked. Hearing heavy footsteps in the hallway outside he closed the door behind him and descended the narrow staircase between walls damp with mould that brushed his shoulders.

He reached a rock-hewn chamber – more a cave than a room – with a masonry wall on the side facing the valley and the sea, in which a tiny aperture high up was the only source of light. He let his eyes wander over the rusted metal implements laid out, as if ready for use, on a stone bench and on the floor. Terrible though the scene was, he had, somehow, known what to expect. He fingered each object in the sure knowledge of what had been its purpose and how it had been used. Waves of remorse swept through his body. He needed air, but knew he could not return to the room above, having no believable excuse to be found there. He took hold of a stool – the stool on which…? – and placed it against the masonry wall. Stretching his body upwards he could just apply his face to the aperture. He could see below him the headlights of what must have been Emma's car returning and down the valley to the little fishing village, beyond which the solitary pale blue light seemed to burn with greater intensity. Then, for what reason he would never be in a position to know, the structure of the wooden stool on which he was standing gave way, sending him crashing to the floor.

An hour after her return, and having searched the house desperately for a note, Emma's predicament seemed dire. Hugh's absence was inexplicable; however strange his behaviour over the past few days had been she knew he would never leave her by herself. It was the nightmare scenario she had raised with him time and time again when they were still contemplating buying the house, because of its remoteness and lack of a telephone. Her first reaction had been to drive back to the village she'd left, but the petrol guage showed empty – her own fault for not filling up when she had the chance – and she had no idea were Hugh kept the spare can, even if there was one. Worse still, when she'd made the decision to risk it, she found one of the tyres was flat. Believing that these elements were conspiring against her in a way somehow ordained she poured herself a whisky and sat on the veranda, drumming her fingers on the table surface. Then, just as she raised the glass to her lips there was a frisson in the vegetation beside the old trackway. She felt the presence of the figure she had seen a week before. She needed help, and the only help available lay two hundred yards further up that abominable track. She walked around the house and let her eyes follow the cliff face upwards to where a single faint light – surely in Father Petros' cell – was burning. For all its terrors, that was a better option than remaining where she was. Taking a torch she set off up the track.

The ruins of the chapel came upon her jagged and threatening in the torchlight. But her terror was suddenly magnified by something worse. At first it was just a faint movement on the track ahead. Then, silently, there emerged from the darkness a figure leading an animal whose shape at first had no meaning. She shrank back into the vegetation beside the track. The torch slipped from her hand, sending its useless beam deep into the undergrowth. As the pair came closer she saw that the animal was carrying across its back something heavy and bound in sackcloth. Still there was no sound. It had to be that they would stop, having seen her torch, but they pressed on, as if not needing light, taking no notice of her. She tried to call after, but the words were stifled in her throat. Then the pair was gone.

Scrabbling in the undergrowth she recovered her torch and continued up the track. Father Petros must have seen the light from his cell, for he was waiting for her at the open door of the monastery.

Emma woke the following morning to find herself lying on a simple straw mattress covered by a single blanket. The curtains were being drawn back by a woman dressed in the black habit of a nun. Light flooded into the room, hurting her eyes.

'We thought it sensible to let you sleep,' the nun said. 'When you're ready we can go across to Father Petros. He's waiting to speak with you.'

Father Petros handed her a mug of tea. 'I asked Sister Melina to come and look after you. It's lucky the convent is so close. The police are still searching the monastery but so far there's been no sign of your husband. With daylight we should be able to find him.'

'You think he came here?' she asked.

'Well, that's the puzzle. He may have done, but we can't be sure. If you're feeling brave there's something I need to show you.'

In the cellar beneath the inquisition room Emma saw the scattered fragments of the broken stool. 'That's difficult to explain,' Father Patros said, 'but what's more odd is this.' He handed her the fragment of parchment from the codex. 'It was lying on the floor here.'

Emma stared at the piece of parchment, dimly recalling its origin. She handed it back to him. 'Can you tell me what it says?'

'It recounts the fate of the young monk, Antonis Stavros, who was... well... died here. It seems that after his death his body was taken by boat to his home village on the island of Evia, which you can see across the water from here – and from your house. For some reason neither the boat nor Antonis reached their destination. Can you think why that might have interested your husband?'

'I've no idea,' she said. Then it occurred to her to ask, 'If my husband was here, wouldn't he have been seen coming out?'

'You'd think so, especially as there were people in the

hallway most of the time. Perhaps I shouldn't tell you this, but one of the monks said he thought he heard a noise, possibly a scream. But of course he could have been mistaken. After that there were people about all the time.'

The police search continued, but Emma knew there was no point in telling them what in her heart she knew would never be believed. The investigations would have to run their course, then be quietly forgotten amongst the records of lost persons. Sister Melina stayed with her that day and into the evening, by which time a friend from Volos – Carol Jackson – had arrived to keep her company. They stood together on the veranda, looking down the valley.

'You mentioned a light out to sea,' Sister Melina said, 'but I don't see anything now.'

'I don't suppose you will,' Emma replied.

When Sister Melina had gone Carol said, 'I'm sure the police will find Hugh in the morning.'

'Perhaps,' Emma said, not really listening. Instead she was thumbing through a notebook she had picked up from the coffee table.

'What's that?' Carol asked.

'It's Hugh's address book. You may not remember Graham Spooner...'

'The barrister?'

'Right. He was the chief prosecutor at Tony Savage's trial. The conviction against the odds threw him into the spotlight. It boosted his career – which is more than can be said of my husband's. As it happens they were close friends, in spite of Hugh being heavily in debt to him. I thought I'd invite him to the memorial service, assuming we have one.'

'Memorial service? Isn't that a bit premature?'

'Maybe.' Emma paused, at first uncertain whether to continue. 'I think Graham Spooner might be interested to look around the monastery.' She got up and walked to the window, then stood staring out towards the sea. 'I must remember to mention it to Father Petros.'

WINDOW ON THE MIND

The flick of the switch, rather than extinguishing the lights of the primate room, only resulted in a barely perceptible dimming – the simulation of dusk – that would take another half-hour to reach extinction. Alex Parker lingered in the doorway, his finger still on the switch. He stared into the void between the cages banked on either side of the central gangway. Tiny hands clasping the vertical shiny steel bars were all he could see of the monkeys within, but he could still recognise each of them. 'Goodnight Vanessa, Charlie Boy and the rest of you,' he called. He could not tell whether the sudden rattling of the bars was in answer, but he chose to think that tonight – of all nights – it really was.

He had known some of these monkeys since he joined the company as a raw graduate in toxicology almost a decade before. In the early days he had flexed his young muscles, and management, over the years, had made the cages larger and their contents more interesting. As the lot of the animals improved, some of the anger seemed to go out of their eyes. Alex liked to think it was gratitude, but experience told him that for wild animals such as these that could not be so. Still, given the constraints of his work, he thought he had not acquitted himself badly.

Down the corridor his fellow scientists were still busy logging data into their computers. More disciplined than they, he had cleared his own work and closed his terminal. But tonight he was drawn back to it and switched it on. As the dense columns of figures reappeared he flicked the screen with his finger. 'Just has to be,' he whispered to himself. Then he copied the results to disc, switched the machine off and went home.

Alex knew that this departure from his usual routine – fifteen minutes of inconsequential time – would not go unpunished by his wife. The food was already getting cold on the table.

'Have you forgotten Jessica's got her first exam tomorrow?' Margery demanded.

'There were some unusual findings,' Alex said. 'I had to stay.'

Across the table his daughter was sketching aimlessly, from time to time chewing at her pencil. She seemed oblivious to her parents' bickering.

'So what's so new?' Margery persisted. 'The drugs you feed those animals either make them sick or stop them getting that way. What's so different this time?'

Alex swivelled in his chair to avoid the angry eyes that every mealtime now seemed to find a different fuel to burn. The day before it had been their forgotten wedding anniversary, the day before that keeping her waiting in the supermarket car park – trivial things that a more reasonable person might take in their stride. No way would he tempt providence by telling her that he had discovered something quite remarkable, something so unusual that he had even – and for the first time – withheld it from his colleagues.

He studied Jessica's clouded face, then looked at the tense hand clutching the sketch-pad. The pallor of the knuckles almost merged with the whiteness of the paper. 'What's the problem, Jessica?' he asked.

'It just doesn't come,' she replied, her voice trembling with frustration. 'And it's for the bloody exam.'

The rending of the paper as she tore it from the pad echoed his own frustration when his experiments didn't go right. Was it dedication to a subject she loved – or confrontation of an obstacle too difficult to surmount? It was hard to tell. But when she looked at him, the fear – the same primal fear that he had seen in the eyes of his monkeys – told him which it was. At school she had been the most gifted in her year, but they both knew that relinquishing the Oxbridge place that had been within her grasp to study at art college was becoming an unwelcome spectre at the door.

Margery refused to make his usual coffee. He made that an excuse to leave the table and the room.

In the attic, where he kept his computer, he took the disc containing the copied data from his briefcase and inserted it. He stared at the now familiar figures. The monkeys on the highest dose of the drug – developed to restore memory loss in ageing people – had performed the tasks quicker and better. That was not unexpected. But there was something else there, something that suggested more than just an improvement in mental agility. The objects that the animals had been required to position on the touch screen seemed to have been grouped in ways that Alex could explain only in aesthetic terms. The animals appeared to have become creative.

Alex pulled at his desk drawer. Rummaging behind the pens and packets of envelopes he withdrew a bottle of Scotch. Smiling to himself he patted its flat face and replaced it in the drawer. 'Later,' he exclaimed. 'Tonight you have a rival.'

He placed a blank sheet of paper on his desk. From his briefcase he took an unlabelled amber bottle and carefully broke the seal. The pale yellow contents fell like flour onto the paper. With the edge of another sheet he divided the pile, first into two, then into four, and so on until he had many equal mounds. Then he transferred the powder to transparent plastic envelopes, of which he had a copious supply. He half-filled a glass with water intended for the whisky and emptied into it the contents of one of the envelopes. Against the light the scintillating particles rode the vortex, then disappeared. In one determined gulp he drank it down.

Alex was not unprepared for what came next. Only two years before, the company had developed a drug that had reached clinical trials – that is to say it had been tried for the first time in people. But no sooner had that got underway than the long-term toxicity studies in rats showed that the drug could cause blindness. Further development was stopped, but by then Alex had tried it on himself. One morning he had woken to find he could not dissociate his thoughts from the dreams of the night before. For nearly a whole morning he had inhabited a surreal and terrifying world, in which violently complex images fought for possession of his head. When he emerged from his study he could not explain – even to himself – the abrasions on his face and bruises on his body. After that he devised tests to assess his own responses to small doses. One involved the resolution of complex patterns into simpler geometric forms – in which he was surprised to find the classical golden ratio figured prominently – and in another colours and shapes were juxtaposed. In the early days he had tried these tests on his colleagues. But without giving sufficient explanation he had been ridiculed for his efforts.

He withdrew a test sheet from another drawer and began to complete it. He did this with a different sheet every half hour for the next three hours. When he knew that the levels of the drug within his body would be starting to fall he went to bed. To his relief he found Margery asleep. The following morning he felt fine, as if nothing had happened.

Except that it had. In each of the tests he had scored higher than when he had taken similar tests without taking the drug. For the next five days he repeated the exercise each evening, always with the same result. 'You look a bit flushed these days,' Margery told him one morning, but he attributed this to the success of his experiments.

Margery seemed to be recognising other encouraging changes. For example, she had looked at him in bewilderment on finding him glued to the radio and humming along to Messiaen's *Quatuor pour la fin du temps*; and, later, while reading the paper at the kitchen table, tapping out the more complex rhythms of Boulez's *Third Piano Sonata* with his left hand while executing complicated doodles with his right. When he smiled up at her she shied away as if the devil was lurking in his soul. 'What I have to put up with! Will it never end?' he heard her mutter to herself.

At the laboratory he became secretive about the work he was employed to do, then tried to hide his findings. Each day he would get to work before his colleagues to massage the data, at first by changing the odd digit here and there; then, when that didn't seem to make much difference, by repositioning decimal points in a way that could be interpreted as copying errors. He unearthed earlier toxicology data, but there were no records of effects on rats or dogs that even hinted at what he had found in his monkeys. One morning there was a meeting to review progress, and he stayed away feigning migraine, while sending an e-mail to say that his studies had shown nothing of interest. Then, out of the blue, the company ceased development of the drug in a rationalisation of company initiatives. But by this time his attic drawer was well stocked with tiny envelopes containing the pale yellow powder. That evening he felt quite light-headed, as if a weight had been taken from his shoulders.

Each morning during the following weeks Alex rose early to be first in the kitchen. Having taken one of the envelopes from the drawer on his way to breakfast, he would stop on the stairs to inspect Jessica's increasing output that was now spilling into the hall and downstairs rooms. He peered at each new work to judge whether it was better than what had gone before, but usually walked on bemused. He regretted his inability to recognise true artistic merit, having long accepted that Margery – not he – was the likely source of Jessica's ability, limited though it might be. Still, he could see that there were changes, and that at least was good.

Jessica entered her second year at college with an offer of a shared exhibition in a West End gallery. Alex, with a meeting in town, decided to walk past the windows. Then he retraced his steps and went in. 'Abstract modern,' he said, in reply to the salesman's enquiry. 'Then you may just be interested in this, Sir.' 'And the price?' 'Just five thousand guineas. The artist is still relatively unknown but shows *great* promise.' That afternoon, with Jessica and Margery both out, he gave special attention to the contents of Jessica's room.

The light falling from a high window illuminated a grey and hostile interior. To Alex's surprise the bed had been shifted and cringed, unmade, in a corner of the room. A trestle table in the centre was piled high with artists' materials. The curtains from the windows lay crumpled underneath, as if they too were destined to be cut and daubed. The familiar easel now rested forlornly against the wall, giving way to an expanse of floor on which lay stretched a broad sheet of hessian encrusted and pustulous with globs of red and ochre flecked with grey. It reminded Alex of a particularly violent traffic accident. He looked for the conventional painted canvasses and eventually found them face down under the bed. No longer in doubt about his daughter's ability, he still could not see the direction her art was taking. That did not matter though. So long as others could see it, then it was worth going on. Hearing voices in the hall below, he closed the door quietly and crept back up to the attic.

Then, one day, there was a change in the morning ritual. To his surprise he heard Jessica's voice in the kitchen as he made his way slowly past the now diminishing frames on the stairs. He found Margery tipping cornflakes into her bowl. Jessica was already dressed in her long brown smock and seemed to be in a hurry.

'Is coffee ready, dear?' he asked his wife, trying to control his annoyance.

'There,' she replied, waving vaguely in the direction of the pot.

He took the milk from the fridge, put some in his coffee, and stood with his back to them while he filled the jug. Then he placed the jug on the table in front of Jessica. 'Why up so early?' he asked.

'I can get a whole hour in before I catch the bus to college,' she said.

'So things are going well then?'

'I should say! I've got this fantastic idea for a mural – well, more stucco than painting really – in the college hall.'

'And what will it represent?' Alex asked.

'It'll be called *Penitent Care*. You know how the students stand there in order of year. The figures embedded in the wall will show how influences – social pressures, drugs, that sort of thing – are brought to bear upon their sweet and innocent little natures. The figures won't be recognisable as such, just forms expressing their psychophysical degeneration.'

'Has the college commissioned such a thing?'

'No… But it will, when they see the designs. You see…'

'That's enough, Jessica,' Margery interrupted. 'Your father has work to do and so do I. Tell us over dinner.'

Alex wondered how such a work might be executed, and in the days that followed looked in Jessica's studio for clues. The floor became covered in wooden boards bearing clay models which he presumed were forerunners of the figures in her mural. As the days passed, the space became more and more cramped. Then there were signs of frustration and anger. One wall was half covered in a spattering of paint which Alex tried to interpret as a 'work', before realising that it had had the contents of a can thrown at it. Jessica's request at breakfast therefore came as no surprise.

'Things are going so well that I would like to use the spare bedroom,' she announced.

'Well, you can't.' Margery's response was unequivocal.

'But I have to. The college has said I can go ahead.'

'You should have told us,' Alex said. 'That makes a difference.'

'Don't encourage her,' Margery said. 'It's all nonsense.'

'Then just phone the college,' Jessica replied, getting up and leaving the room.

Margery turned on Alex. 'Why do you have to egg her on all the time? You're just an unhealthy influence.'

At Margery's insistence the move to the spare bedroom took place when she and Alex were away for a weekend, and on condition that all was tidy on their return. That condition had been fulfilled but the pair did not anticipate the extent of the changes. The wall between Jessica's room and the spare bedroom had been removed to form a single studio. On the floor lay the design for Jessica's mural. 'It's only a tenth the actual size,' she explained when they returned.

With the construction of fibre-glass moulds and importation into the studio of a miscellany of metal, glass and ceramic fragments, it seemed to Alex that Jessica had at last determined the materials she needed. But there was another aspect of the project that began to concern him. The first intimation came one evening at dinner.

'I would like to see your monkeys,' she told Alex, while pouring gravy over her lamb chops.

'Whatever for?'

'I'm just… well, I'm a bit into neuropharmacology at the moment, what with my project and all that.'

'Well, I suppose…'

'At least it gets her out of the house,' Margery exclaimed. 'All that banging and clattering she does up there.'

It surprised Alex that Jessica's visit to his laboratory was a success. She seemed to captivate his colleagues with her knowledge of drugs and their actions, and impressed them by the time spent with the company librarian. 'That's a gem of a daughter you've got there,' one told him afterwards. 'Following in her father's footsteps?' another asked. He went home with a weakened resolve to indulge his daughter no further.

Not long after, Alex began to have doubts. It was signalled by the installation of several CCTV cameras around the walls of the studio, with their terminal behind a screen in the corner – and a lock on the door. On several occasions he caught his daughter on the stairs carrying a large box – or what he presumed was a box – covered completely in black plastic sheeting. Once he was sure he heard a scuffling noise from within, and he thought instinctively of the bottles of worms and snails that he had seen on the table a fortnight before. Yet, if his hunch was right, these were nothing as lowly as worms.

'I guess you're wondering what I've got in here?' Jessica challenged.

Afraid to be told the truth, he replied meekly, 'More materials, I suppose.'

'Right,' she answered, grinning broadly.

From then on the door of the studio was always locked. 'I'll show it to you when it's finished,' Jessica said. 'Only then will you understand it.'

Alex seldom, if ever, thought about his birthday. He couldn't remember the last time he'd received a present from his wife or daughter, although each always gave him a card. So when the day came he was delighted to get not just a card – this time a futuristic creation by Jessica, with endearing messages from both of them – but the promise of a cake as well. It seemed out of character for them to have combined their efforts in this way, especially given their usual antipathy. That was a little strange, he thought.

They warned him at breakfast that he was not allowed to see the cake until he returned from work. At the kitchen door he looked back to find them exchanging wild glances, silently choking back laughter. When they saw him they waved him away. 'We've still got to make it,' Jessica joked.

That evening, turning the corner of the street, Alex saw a number of passers-by gathered on the pavement, staring at the front of the house. He ran towards them, thinking there had been an accident. Then – just as they had done – he stopped in amazement. The cake stood upon the table in the bay window of the living room, like a Bavarian castle embellished by Disney, its faceted surfaces rising up, reflecting the light of the forty-one candles burning brightly around it.

It would occur to him in his final moments that they knew he could not bring himself to mutilate something so magnificent. That that was why they had made him a miniature version in the form of an exquisite single turret, too small to share, yet… well… expendable. From their chairs across the room they watched him take his first bite, and then another as the excellence of the confection challenged his senses. Against a background of cinnamon and other spices there was another familiar – he could not place it for the moment – taste, smell, whatever. It gave him a sense of well-being and contentment.

Margery looked at him benevolently. 'Now, as an additional treat…'

'As if this isn't enough,' he interjected.

'… Jessica will show you her creation. Actually, she's been waiting for a suitable occasion and decided this had to be it.'

'I'm just sorry it didn't come sooner,' Jessica said.

'That was delicious, thank you.' Alex said, wiping his mouth. 'I'll just go upstairs and put my papers away, then I'll be with you.'

Alex climbed the stairs. The bare walls told him what he had achieved and he began to relish the prospect of being father to so prodigious a talent. He reached the door of the studio and turned the handle, but it was still locked. He walked on, then climbed the final stairs to the attic.

The taste in his mouth, that familiar distinctive, not unpleasant, intensifying taste, not cinnamon, not other spices, not anything known to the culinary repertoire, suddenly drove him to his desk. A sensation just as familiar was creeping into his head, subtly colouring the walls, distorting the straight lines of the furniture and making the room seem to curl and sway. Frantically he pulled at the drawer of the desk. Its contents spewed onto the floor. The whisky bottle rolled away with a clatter that resembled cackling laughter. He scrabbled about amongst the papers, throwing them into the air in desperation. But of the dozens of little polythene envelopes he expected to find, there were just two, as if they had been left deliberately to say that it had all been planned. A kind of 'thank you.'

Staggering now – because he was losing control of his muscles and it was becoming difficult to keep his balance – he clutched the stair rail and somehow reached the floor below. The door, previously so resolutely locked, now stood wide open. He entered cautiously, almost creeping, looking around fearfully, down at the bare floor, then up at the lights that illuminated it. He saw the cages that lined the walls, with their demented occupants. Then he saw the cameras that, from their flickering red lights, he knew were activated, and heard the catch of the door click shut.

THE TUNNEL

The taxi bearing Thomas from the bus station swept up the drive and stopped in front of Laurel House. While the driver unloaded his case, Thomas waited patiently for someone to appear, but no-one did. He stepped back on the gravel and looked up at the creeper covered walls and white lattice windows, awed by a manifestation of wealth that set to shame his parents' terrace house in Putney. A slight movement at one of the upper windows caught his eye, but he gave no further thought to the pale face of a woman he did not recognise watching him through the gap in the curtains.

As it had been throughout his journey, his mind was occupied by the prospect of greeting his Aunt Harriet, whose dark image had lingered in his memory since his last visit five years earlier, when he was just nine. That was before his mother and her sister stopped speaking to one another, a situation that had continued unresolved until his mother's recent traffic accident and hospitalization. It was only through a perceived duty on the part of his aunt that he was here at all. But while he expected problems with Aunt Harriet, there was no way he could have foreseen that the bane of his stay would be his cousin Mirabelle.

Unable to find the banknote his father had given him, and thus placate the taxi driver, Thomas opened the door and ventured inside.

He found them in the drawing room. Mirabelle was seated in front of an easel, twirling a paint brush in an attitude of deep reflection. Aunt Harriet was standing behind with a hand on her daughter's shoulder.

'Thomas, did you remember to tip the driver?' His aunt's first words as were hardly welcoming.

'Well, I only had…' Thomas stuttered.

'Then I suppose I'd better. While I'm busy with that Mirabelle can show you to your room.'

'He'll have to wait until I've finished.' Mirabelle said, slowly unscrewing a new tube of vermillion and squeezing a long worm of paint onto her palette. 'Then I'll see.'

Despite his embarrassment, Thomas' powers of observation had not diminished. Brightly coloured and incomprehensible paintings – presumably Mirabelle's – had displaced the original family portraits. The old upright piano had been upstaged by a baby grand that now basked in the light of French windows opening onto the lawn. Thomas only later realised that this extravagance, so clearly aimed at nurturing the gifts of a prodigal daughter, was quite misplaced. From that moment, and until it was unexpectedly ripped asunder two days later, a fine veil of unreason had fallen in front of all he beheld. Now he could only contemplate Mirabelle's fair face, trying hopelessly to reconcile it with that of the tomboy he had once fought – and succumbed to through lack of interest – on his last visit. For the moment Mirabelle and all her doings were wonderful.

'Bloody man's a crook,' Aunt Harriet said, returning to the angry scrunch of tyres on the gravel outside. 'How can a fishing rod possibly be a second piece of luggage?'

'I think fishing's cruel,' Mirabelle said, idly toying with her brush.

'Yes, I quite agree. A stupid thing to bring.' To restore her equanimity Aunt Harriet stepped behind Mirabelle, bunching the girl's raven hair in her hands and looking at the painting. 'What heavenly camellias. Do you have such glorious things where you are in London, Thomas?'

'Dad's got some marigolds and Michaelmas daisies.'

'Has he really? Poor Samantha. What a destiny.' She turned to her daughter. 'Would you wish to paint marigolds, Mirabelle?'

'I would never paint marigolds, Mother. Aunt Esther told me only yesterday that people who grow marigolds also eat turnips – or look like them – I can't remember which.'

'Aunt Esther couldn't possibly have said that, Mirabelle. That would be too much of a coincidence. You're naughty to tease Thomas.'

'Then it was something equally stupid,' Mirabelle replied, feigning intense boredom while delivering a large blob of paint to the canvass.

As she was later to tell Thomas, Aunt Esther was listening intently to this exchange from behind the drawing room door. She was in an agony of indecision, uncertain whether to enter. The boy's appearance from her window had rekindled thoughts that she had immediately dismissed as fanciful. Now, hearing his voice, they had returned with a force that set her heart pounding. Withdrawing her hand from the doorknob and grasping her stick she returned silently and thoughtfully to her attic room.

In her wardrobe mirror Aunt Esther contemplated a face that had managed to keep at bay a little of its seventy-five years span. She followed its lines with sensitive fingers, as if to brush them away, and parted the grey hairs at her forehead that seemed not so far removed, in this dim light, from their original gold. Not quite realising why, she crossed to the window to survey the landscape, letting her eyes dwell on the embankment at the boundary of the garden, where trains had once passed before Dr Beeching closed the line. Beyond that was the village of her childhood, its church now no more than a point of reference in the brown blotch of development around it. Then she did a curious thing. From the drawer of her dressing table beneath the window she withdrew a single penny piece and sat there, idly turning it over and over with her fingers until the daylight had quite gone. When Harriet knocked on her door she excused herself from dinner, claiming a headache. She needed that much time to think.

By the time he went to bed Thomas had begun to feel sorry for Aunt Esther. She was isolated in this household and in that respect at least it seemed he shared a kindred spirit. When she brought his breakfast in the morning and he saw her for the first time he knew he had found an ally.

But if an ally was needed, it was less for defence than to achieve a certain – though as yet indefinable – end; the same that had kept him turning, sleepless, in his bed until, with the dawn light, sheer exhaustion at last secured release.

'They've had breakfast,' Aunt Esther said from the door. 'So I've brought you yours.'

'They could have woken me,' Thomas said, blinking angrily.

'Mirabelle said she tried. She told me to tell you.'

Aunt Esther placed the tray with great care on his bedside table. Thomas thought that the decapitation of his egg was masterly.

'I'd get up as soon as you've finished. Apparently Mirabelle wants to show you the garden.' She paused. 'I would keep on her good side if I was you.'

Mirabelle was waiting for him in the conservatory, her raven hair gleaming from a monotony of brush strokes. Its length over her shoulders equalled that of her body, but both were exceeded by the splendour of the legs that emerged from her white and very short skirt. It took several seconds for Thomas to notice the black and white rat perched on her shoulder; its presence there seemed only incidental.

'There's one for you. Mummy bought two. But that's for after we've seen the garden.'

To Thomas gardens were rectangular flat constructions with geometric subdivisions and grass tailored to resemble a carpet. Here, from the conservatory window, there was a dynamic, almost limitless, sweep of green, cupping all manner of vegetation quite unfamiliar to him. The ground shelved irregularly downwards until halted by the rampart-like bar of the old railway embankment. The warmth of Mirabelle's hand in his set him forward towards it, and the gentle seductive pressure of her fingers controlled his steps. He felt like one of those radio controlled cars that his Uncle Ken sometimes let him play with: he was under the same irresistible control. At another level it seemed like drowning in a sea of the most fragrant ice-cream.

As they approached the bottom Mirabelle prised a path between the bushes. Thomas could hear the metallic tinkle of running water. Then he saw a stream that widened into a pool skimmed by blue dragonflies, and beyond that a gentle cascade where the water glistened over yellow sandstone rocks.

'Perhaps I will let you fish after all,' Mirabelle said. Thomas stared at her, wondering what condition might be implied by this change of manner.

'You'd never guess that above us was the old railway. Daddy planted all those trees to hide it. Then they decided to close the line.'

'Oh, I see,' Thomas replied, with his mind on other matters. The black pinpoint eyes on Miranda's shoulder were already accusing him, but not of indifference. He looked away. 'That's a fine rat you have,' he said.

'Rats are lovely,' Mirabelle said. 'They're mysterious but can be quite evil. Except Horace. Mummy says he's an aristocrat.'

'Or an aristorat,' Thomas said, but without sufficient conviction to make an impact.

'That's a stupid thing to say.' She turned away from him, but not quite fast enough to deny Thomas a glimpse of her attempt to hide a smile.

He followed her doggedly along the path by the stream, his attention divided between the bright white folds of her skirt and the lapping water. Then, without warning, the stream seemed to disappear. He looked closely at where she was pointing, to an arch of red bricks, less than a metre high, almost obscured by hanging fronds of ivy. The gurgle of escaping water told of its function.

'Aunt Esther said that when they built the railway the stream had to go underground to get to the other side.'

'Have you been to the other side?'

'Silly boy! It's far too overgrown. All brambles and nettles.' She paused. 'We must go now. Horace is hungry and needs feeding. After that you may get some lunch, although I don't think you've earned it.'

Thomas flushed red. 'Why do you say that?' he demanded.

'Girls like me like to be… excited.'

'Tell me what I should do then.'

'For a start stop asking silly questions like that.'

She raced up the grass to the house. At the conservatory door the white flame of her skirt was extinguished like a snuffed candle.

Thomas realized it was pointless to follow. Idly he turned his attention to the black orifice of the tunnel. He stayed because the place had assumed a dark aura of fascination that was strangely and deliciously familiar. There was a riddle here that demanded resolution, expressed, for the moment, in starkly physical terms. He had felt the same when his neighbours in London had shown him a dark, forbidding passage leading from their cellar towards his own house, and again when he had cast a stone into the depths of his first well. From the path he was too high to see inside, even with his body flat on the ground. He tried to stand on the wet stones with his head held low, but succeeded only in slipping and getting water in his shoes. Then he found a fallen branch, which he placed across the water. With his toes on firm ground and grasping the wood with both hands he was able to bring his eyes level with the entrance. For a metre or so he could make out primordial stalactites at the apex of the glistening brickwork. Beyond that was nothing but blackness, and distant muted sounds that only imperfectly echoed his own movements.

After lunch the children sat at the kitchen table and played with the rats. Mirabelle presumed Horace to be a willing subject, having fed him copiously with chocolate drops. Horace's less engorged companion was called Henry.

'Henry is yours,' Mirabelle said.

Thomas had never owned an animal before, but the bond between them, from the first touch of its twitching whiskers against his nose, was immediate and serious.

'The game,' Mirabelle said, 'is to race them.'

Thomas now appreciated the purpose of the household objects littering the table top.

Contrary to expectation Henry negotiated the course rather well, of the two being the more eager to reach the promised reward of a chocolate drop. Horace managed the cornflakes packet but refused to enter the cardboard tube that had begun life in a roll of wallpaper.

'He will go in,' Mirabelle hissed, squeezing his tail.

'You're hurting him.'

'Nonsense, he's used to it,' Mirabelle said, taking the animal in her hand and stuffing it into the tube.

'You can't do that.'

'Mind your own business.'

'No.'

'Try to stop me.'

For the first time in their relationship Thomas took the initiative. He tried to wrest the tube from Mirabelle's grasp. With the rat still inside, the tube executed spectacular aerobatics above the table top.

Whether by design or accident – Thomas was never able to tell which – Mirabelle let go. The tube swung backwards over Thomas' shoulder, expelling the rat onto the floor. It looked up at them once with an expression of amused pity, then scampered behind the Aga. Attempts to locate it occupied the children for the next hour. It is sufficient to record that the animal was never seen again.

When Aunt Harriet appeared the children were again sitting at the table. Mirabelle, who was now stroking the surviving rat, was first to break the silence.

'Mummy, Thomas has killed Henry.'

'That's a lie,' Thomas said.

'Mirabelle doesn't lie, Thomas.' She turned to Mirabelle. 'Tell Thomas why you know that rat is Horace.'

'From the markings. This rat is definitely Horace.'

'It seems to me, Thomas, that you are being deceitful,' Harriet said.

Thomas confronted the two pairs of eyes bearing upon his: Aunt Harriet's possessive, protective and blind, Mirabelle's beautiful, scheming, triumphant. He could see that neither would shift her position until he had capitulated. Hurt and confused, he fled the kitchen and for the next hour lay on his bed, trying to draw an arrow that had been tipped with the most intoxicating and seductive of poisons.

Later, in the bright evening sunlight, the children again found themselves at the place where the stream disappeared into the tunnel. Retrieving the branch he had used before, Thomas put his head inside. This time, in the far, far distance, he could make out the tiniest pinpoint of light. Mirabelle followed his example and stretched her lithe body along the length of the wood. But her objective was different and her efforts were not wasted. Thomas was not reluctant to accept her instruction to grasp her ankles to steady her. Neither was he aware of the water flowing over his feet as he helped raise her body from the log. Before they left he looked one more time into the tunnel, but a cloud was passing and there was only darkness.

Inside the house Aunt Esther was waiting for them. Mirabelle passed by without a word, her lips taut and her expression vindictive. Had she bothered to look back she might have seen Thomas being guided secretively into the drawing room.

It was getting dark and the woman's features were indistinct. Thomas wondered why she did not put on the light.

'Thomas, can you give an old woman credit for remembering her youth and all its problems?'

He was immediately out of his depth. 'I don't know. Well, I suppose so. Why?'

'Because I was watching you both at the stream. Oh, let me be honest – as I believe one must be with children – I deliberately followed you. Does that surprise you?'

Thomas had already learnt that dreams are made only to be shattered. Without thinking he answered sullenly, 'no.' But, as he said it, he was aware of an incongruity. He should have been resentful and angry. For a fleeting moment it had seemed that the woman was involved as if by right; even that he welcomed her intrusion, as one might heed the advice of a long-departed friend. But the moment passed as the door to his subconscious mind closed. He was suddenly resentful. 'You've no right…'

'I admit it was slightly underhand. But it's done. I just wanted to remind you that girls and boys of your age are not necessarily – how can I put it simply – at the same stage of growing up. Your cousin is a determined young lady. And other things besides.'

'I can look after myself.'

'It would not be impossible for you to return home now, if you wished. Your mother is not well. With your father away she would appreciate having you back home. I can easily say she rang.'

'No!'

In the fading light Thomas could just discern the transient whiteness of a smile.

'I didn't expect you to agree.' Suddenly she was serious. 'But Thomas, I did want you to think about your position here. Just promise me you will consider everything you do and not do anything foolish.' She paused, withdrawing into the darkness behind him. 'My, the moon has risen. Do you see it, Thomas? Beautiful things can still be found outside mere relationships.'

Thomas looked at the yellow orb in grateful relief, hardly aware that she had taken his hand and pressed something into the palm. 'Yes,' he replied a moment later, into an empty room.

Although Mirabelle's fair image returned to dominate his thoughts, he could not quite expunge Esther's admonition from his mind. And he was puzzled, as well as delighted, by her apparent gift of a double headed penny.

Thomas did not wish to sleep. He wished to dream in a state of sensual wakefulness. He left the curtains open, so that the light could stream in, and the window ajar to subject himself to the sounds of the night. He tried to scheme, to devise strategies, to construct rigorous arguments. He prepared fine speeches with which to impress and once he leapt from his bed to practice appropriate gestures in front of the mirror. Then he lay in quiet despair with his second pillow a pale imitation of her beside his restless body. I would do anything, he told himself, forgetting Aunt Esther's warning. By the time the door opened hope had all but gone.

'Are you awake?'

'Yes.'

'I thought we ought to talk.'

This may still be a dream, he told himself. Keep control. 'What about?' he asked. It was difficult to suppress the tremor in his voice.

'About things. About you and me. It seems you don't like me, Thomas.'

Was this the opportunity that he craved? The item of advantage that could be turned to useful effect. 'I tried not to let it show,' Thomas said. 'Perhaps I could get to like you.' He hoped desperately that she could not hear his heart pounding.

'It's what I feared.' She sniffed twice and grasped Thomas' hand, placing it on her thigh. 'I think I'd better go.'

'No! I mean, no, there's no need to go.'

'Mummy would be awfully cross if she found me here.'

'You can stay.'

'I thought we might talk about Horace.'

'Henry.'

'Whatever. I thought I might give him to you.' She waited for a response that did not come. 'You don't want him then?'

'I could just take him off you,' Thomas said gruffly.

'Of course, you'd have to prove to me that you're serious about him.'

'What do you want me to do?'

'It's something I've always wondered. Nothing difficult. Something you can help me to find out. Will you do it for me? Please.'

'If I can I will.'

'Promise?'

'I promise.'

'On this bible?' She had a book in her hand.

'On this bible I promise. Now tell me what it is.'

'To crawl through that tunnel to see what's on the other side.'

Thomas chose not to interpret her cough as she left the room as suppressed laughter. But he tried desperately to recall having seen the bible on his bedside table.

In the early hours of the morning Thomas' dilemma assumed gargantuan proportions. Fear of the unknown was dwarfed by a more focused dread of being confined in a small space that had first come to light two years before in a traumatic encounter with Crighton, the school bully.

There was also the problem of when. If he went early it was just possible he could overcome his fears by being alone, but he would be missed; if late... well... all manner of unforeseen difficulties might be put in his way. In the end he decided on a compromise: he would slip away unseen just after breakfast, having misled Mirabelle as to his intentions. To his surprise it worked. 'But you mustn't leave it too late,' she said. 'The weather forecast said more showers.'

Under a dark sky only partially visible through the swaying branches above Thomas contemplated the swirling water. It must have rained during the night: what had been a benign trickle the previous day now seemed a cauldron of mutually hostile elements frantically competing to escape the light. By pinching his arm he forced himself into the tunnel entrance – just to see, nothing more. If he had to he could still swallow his pride, catch the next train home and never make contact with this wretched family again. Except that not seeing Mirabelle again was not an option.

The bite of the water across his feet had the same cold cruelty as its appearance. It filled his trainers and surged over his hands as he groped his way forward. To his dismay he found it was not possible to kneel. Worse still, he could not turn around. Any further progress depended upon squirming, eel-like, with lateral undulations of his shoulders and hips. Suddenly he panicked. He emerged backwards out of the hole like a piece of excrement.

In the rising water he cried bitter tears of frustration, unable to make any decision that might relieve his situation. For the first time in many months Thomas prayed.

The Almighty's response began with a crackle of twigs on the embankment above. At first Thomas thought it was Mirabelle selecting a favourable position of vantage from which to crow. But a moment later a youth of about his own age and appearance, with torn clothes and bleeding scratches on his cheeks, climbed – or rather slid – down the bank towards him. Thomas stared in disbelief.

'You've set yourself a difficult task there,' the boy observed.

'Yes, haven't I just,' Thomas replied.

'Think you can make it?'

'I don't know.'

'Then why are you doing it?'

'I promised someone I would.'

'And what do you get in return?'

'My self-respect… and a rat… and…'

'A rat! Heavens, there are enough rats in that tunnel.'

'Not seriously?'

'Seriously.'

Thomas looked at him suspiciously. 'How do you know?'

'I know someone who went through once. Don't worry, they leave you alone.'

'I can't decide.'

'I know that feeling. Want to know what I'd do in that situation?'

'What?'

'Let chance decide. Got a coin?'

Thomas withdrew from his pocket the penny Aunt Esther had given him. 'Ye…es,' he stuttered

'Toss it. I'll call.'

'I'd rather call myself.' Thomas was becoming flustered.

'Then it wouldn't be chance, would it?'

'I suppose not.' Reluctantly Thomas threw the coin into the air.

'Heads you go through. Heads it is! Best not to wait. Do it now.'

'I can't.'

'If you don't I shall have to make you.' The boy's laugh held no humour.

'No.'

Thomas bent double as the boy's fist embedded itself in his stomach. A moment later he was in an arm lock and being propelled towards the gaping orifice. His face was in the water. He had difficulty retrieving his twisted arm. A stone clattering after him came to rest just in front of his head. In panic he squirmed his way forward.

That was the moment – as Aunt Esther was to tell him later - that Mirabelle's voice floated sweetly across the lawn. 'Thomas, Thomas. Where are you? You don't have to do it.'

The water rushed past with a desperation that seemed to match his own. Its currents might have been kindred souls fleeing a fire or an insurgent army. It was how it had been that day in the playground, with the mob upon him, when the classroom had offered no refuge and Crighton was leading the pack. Now, like in his recurring dreams, they seemed once more behind him, their exchanges just as vicious. 'Lock him in the cupboard.' 'Christ, Crighton, can't you shut him up.' 'We're going to shut him up.' 'He won't fit in.' 'Know what a coffin is, Thomas? Here, Midgeley, give a hand and push. Over she goes, mind your toes.' 'Look, there's a hole. Can you see him?' 'I can see an ear.' 'What does Beaky say?' 'I don't know, what does he say?' 'Beaky says, wash your ears out, boy.' 'Crighton, no! Not ink!' 'Bullseye!' 'Let's get out, please Crighton.' 'So much as a squeak, Thomas, and you bloody know what will happen.'

He imagined the ink flowing down his face and dripping into the water beneath his body. Yet when he felt there with his hand there was only dampness. As he opened his eyes the brightness of the janitor's torch was consumed by the brighter ball of daylight that was almost upon him. The clockwork of his squirming body wound down.

The nightmare over, he felt relief and a sense of achievement as the tunnel end came nearer. And there were noises: chipping, knocking, veritably human noises. He noticed that the floor of the tunnel was now dry. Already he could smell the fresh earth outside. His thoughts returned to Mirabelle.

But, in rapid succession, the sky, the sunlit meadow and human faces spun in a mêlée of pain and confusion. From where he came to lie he could see the jagged, broken end of the tunnel. Around him lay the scattered bricks, each with its buttering of fresh mortar.

And then the two men were circling him with shovels held like jabbing spears, as if waiting for a vulnerable part of his body to be exposed.

'See what you bloody done?' one said.

'How long you bin hiding in there?' the other demanded.

'Hiding?' Thomas said. I wasn't hiding. I crawled through.'

'You what? You lying bugger! Other end's blocked. Has been for days.'

'You shifted the logs, did you?'

Then Thomas remembered the dry floor of the tunnel as he approached its end. Inexplicably the man was credible. Perplexed, he said nothing. He felt the flat of a shovel pushing viciously against his head.

'Course you didn't. Couldn't. Take an 'orse to shift those logs.' He turned to his companion. 'You get his legs.'

'You be careful, Jed!' This was a third voice, thin, musical, undeniably feminine, piercing the confusion like a shaft of light.

'We've only just started.' Jed growled.

'I said be careful of him.'

'Look, you don't…' But the admonition was converted into a rearward thrust of the shovel handle that caught the girl – for Thomas, with his body suspended between the two men, could now see her – just below her ear. She reeled backwards, clutching her face.

'Now I've got an idea,' Jed said. 'Let's put him back inside.' He laughed. 'So he can crawl back to the other end. Backwards.'

The sharpness of each brick was a knife in Thomas' back as he was dragged to the tunnel and flung inside. But the real pain came from the manic laughter as the bricks were rebuttered and piled on top of each other until only a space the size of a letterbox remained.

'We're off,' Jed told the girl. 'If he tries to break out, hit him hard.' From the clang of the blade it was clear to Thomas that he was instructing her in the use of the shovel. The scrunch of boots on the scattered bricks resolved into silence.

Thomas' plight was horribly apparent, but its explanation still eluded him. It seemed at first that he was acting out a part in a set-piece drama devised by Mirabelle, or even Aunt Harriet, to force him back through the tunnel to face further humiliation on emerging rearwards and bloodied into their laughter. On the other hand, what Jed had said about the logs had the greater resonance of truth. Thomas sought guidance from the only possible quarter.

The girl sat with her back arched towards the space that was his window on the world. Her head was inclined backwards, the listening ear exposed now and then as the wisps of sunlit hair shadowed her cheek in the breeze.

Thomas pushed gently at the bricks. The mortar had not

yet set and for the moment there remained a possibility of escape. If he dared. He needed to know more about the girl.

'What's your name?'

'Tessie.'

'I'm Thomas.'

'Well Thomas, you've got yourself into a fine pickle. Why did you lie to them like that?'

'I told you, I crawled through.'

'If you lie to them again they'll kill you. You wouldn't be the first.'

'When will they come back?'

'They take an hour, usually.'

'Then what'll they do?'

'I really don't know.' The impatience in her voice was a warning, but he persisted.

'But what do you think?'

'Beat you probably. They'll enjoy that.' Something seemed to amuse her. 'But they've got to finish the tunnel today, so it will be over quickly.'

'What if I tried to escape?'

Suddenly the girl's face filled the aperture, the eyes wide with apprehension. The blade of Jed's shovel passed slowly before her face. 'Then I would have to stop you with this.'

'But just suppose, what if you were to let me go?'

'Then they would beat me. You saw what happened just now.' With her face inches from his the swelling of her cheek confirmed that her position was as precarious as his own.

Thomas placed his hand on the topmost brick. The response was a shower of sparks as the shovel struck, narrowly missing his fingers. For more than a minute neither child moved nor spoke.

For the second time Thomas prayed for guidance. It came in the form of scuffling tiny feet in the passage behind. Looking beyond his body into the gloom he could just make out a convulsing grey sheet from which arose a multitude of pin-point squeaks of anger. Had they too resented their new captivity, or was he their target? 'I'm coming out,' he shouted. The bricks flew from the violent thrust of his shoulder, dancing in the sunlight and choosing one from their number to be hooked like a cricket ball far into the distance by the force of Tessie's shovel. But Thomas was ahead of the implement and his face and shoulders were already engulfed in the folds of her skirt. Locked together the pair fell backwards into the black and freshly dug channel that led away from the tunnel entrance.

His body thrilled to the struggling mass beneath him, but his mind was pierced by its desperation. When the writhing stopped he felt only the wetness of her cheek against his own.

He helped her to her feet and wiped the dirt from her mouth with the corner of his shirt-tail. Silently she took his hand and they crawled within the black channel until they were out of earshot of the men that must surely be returning.

'Will they follow?' Thomas whispered.

'They know I have to go home. They'll tell themselves they can wait. But I'll stay out until they've drunk themselves silly. By morning they'll have forgotten, or at least I can handle it.'

'Are you poor?' Thomas asked, without really knowing why.

'The whole village is poor.'

He pulled out the two coins in his pocket and held them out to her.

'What's that?' Tessie asked, intrigued by the smaller and brighter of the two.

'A pound.'

'Pounds are paper.'

'Not anymore.'

'Liar! I know because I had one once, after Aunt Ethel died – but they soon took it off me.' She rummaged in her own pocket. 'That's what I've got. Three farthings.'

Their brief absorption with one another was interrupted by shouts of malice and retribution ringing across the meadow. Thomas thrust the coins into her hand, but the smaller one fell into the mud. Ignoring it, she tugged him down onto the floor of the channel and together they squirmed their way towards safety. After a hundred yards or so the channel ended abruptly in a vertical earth wall. Beyond the obstruction Thomas could hear the soft gurgle of running water.

'They'll have to dig this earth away when they let the water through the tunnel,' Tessie explained.

The men's expletives continued to swoop and dive through the still summer air, but there was no attempt at pursuit. Through the waving grass Thomas could see them repairing the damaged brickwork with demonic energy. 'I think they really would kill anyone who broke it now,' Tessie said. Thomas believed her.

They climbed the bank and made the greater safety of the stream. To Thomas' surprise the water was not cold. For the first time he could take stock of his position.

Tessie stood with the water almost to her knees. To Thomas the damage to her face was apparent even in her reflection. He raised his eyes slowly, fearful of what he might see.

'They could do that to you?'

'It will heal. It has before.'

'Would you let me... touch it?' His embarrassment was acute.

He took a step forward in the water and raised his hand to her cheek. This time he could see the tears that flowed. He tried momentarily to substitute Mirabelle's fair image but instead saw only injustice written there. 'I shall have to go back,' he said.

'Why don't you stay?'

'Because they will come looking for me.'

'Who?'

'My aunt from Laurel House. And my cousin Mirabelle.'

'House? I know Laurel Cottages. I don't know of any house. I think you're strange. But I wish you would stay. When the sun begins to go down, then you can go. At least that will give us time to wash our clothes.'

'Here?' Thomas was alarmed.

'There's a backwater where no-one can see.' She took his hand.

The reeds opened upon a limpid pool, its banks a patchwork of mosses of the most subtle green, the winged life above its surface vibrant in the warmth and brilliance of the light falling through the trees. Its charm imposed an irresistible urgency on the two children. They entered and the reeds closed decisively behind them.

Later they climbed the new embankment of impacted earth. The girl's hand was warm in his as they neared the top. 'You still don't believe? Look around. What do you see?'

'There are no rails,' Thomas said.

'And that surprises you? The rails can't get here until the embankment is finished. And your tunnel. Look at me.'

Her eyes were as blue as the sky and her hair the colour of the distant cornfields. 'I think it might rain,' she said.

'But it's bright sunl...' Thomas' eyes were drawn upwards, against his will for she continued to fascinate him.

He felt her hand slipping away from his. There was a sharp bite of air against his cheek. A cloud as if from nowhere passed across the face of the sun. With sinking heart he saw others following, swirling across the sky until, in what seemed like seconds, the whole expanse was uniformly grey. Then Thomas looked down.

The rails were there, a little rusty, but solid against his toe. Weeds growing amongst the shingle had had time enough to encroach upon the wooden sleepers. Beside the track were dense thickets of brambles. He turned to look back. Far down the track, beyond the limits of certain recognition, a small figure hobbled upon a familiar stick. Thomas began to lift his hand to wave, then thought better of it: the matter could be resolved later.

The brambles clutched at his body as he forced his way down the embankment. The path became precipitous, seeming to lead nowhere. He followed its near vertical descent with a sureness that in other circumstances might have been suicidal. He had a new-found confidence that made him feel invulnerable. When he reached the bottom it set him apart from the youth standing distraught in the stream, contemplating the black orifice into which the waters flowed.

When the boy prevaricated it was no chance thing that directed the toss of the coin and his choice of call. The power of the arm that doubled the boy had only purpose, and held no malice. He regretted throwing the stone but, if the end had been determined, what point was there in not hastening it?

The force of the stream seemed to lessen and the elements of the water began to assume more harmonious murmurs. Thomas looked up to a new quality of light filtering through the swaying branches. A fresh gust brought down a shower of drops. He felt it as a ritual cleansing, washing away inhibition and bestowing purpose. In the reflection in the pool he noticed for the first time the width of his shoulders and the rake of his jaw. He smacked a fist into the palm of his other hand.

The owner of the voice that carried sweetly across the lawn was no longer invincible. She would deserve his answer, and he was set to deliver it. And then? Well, then there was the matter of Henry...

A JERUSALEM TRILOGY

LAZARUS
JUDAS
JUDAS THOMAS

LAZARUS

Paul Southery, having finished his mid-morning coffee, peered through the glass window of the library door, over the notice in Hebrew affixed to it – which he could just translate – requiring silence from its readers and consideration for others. The rule had been flagrantly broken: even through the closed door he could hear the animated voices of those clustered around the reception table within. Intrigued to know what the excitement was about he opened the door and went in. There on the table – the focus of attention – was a single page of script in Greek.

Standing beside him was Maria Goldman, a postgraduate like himself specialising in New Testament studies.

'What's the fuss about?' he whispered.

'Apparently it arrived in the post yesterday,' she replied, 'but what it is and who sent it no-one seems to know.' She picked up the document. 'You can read Greek, you tell me.'

'The hand looks post-reformation,' Paul said.

'Well, the egg-heads here think it's a copy of a letter from a second century church father – Clement of Alexandria. Apparently its warning someone to be suspicious of the authenticity of an unknown version of the gospel of Mark. It quotes a passage that our friends here can't find in the canonical version – about the raising of Lazarus.'

'But that's only in John, not the other gospels.'

'Exactly,' Maria said.

When the excitement had died down and the library had assumed its usual sepulchral feel Paul looked at the document more closely. The relevant section began: *And they came to Bethany. And a certain woman whose brother had died was there. And, coming, she prostrated herself before Jesus...* 'The story's familiar, but not like in John,' he said.

'No,' she replied, 'but if you look at Mark chapter ten you can see where it would fit.'

'Edited out, you think?'

'Looks that way.'

Paul looked out of the window. In the distance he could see the road following the Kidron Valley around the foot of the Mount of Olives on its way to the Judean desert, Jericho and the Dead Sea.

'Bethany's just round that bend, where it happened,' Maria said.

'Come with me, to take a look?'

'If we're quick, with the Sabbath starting later. So I'd better drive.'

The entrance to the tomb from which Lazarus was alleged to have risen turned out to be a low aperture in a featureless stone-built wall flanked by the mosque of al-Uzair. 'Why do you think it's authentic?' Paul asked.

'There's been a continuous record since the fourth century, and before that an oral tradition. Unlike many of Jerusalem's sites, this was far enough out to escape damage by the Romans. There's no reason for it not to be genuine.'

'I believe you,' Paul said with a supercilious smile.

From the entrance they descended a flight of twenty or so rough steps to reach a square vestibule. They saw that further steps led down into the vaulted chamber of the tomb itself. In a hushed voice Maria said, 'We believe this is where Jesus stood when he ordered Lazarus to come out. Then there would have been a stone covering the entrance to what at the time was little more than a cave.'

'So who moved the stone?'

'I think there would have been quite a gathering – and no shortage of hands. The family was well-off and Lazarus' death had attracted many well-wishers.'

'Did they know in advance Jesus was coming?'

'I think they must have done, don't you?'

Leaving Maria to get fresh air outside Paul descended into the tomb, where there were still niches to take the bodies of the dead. Becoming accustomed to the gloom he ran his fingers over the stonework, feeling the dampness there.

Maria called down to him, 'The Sabbath begins at sunset and its already beginning to get dark – we need to be quick.'

But Paul had no intention of leaving. His mind was full of imaginings of what had taken place here, growing more powerful as the minutes passed.

'Paul!'

'You go on without me. I can easily walk back to the city.'

'You be careful then. This is not a safe place to be, especially at night.'

He emerged from the tomb to see Maria's car disappearing round the corner. Nearby was a stall selling snacks and drinks and he sat there for a while, cup in hand, on a low stone wall. When it began to get dark he looked stealthily around him and re-entered the tomb. He squeezed his body into the largest of the niches and asked himself why the apostle Mark had not thought to record what had happened here – or, if he had, why it had been suppressed.

In the end it came down to a matter of timing. He'd assembled his thoughts, re-read the scriptures and tested out his ideas – admittedly in an oblique way – in the few synagogues where he'd been invited to speak. But few had understood his message. And that included his own disciples, now blissfully sleeping in chairs or on rugs on the floor around him. He asked himself if any shared his dream. Perhaps that was too much to expect. To be in sympathy, to have a vague awareness of where it all might lead, that was about all he could ask. More than once he'd been direct: 'Who say you that I am?' And back had come the reply, 'You are the Messiah,' because that's what people were saying about him, in the markets of Galilee and now in Jericho and other settlements in the Jordan valley. Sometimes he did not know whether he was leading their expectations or assuming a mantle that had been thrust upon him. He saw stretched out around him absolute loyalty and trust, of that there was no doubt, but aside from Mary – his beloved Mary, who feared for him – it was beyond this little band that he had to look for understanding.

They'd been in Jerusalem in the middle of winter and the unusual cold had not favoured the delivery of his message. Or if it had got across it was only the Temple police who had been excited by it. In a gathering on the portico steps he'd heard for the first time the threat of stoning and it perplexed him that his words were falling on deaf ears. The lodgings in Bethany provided comfort only for himself – in the house of Lazarus and his sisters; the twelve had to make do with unheated stables and cattle sheds. It pricked his conscience that he had insisted on frugality, as was their rule.

He spoke of it as Lazarus' house, though the two sisters of this seventeen-year-old boy – Mary and Martha – were both several years older. With each visit to the city the bonds between them strengthened, but it saddened him that Mary – his Mary, as distinct from the sister of Martha – could not slip so easily into the relationship. Now, as he looked at the beautiful face of the sleeping figure beside him, he still felt unable to take her with him. So he wrote her a note saying where he was going and placed it with an orange blossom in her hand, gently closing her fingers over it. Then he kissed her goodbye and went out into the darkness.

He had waited for a full moon, without which the walk – perhaps climb would be a better word – would be hazardous if not impossible. He had with him his long staff to protect himself, if the need arose, as well as to help him negotiate the rough track. Bethany came into sight as dawn broke. It was too early to disturb the family, yet he had to remain unseen, so he settled on his haunches in a nearby straw barn and ate a crust of bread and some cheese. When the sun was fully up he made his way unseen to the house.

They sat together at the table, as they had done so many times before. From them he learnt that his name – in different contexts – was still mentioned in the city. Out of consideration for their sensibilities he refrained from explaining his grand and desperate plan, whose culmination would be at the coming Passover. And of his planned death he said nothing, speaking only in terms of demonstrations and rituals. Mary asked him what he hoped to achieve. He smiled and said, as if a joke, the kingdom of God of course; but knew they could see beyond his levity.

'I'm here,' he said at last, 'to ask you to help me prepare the way. My works you know about by repute, but of my methods you are completely ignorant. There is something I must do, necessary for my purpose, and for that I need your complete trust. You will not fully understand what I am about to ask.' He raised his eyebrows, inviting dissent, but Mary just said, 'Tell us what we must do.'

They walked down the hill to the cemetery. 'This one belongs to the family,' Martha said, pointing at what was little more than a flat stone covering a hole in the ground. Together Lazarus and Jesus moved it away and squeezed inside. Jesus said, 'You will need warm blankets and enough food, and a means of ticking off the days.' 'I'll pass by frequently,' Mary said from above.

When they were back around the table he handed Lazarus the glass vial. You will have four hours of unconsciousness, so have the shrouds ready. To the women he said, 'Only send word to the city when you're sure of the effect, so that some may arrive in time to see the tomb closed.' 'Risky,' Lazarus said. 'What's new,' Mary replied.

The next four days Jesus spent in the Judean desert, as he had many times before. When word came by messenger that Lazarus had died the awful thought occurred to him that something might have gone wrong. But he fought the urge to go there and stuck to the plan. It would take him two days to mobilise his little army and make the journey back under less than a full moon. It was critical they arrived with hours of daylight in hand, so that their presence in Bethany would draw in the curious and the hostile from the city.

He took with him only Simon Peter, his own Mary, and James and John. A sombre Martha was waiting for them on the Jericho road, just out of sight of the village. 'Mary needed to stay home to guard the house.' she said. But as they approached the tomb Simon Peter ran ahead to fetch her.

Mary's head and body were draped in concealing black cloth. Her stooped walk suggested tragedy. She lifted her veil a fraction and brushed her cheek, as if to wipe away a tear. Jesus' doubts became indubitable fact: Lazarus had indeed died. His foolish self-confidence had again led him into another disaster of his own making. His own tears welled up and he let out a violent scream that engendered pity from all around. He looked towards his own disciples, all heads bowed, and at his own Mary, whose expression was of deep pity. Even the normally inscrutable faces of those he knew to be in the employ of the high priest were lowered in sympathy.

Jesus raised his eyes skywards. This was the biggest test of his faith he had ever been called upon to make. He fell to his knees and prayed, then slowly rose to his full height, motioning to his disciples to roll away the stone. Facing the aperture in the ground he shouted, 'Lazarus, come out!'

A minute passed. There was a movement within the tomb. Shedding his shrouds, Lazarus emerged, blinking in the sunlight.

They had to help Jesus to the house, so great had been the effect upon him. Slowly the crowd dispersed, some returning to the city along the road, others walking over the summit of the hill of olives. One of the last to leave was a young priest called John, who had helped guide Jesus back to Lazarus' house.

It was two days before Jesus' fever abated. By that time his disciples, except Simon Peter, had returned to the Jordan valley. Afterwards, those well-wishers favoured enough to see him commented on the blazing conviction in his eyes and the fervour of his arguments. To some he seemed a changed man. Meanwhile Lazarus and his two sisters reflected upon their deceit. But as no harm had come of it – and Jesus' standing had clearly increased – they chose to remain silent, knowing that to reveal the truth would be devastating. 'An honest man knows not how to act,' Martha had told Lazarus in justification, and there the matter had ended.

After six days had elapsed – with rumours of the Sanhedrin's hostility towards him emanating from the city – Jesus, with Simon Peter and Mary, prepared to leave Bethany. His last act, in a session lasting well into the night, was to explain his teachings to Lazarus. But neither Jesus nor Lazarus was to know how instrumental this young man and his sisters would be in shaping Jesus' destiny.

Paul threaded his way through the tables to where Maria was waiting. Her eyes were wide with mock expectation, her lips pursed with a hint of derision. He took the seat opposite her.

'So what happened to you?' she said.

'Before or after they complained to the dean?'

'Being caught in a tomb sounds rather pathetic to me. Was it worth it, did the walls speak to you?'

'Perhaps they did.'

Maria sat up sharply. 'That sounded serious! So what new insights can you give me?'

'I dreamed. I can't remember the details, but when the custodian came for me – he actually shouted at me to come out, would you believe – there was one thought uppermost in my mind. And it's stayed with me since. It's so bizarre I hesitate to tell it.'

'I'm your best friend – in this place at any rate. I can handle anything.'

'Between us, then? For the moment?'

She clamped her hand over her mouth in a gesture of promised silence. Paul saw it as the stifling of a laugh.

'Let me say first that I don't believe in miracles, biblical or otherwise,' Paul said. 'And I don't believe half of Christendom does either.'

'So the raising of Jairus' daughter, and the young man from Nain – those were not miracles?'

'I think Jesus allowed people to think so. As with the other miracles. I don't think it was deceit – more a demonstration of power in the service of his God. True or not, such acts would have been impressive. But at the time he was not the only person making such claims, and they, too, were believed. He was not unique.'

'So then why was the raising of Lazarus so special? You've said yourself it stood out as the greatest of all the… well… miracles – except, of course, for the resurrection itself.'

'I believe that Jesus went to Bethany to perform a symbolic ritual act that would facilitate acceptance of what he believed would happen after his own death. A softening of minds, if you like.'

'Go on.'

'So when he went to the tomb he didn't expect Lazarus to be physically dead.'

'But that's nonsense. We know from John's gospel that Jesus was devastated to hear of Lazarus' death when news reached him in the desert. And then showed real grief at the tomb before Lazarus emerged.'

'As I believe was truly the case.'

'But that could only mean that Jesus had been deceived, that somehow Lazarus or his sisters had deliberately allowed him to believe Lazarus had died. Why on earth would they have done that?'

'So that Jesus' response would have been accepted by everyone present as genuine grief.'

'That sounds a wild theory to me,' she said, smiling. 'Now, I've got a lecture to attend. I'll think about it and let you know, but don't hold your breath.' She got up to go.

'Just hold on a moment,' Paul said, taking her hand. 'I believe also that Jesus never realised he had been deceived. He would have prayed to God in good faith and when that prayer was seemingly answered – by Lazarus emerging from the tomb – the effect on him would have been profound.'

'I'm sure it would have been. But why, in that case, wouldn't they have disillusioned him?'

'To what advantage? To destroy a man who believed himself to be on the brink of realising his destiny? Though it must be said that they would have had no clear idea then of what that destiny entailed.'

'Death on the cross, you mean?'

'Exactly. So he would have left Bethany with any lingering doubts as who he was resolved – and his disciples no longer sceptical. If God had permitted him to bring Lazarus back from the dead surely he would have allowed Jesus to survive death also.'

Maria had become thoughtful. 'It would certainly explain why Jesus' belief in himself was so absolute when he returned to Jerusalem for Passover – for one last time.'

'And maybe why Lazarus and his sisters were so hospitable towards him. How mixed their feelings must have been: hidden guilt for the past and elation at being part of his fantastic journey.'

'We have a tea-club meeting coming up next month, and still lack a speaker,' Maria said. 'Why don't you air your theory then?'

Which is what Paul did. But he failed to convince anyone there that the Saviour who was God's son and saw everything, was capable to the least degree of being hoodwinked. 'What you're saying,' said a wag in the audience, 'is that Lazarus killed Jesus.'

And there, at four o'clock in the afternoon in the Institute's smaller lecture theatre, on a dismal March day in 1972, Paul's great idea died.

JUDAS

Judas closed the door carefully behind him, but he could not prevent his hand from shaking or the catch from rattling. He stood with his back to it, breathing hard, while the pasty fragments of crust sticking to his palate released juices that seared his throat and tongue. Through the door he could hear muffled conversation. He pondered who – besides the Master – might know the reason for his leaving. Then he went below, his sandals clattering on the stone steps, and out into the moonlit street.

From here in the upper city he could see the vast silhouette of the Temple. Beyond it, black storm clouds gathered over the hill of olives. It was a scene familiar to him from the past, before he sought refuge and obscurity in the remote and quieter Galilee. Here, more than anywhere else he knew, the elements seemed able to organise themselves into an ordered canvas, the perturbed sky mirroring the afflictions of the souls trapped within the mass of the city below. Sometimes, even, instruction might be written there in God's hand. And once, in a moment of rapt contemplation, it had offered a solution, and turned the heart and mind of this previously troubled man.

He found a low wall and slumped onto it, trying to make sense of his predicament. He yearned for solitude, something not easily had in the now seething city. Some of the passers-by were newcomers, walking the streets in wonder, climbing higher and higher to gaze at the Temple and finding themselves in this place by accident. Others seemed here by design, walking furtively. A few looked down on him in pity, for he was not well-dressed. He longed to have them stay, to tell him that they, too, could not see things remaining as they were. Two young men came by, Pharisees both. One pointed out to the other how, by squinting along the Temple precinct wall, the black mass of the Antonia Fortress could be seen blemishing the lines of the Temple. They joked about it, then, seeing him, became quiet, as if he might be in the employ of the Temple Police – or of Rome itself. He wanted to shout out that he was no threat, no spy, just a foot soldier of an obscure little army of the mind advancing to nowhere he could determine.

A week earlier – before their little band had plucked up courage to emerge from the desert and enter the city – it had all seemed clear. They had purpose, a message, prospects of influencing by example and deed. To their surprise, the crowds coming for Passover had multiplied their band a hundred-fold. Then, suddenly, the direction had changed. What had become of the humility, where the place of the poor and the sick? More puzzling still, why did the Master appear to have another agenda, involving shadowy persons and influences unknown to the Twelve? Perhaps he, Judas, was just the first to see – or the one most likely to snap through indignation. When they came there were people with whom he had spoken too freely – that he now realised. But then, what can a man from Galilee know of intrigue in the Temple and the city?

Yet the Master had known of his disquiet, somehow, and had sought him out, alone, to divine his thinking.

It happened on the evening of the third day, as the band tramped back up the hill between the olive trees, their minds bereft of useful thought because of the battering they had received in the Temple. For Judas, a little older and more corpulent than most of them, progress was slower and he lagged behind. Anticipating this, the Master had chosen the place carefully.

Judas came upon him where the olives gave way to a small grove of larger trees offering deeper shade. He was sitting on an ancient stone seat from which the vast panorama of the city could be seen across the valley. He was quite still, his face dappled with pale sunlight that for the moment obscured the strain. His voice cut the air – paradoxically, Judas thought, because it was never loud or harsh.

'Look back, Judas,' he called. 'The city is beautiful, is it not?'

Judas stopped and turned to look. 'You were waiting for me, Master?' he asked, still panting.

'From here the balm of the evening can separate us from our tribulations so that we see them more clearly from a distance. The others have gone on ahead and won't come looking for us. That was my thinking. Come, sit beside me.'

Judas did so. He had never sought, or truly experienced, the physical intimacy with the Master enjoyed by several of the disciples; never appreciated the courseness of the cloth garments compared with his own, or thought much about the odours of people on the move that characterised each of them. Now, above the sweat of exertion, Judas detected for the first time the faint but pungent stench of emotion and fear.

'What is it you want to tell me, Master?' he asked.

'You are a thinker, Judas. Perhaps the only one of our band that I would so describe. And things do not generally pass you by. It is something I have valued in you. But your problem – no, don't try to deny it – is that in our present predicament you do not have the knowledge to make judgements. You have looked to me to give you that knowledge. Because I have not done so, you have… well, let us say sought enlightenment by talking to those who may not have our best interests at heart. Am I close?'

Judas smiled ruefully. 'I should have realised little can be hidden from you,' he said.

'My contacts in the city are more extensive than you can imagine,' the Master continued, 'and almost unknown to the others. Perhaps you find that a disturbing admission?'

'It seems against the spirit of our brotherhood. But it doesn't surprise me. It would account for many things that are… unexplained.'

'Then where do you think our problems lie?'

It took a moment for Judas to summon his thoughts and his courage. 'Three days ago, when we came, we passed close to this very spot. People were shouting and waving. They loved you, welcomed you as a leader they could follow. Now, somehow – I don't know why – there is confusion.'

'So when we came over the crest of the hill, just up there, and you saw the city below. Everything seemed clear to you? What we had to do?'

'No, how could it? But we trusted you. We put our faith in you.'

A hint of impatience crept into the Master's voice. 'To do what? To walk into that fortress down there by the Temple and say 'Romans go home' and seriously expect them to, and then when that didn't work create mayhem amongst the Judeans and attempt to overthrow Rome by force? Oh, it will be attempted, Judas, but not with me because it wouldn't work.'

'Not so blatantly as that,' Judas protested. 'Such things take time and careful planning, and require religious solidarity and…'

'Whereas I have been treading a more… obscure… path?'

'You tell us about things that are written, and we are impressed when they happen, but we don't know why they happen, or how they advance our cause.'

'An example?'

Judas thought for a moment, then said, 'Lazarus.'

The Master smiled. 'You weren't impressed?'

Judas was indignant. 'I was even party to the planning.'

'People confuse symbolism with reality, and as often as not choose the latter against their better judgement. It should have given you an insight into… such phenomena.' The Master's face hardened and he added, 'And perhaps, even, why it was necessary.'

'So it was no miracle?'

'A miracle, certainly, in that Lazarus survived. That is to say he did not die when the odds were against him. *That* indeed was the hand of the Father. It is what I asked of him.'

'It was a rehearsal then?'

The Master seemed taken aback, as if a weakness in his strategy had been revealed. 'No, no. Not a rehearsal. What must come to pass will be unique, quite unique. It's just that people may be that much more… receptive.'

Judas was suddenly angry. 'What you are telling me I think I want no part of.'

The Master jumped to his feet and stood before him, his greater height blocking out the sun, making Judas gaze into a shadow where only the white anger of the eyes was discernible. His voice trembled. 'Do you think I want it? To give up this life, my friends, Mary, to continue to work for the common good even? The difference between us, Judas, is that I have no choice.'

'It's all determined?'

'And always has been – at least since my immersion by John in the river. Before then, when I preached around Galilee, and got to know the scriptures, it was coming together. Fragments seemed to have meaning but didn't quite make sense. But that moment with John, that's when it became clear.'

'And you weren't afraid?'

'Terrified. Then and now. Not so much of the outcome – I've lived with that for so long – but in being given the option, slender as it is, to withdraw. That's the temptation. I'm ashamed to admit that the thought crosses my mind even as we speak. Contrary to what some would have you believe, I'm still human.'

Judas rose slowly to his feet and stepped out of the shade. The Master followed, for the first time revealing the extent of his ravaged face.

'Master, am I right in thinking that your question to me is whether I can accept this outcome?'

'My friend, yes. And in accepting it, and pursuing what I believe is in your mind, help ensure that my mission is fulfilled.'

Judas looked into the Master's eyes. He saw there fear – not of humiliation or suffering or death, but of failure in the eyes of his God. And when he thought about it the reason was not difficult to see. They had been to the Temple for three days now. In spite of the Master's belligerency, sometimes violence even, which he knew was out of character and forced, here they were, openly returning to

Bethany, without – or so it seemed – significant threat to their safety. One could see how the Temple elders might be thinking. If Passover came and went and nothing happened, what danger then would there be, with this Jesus a spent force? This was why, for the Master, events desperately needed to take a different course.'

Without a word Judas walked away, amongst the olives, shuffling his feet in the dust in agitation. He looked at the city, with its temple bathed in golden light. He saw that its destiny was this man's destiny, bigger than anything he could understand, in the hands of an intellect greater than his own, deriving from a source that he could comprehend only in terms he could not define. And in it all he saw only his own smallness and insignificance. Whatever his fate, it would not matter to anyone except this man standing by his stone seat in the leafy shade, waiting for his answer. Slowly Judas returned. 'I will consider it,' he said.

They said no more to one another as, master and servant, they trudged to the top of the hill. They sniffed the dry, clean air and saw the arid yellow of the desert fall away towards the Jordan River and the salt sea. In this vast wilderness, so beloved of the Master, ideas could grow unfettered and dreams turn into deeds.

In the days that followed Judas realised he had emerged from the encounter without guilt. If anything, he had become a more willing party to the Master's great, unbelievable scheme. It was as if the Master had said, 'You and I are in this together. If your role is not what you would choose, it is in the service of my greater need. What you suffer – the hate and condemnation you will bring upon yourself – will be recognised by others only as what it seems. The truth will be known only to me – and to the Father – and that must suffice for you.'

Judas watched the two Pharisees descend the street towards the Temple. Their words seemed to flutter like moths in the lamp-lit street. Faith in God – or faith in a man whose faith in God was so absolute that it permitted only blind acceptance or absolute denial? He raised himself from the cold stone. Even now there was choice. Not to go back to the room, of course – that was impossible – but simply to go home, to his lodgings in Bethany across the hill of olives, to take supper with Mary and Martha and wait for them all to return.

But what, then, of that return? He saw in his mind the Master's scorn and rage, because a path that had been determined – had been planned meticulously all these months – had come to nothing and was unsalvageable. For a moment he glimpsed relief, too, in those imagined burning eyes, that turned immediately to hatred because temptation might not now be overcome. The poisoned cup would indeed have been taken away.

But still Judas could not do it. His grip tightened on the purse in his pocket so that the coins crunched within. He walked down past the fine houses of the rich and influential to the one where he knew he must go. But he walked on, skirting the Temple until he reached a point high above the valley gate. There he positioned himself so that he could see who might come and go before it was closed for the night.

It was not difficult to recognise them. They emerged with heavy tread, in single file, as they always did when their thoughts were too profound for speech. He looked at the figure at their head, and saw in his bearing a man with no future other than that of his own choosing, enmeshed in his own dreams and fantasies. And he, Judas, had to decide: were those aspirations – and Judas now realised what they portended – more important than leaving the Master a shell?

What artist, he asked himself, would wish to be blinded, or craftsman become an amputee?

As the twelve bobbing heads descended into the darkness of the Kidron Valley Judas saw his own future in these same terms. There would be ridicule and hate, perhaps even to an extent he could not bear. Yet, what was the alternative?

Time was not material. They would wait in the garden. He knew they would wait as long as it took. He had to fulfil his role because, had it not been needed, they would surely have opted to find safety.

Two men with destinies: that was all there was to it.

Judas took the purse from his pocket, tossed it into the air and caught it with a snap of the wrist. The course was clear because he realised at last he was no longer a party to the decision.

A light rain began to fall as he set off back into the higher quarters of the city.

Outside the house of the High Priest he waited for many minutes in the darkness and freshening wind. Not until his tears had ceased to flow did he enter.

JUDAS THOMAS

The door inched open, then a fraction more. Thomas caught sight of a woman's eye before her head turned from him and the door opened fully. Not a word was said as he followed the cloaked figure up the stairs to a landing, then into a tiny apparently windowless room with floor to ceiling sackcloth drapes at the rear. The sparse furnishings included a table, two chairs and a stand bearing a number of parchment rolls and codices.

Reading at the table was Thomas' brother, James, leader of the Nazirite community in Jerusalem. The unkempt figure in a brown cloth tunic rose to greet him, the frowns at his forehead transforming as if by magic into an expression of delight. The woman said, 'Your visitor, Father,' bowed slightly and left the room. It seemed to Thomas that all the while she had deliberately avoided looking at him.

'Brother Judas Thomas!'

'Brother James!' Lowering his voice and keeping a straight face, Thomas said, 'Was that a fraternal or an ecclesiastical greeting?'

For a second James didn't know how to respond, then broke into a grin. 'You haven't changed, have you? I thought after eight years you would have grown up at last.'

'Can it really be that long?'

'At least. But Jerusalem welcomes you, and I thank you for coming.'

'But you haven't answered my question. Your invitation hinted at a family matter.'

'It's perhaps a bit of both. But first things first. You are well, obviously. Our brother Joses likewise?'

'He is, as are Miriam and the three children. They send their greetings.'

'And the family business?'

'In Galilee? I thought yours here was the family business.'

'This? Well, I've done my utmost to involve you all but…'

'And we are *all* contrite. But at home the firm's…' With his hand he signalled so-so. 'Actually it's been saved by a bit of work in the town. Some stonework in the amphitheatre. And – you'll appreciate this – you can see it from the village.'

'But Sepphoris is three miles from Nazareth.'

'True. But the evening sunlight catches the new stone. You should come to Galilee to see it. And other things.'

'I will, I will.' James paused to engage Thomas' gaze. 'Do you remember when we three – Jesus, you and me – used to slip away as darkness was falling to explore the big city?'

'And crept about in the shadows lest we village urchins would be mistaken for thieves.'

'You're sure we weren't? In a very minor way, of course. I remember the oranges in the gardens of the Via Maxima were particularly delicious.'

'How we ran! And then the girls. James, are you sure you want to pursue this?'

'You're right. I'm supposed to be above reproach. Funny,

though, how we followed him, even then. And though I was the middle one I always seemed the odd one out.'

'That never occurred to me.'

'Because you and Jesus were so alike. You, Thomas, were tall for your age – not like me – and you both had our father's hang-dog expression. When it suited you.'

'What?'

'Isn't that why they nicknamed you Thomas? Judas Thomas – Judas the Twin. Jesus' twin.'

'New to me. But if people thought we were twins I could never hold my own against him. Even then there was something of the magician about him. We'd argue and he'd win a point. Then he'd hold you with those piercing eyes…'

'Just like yours.'

'…and relish the advantage. But only for a second. Then his face would crease into a smile and he'd slap your shoulder. But not a trace of malice there. That was curious.'

'But something was driving him, even then.'

'He could be cunning, too.'

'Surely not.'

'Like – here's an example. He'd say casually, the chickens laid three eggs this morning. Then that evening he'd challenge you to say which cup he'd hidden a stone under. And you'd go, one, two, *three*, without realising it. And there it was.'

'That was thirty years ago, Thomas. And we still miss him.'

'So that's why you must come to Galilee. Imagine visiting all the old haunts.'

James ran his fingers through his tangled hair. 'But look at me – I'd be arrested as a vagrant. Perhaps when it's safe to leave here.'

'I thought things had gone quiet.'

'Superficially. But there's trouble brewing. Look out of the window.'

'Roman soldiers.'

'They've doubled the fortress guard. It's mostly paranoia, of course. They think it's time something happened. And once they start thinking that… it will.'

'I thought the new procurator was quite tolerant.'

'Compared with Pilatus, I daresay he is. But being tolerant implies something to be tolerant towards.'

'The high priest in the line of fire?'

'They don't give a toss about the high priest. He can gorge himself on pigs blood, so long as they can control things through him. But any dissent within the Jewish ranks – that's a potential flash-point. And you know our appetite for dissent.'

'Tell me about it.'

James threw up his hands in mock alarm. 'But where's my hospitality? I'm sure I asked Mary to prepare some refreshment.' He clapped his hands together. Mary, who must have been waiting at the door, entered. 'Did you forget?' he said, not unkindly.

'Oh… no.'

'I think probably yes.'

Thomas had to strain to hear her reply: 'Yes, then. Sorry, Father.' She left the room and returned with cups and biscuits on a tray. Then, without looking at them, went out again and closed the door.

'You recognise her?' James said.

'James, I've not been in this house for eight years.'

'She goes back even longer than that. I'll tell you shortly. A troubled soul, but devout. And devoted to me.'

'As are many others, so I'm told.'

'Really?'

'You've kept the community together.'

'Not easily. And it's... well... grieved me that I've never been able to tempt you back into the fold – with your obvious... connections.'

'There have been... reasons.'

'Well, I suppose a roomful of us praying and singing psalms is not that much of a draw. Last week I had Paul here. His first visit for goodness knows how long – almost as bad as you. He had the grace to call us the Jerusalem Church, but I could see that he was itching to call us the errant Jerusalem branch of *his* Messianic Church.'

'You're exaggerating, surely.'

'Maybe. But it does lead us back to why I've asked you here, Thomas.'

'Not brotherly love, then?'

'Ye..es. But not in the way you think.' He paused to take a sip from his cup. 'What that man Paul has achieved is tremendous. But... is it what our dear brother intended? Did you ever hear him say we should operate outside the Jewish faith, circumvent our dietary laws and circumcision? Oh, I know Paul pays lip service at the moment, but the conversions are incomplete. And Simon Peter, who's visited these places, has been weak in countering it, as I told him to his face. We're on divergent paths, Thomas, and I'm mightily unhappy about it.'

'I thought Jesus made specific provision for you to be entrusted with our community. I was there, I heard it. Surely the implication is that...'

'I'd got it right. Well, apparently not.'

James reached across to take a couple of documents from the stand. Look at these. Copies of Paul's letters to the community in Antioch. Where they've started calling themselves 'Christians' would you believe. But that's by the way.'

Thomas took one of the letters. 'I see you've marked one of the passages.'

'Read it.'

'Mm, mm mm... raised up on the third day in accordance with the scriptures; that he was seen by Peter, then by the Twelve: after that on one occasion by more than five hundred brothers... Five hundred? On one occasion?'

'Give or take a few hundred. Thomas, I'm beating about the bush because I don't quite know how to come to the point; because the issue is so... momentous. Listen. Paul's teaching is founded on belief in the resurrection of our brother, just as he – that's to say, Jesus – told us it should be. The risen Christ, isn't that what Paul calls him? We in the Jerusalem community believe the same. But whereas Paul's Jesus is already here, in metaphysical form, available, as it were, to anybody, we...'

'... are still waiting. The kingdom of God hasn't exactly... arrived. Is that what you mean?'

'Well, has it? Can it still? Oh, this is awful. I didn't mean to involve you like this, to seed you mind with doubts. Or nurture them in my own for that matter. Perhaps it's best if we stop this discussion.' He paused to take another sip of water. 'The thing is, Thomas, we Jerusalem brethren can muddle on within the framework of the Jewish faith. All our members go daily to the Temple. They observe the Law. It's their life. Does it matter much now, to them, whether the coming has been and gone, or has never happened?'

'Or whether Jesus really was the Messiah?'

James turned to face him, deeply perplexed. 'That's a step too far, but I want reassurance.'

Thomas was incredulous. 'From me?'

'You knew him as a brother, understood him, probably better than any of us.'

'So you want to question the past – is that right? I can tell you for a fact...'

James clapped his hands. 'Ha, that could be him speaking.'

'... that it's not wise, James.'

'Whatever the issues, however difficult they may be, the bottom line is that we have to be honest with ourselves. Would you agree with that?'

'What would you have me do?'

'Do you recall that awful day in Galilee when the message came that he was heading for Jerusalem? I was a humble rabbi in Sepphoris. You, if I remember, were nowhere to be found.'

'I had work in Tiberias – the news reached me later.'

'Whatever.' James was finding it difficult to recount something that was painful for him. 'I left as soon as I could, but when I got here... all was over. I went to Bethany. Deserted, but a watchman directed me here, to this house, where I found a young priest called John and a bevy of women, including our mother. The Twelve, it seems, had fled. Terrified out of their wits.'

'Who wouldn't have been?'

'I spent days trying to piece together what had happened. I walked the route taken by Jesus and the cross. I even spent a night in that dreadful tomb, where he'd been, thinking that if there was to be contact beyond the grave that would be the place. Again, nothing.' He paused. 'Then rumours began to circulate, that he'd been seen. Reluctantly, I believed the ramblings – as I saw them then – of his companion, the Mary from Magdala, who thought she'd seen him alive in the tomb. The rest is common knowledge, and the fact of the resurrection is incorporated into our faith.'

Thomas was guarded. 'You looked at all... rational... explanations?'

'I believed so. Until, that is, a few weeks ago. I had business in Tiberias and got talking to an old fisherman there. A thought flashed through my mind that was so bizarre I discounted it immediately. But it's never left me. That's why you're here.'

'Can you share... that thought?'

'Maybe not just yet. See if you come to the same conclusion. It's probably premature senility, Thomas.' Then he added, mocking himself, 'Or weight of responsibility.'

'So where to begin?'

'Tomorrow. We'll walk the path he took, to Golgotha and the tomb.'

'It still exists?'

'Fortunately no longer as a visitor attraction.'

'Quite a trudge up there, I recall.'

'Nonsense, Thomas. That's settled, then. Before you go, let me show you something.' James pulled back the drapes on the back wall to reveal a large sunlit room overlooking the city through an arched portico. A long table occupied the centre of the room. James and Thomas stood within the threshold. 'When you came before... did they show you this?'

Thomas said guardedly, 'They... may have done.'

'You have to imagine this table with the Twelve seated on either side of him. Quite a subdued gathering I imagine. Now look across the city. Temple to the right – beautiful, no? – and then the land falling and rising again to the little hill against the sun. That's Golgotha. The summit's bare now but the crosses would have been clearly visible.'

Thomas was puzzled. 'But that final meal was on the Thursday. Surely the crosses on Golgotha weren't put up until the Friday morning.'

'Others had to be removed to make way. So I was told.'

'Quite a view. So, this was John's house.'

John the priest, who had friends in high places and could pull strings. Most of the Twelve had been staying at Bethany and had fled. But Simon Peter sought refuge here with the women.'

'Wasn't that risky?'

'A headless snake presents little danger.' James stepped back into the smaller room and closed the drapes behind Thomas. 'So, there we go.'

'The feet that must have tramped through this room,' Thomas said wistfully. 'Imagine Judas Iscariot standing right here, wondering what on earth he should do. And all the sandals scattered about.'

There was a long silence before James said, 'You'll stay for some supper?'

'They're expecting me at the inn. But perhaps tomorrow…'

'I'll get Mary to see you out.'

'No need. I can remember the way.' James took a parchment roll from the stand and gave it to Thomas. 'A little light reading.'

Thomas turned it over in his hands. 'I recognise his handwriting. What is it?'

'References to the scriptures – pointing the way. Discuss it tomorrow. God be with you.'

'And with you, brother.'

As soon as Thomas had left Mary entered.

'You look troubled, my child.'

'There's something pressing in my head again.'

'I understand. Shall we break a crust together? We've not done that for quite a while.'

'Thank you, Father.'

The following morning James and Thomas were returning from a walk that had taken them past the gardens around Golgotha. Outwardly the stronger, of the two men Thomas was the more fatigued.

'Look at you!' James said. 'Don't they have hills in Sepphoris?'

'Not like here.'

'Then Jerusalem would suit you better. Make you fitter.' He handed Thomas a cup. 'Have some water.'

'Nothing more... never mind.'

'A clear head, Thomas, is what we need.'

'That was no idle excursion, was it?'

'No.' James paused. 'I'm perplexed, Thomas. And have been for a very long time. I had to summon up courage to get you here.' He slumped into a chair and Thomas followed suit.

'As I explained yesterday, our protestations of faith – Paul's and mine – hang upon the concept of a risen Jesus – or Christos, as he would have it in the Greek vernacular. It was the fulfilment of what Jesus had told us to expect. That event – initially so fantastic – was firmly accepted within weeks of the crucifixion... and has never seriously been questioned. Yet the reports at the time were so inconsistent. On almost every occasion he appeared to his followers, someone had doubts.'

'I vaguely remember that.'

'And if Jesus was truly back with us in the flesh – as he is reported to have said of himself – where was he in between times and – here's the crunch question – what happened between his entombment and his first appearances? Acceptance of the resurrection was at first wholly dependent on the disappearance of the corpse, about which we know nothing. Let me be blunt: I don't believe a lacerated and broken body removed itself. And if one of his followers had taken it... well... then our faith would have been founded on a lie, which is inconceivable.'

'It is said the Twelve believed it to a man.'

'And still do, the ones that are left. But do you?'

Thomas grinned. 'Conveniently I have a meeting in the city. Discuss it later?'

'Think about it, Thomas.'

'I will.'

As soon as the sound of Thomas' footsteps on the wooden stairs ceased there was a knock at the door and Mary entered.

'Has he gone?'

'Did he upset you?'

'I didn't speak to him, Father.'

'And you didn't look at him either. I saw you averting your eyes. It's our custom to welcome visitors, Mary, not shy away from them.'

'I'll try... next time.'

'I know you will. Now, draw up that chair.'

'I really will, Father.'

She sat and James shifted his own chair to face her.

'Mary, you remember Paul, the envoy who was here last week.'

'No... oh, yes.'

'A good man, and zealous in our faith. The resurrection of my brother – your master – dominates his thinking in ways that are not always easy to understand. Much more so than the message that Jesus preached within the Jewish faith.'

'I'm sure you're right, Father.'

'The point is, Mary, that Paul set me thinking about things I'd shut out of my mind. You told me once about certain... events. Would it trouble you greatly if I asked the same questions again?'

'If it pleases you.'

'So, let's go back twelve years, to when your master died. I remember we established that you, Mary his mother, the other Mary and Salome were all present when he was taken from the cross.'

'We were there all afternoon.'

'Was Simon Peter there?'

'No.'

'So who took Jesus from the cross?'

'Roman soldiers. They left him on the ground.'

'And no-one did anything?'

'They wouldn't let us near.'

'Us?'

'The women... and John.'

'And then?'

'Men came.'

'Who?'

'I don't know.'

'How many?'

'Two... no, three.'

'You're uncertain?'

'One was telling the others what to do.'

'What time was this?'

'It was getting dark.'

'But you could still see?'

'Just.'

'And then?'

'They carried him to the tomb in the olive trees.'

'The same that we've seen many times when we've walked there together.'

'Yes.'

'And they closed the tomb?'
'It was dark... but I think so.'
'Were the others still there?'
'No. Just me. John had brought Jesus' mother back here.'
'To this house?'
'Yes.'
'And Simon Peter?'
'When I got back he was sitting there, where you are. Scared, he was. He told me to go. John said I could stay. I told them what I'd seen.'
'And the following day... the Sabbath?'
'Everyone just moped around. Then we brought things for his body. It wasn't allowed, but we did. Next morning we took them there.'
'We?'
'His mother and me. But I got there first. The tomb was open, so I went in. There was someone there, holding up the shroud to fold it.'
'Did this person speak to you?'
'He said Jesus had gone from there.' Mary's voice was beginning to waver and James gripped her trembling hand. 'But he had Jesus' voice,' she continued, 'and looked like him, even in the darkness. I tried to touch him, but he pulled away, and then I knew it wasn't him. I was so frightened I ran back here.'
'And Mary, his mother?'
'She didn't dare go inside.'
'What did the others do when you got back?'
'John rushed out like a madman to go there. Simon Peter followed. When they got back they said it wasn't Jesus, but then thought it must have been, because that's what he said he would do.'
'Which was?'

'Come back from the dead.'

'Now, Mary, I want you to think very carefully. We know from Simon Peter that the Twelve expected something like this to happen, and that when it did it would herald the coming of the kingdom of God – which I'm sure one day will happen. But when Jesus spoke to you before... privately I mean... did you expect... the same?'

'I'm... not sure. I don't know that he knew himself. He said he was following God's will, and was in God's hands.'

'God having the final say?'

'He was God's servant – though I never heard him say that to the others.'

James muttered under his breath, 'I truly wish Paul could have heard what you've just said. And in the days... weeks... that followed, did you experience anything... well... unusual?'

'I heard rumours. But I was no longer with the Twelve.'

'They excluded you?'

There was resentment in Mary's voice. 'They said I was... unclean.'

'And John?'

'He kept apart. But we all worshipped in the Temple together.'

'And then John left Jerusalem for Ephesus, taking our mother with him...'

'That's when you came.'

'You have remembered well, Mary. I'm grateful.' He rose and helped her from her chair. 'Now, for our visitor this evening I've arranged for one or two special dishes to be delivered here. Will you serve them... and then join us?'

'Thank you, Father.'

That same evening Mary drew back the drapes that separated James' cell from the room in which Jesus had held his last supper. In the distance the lights of the city were becoming visible, but the summit of Golgotha could still be seen in the fading sunlight. James and Thomas entered and moved instinctively to the portico.

'The city is beautiful.' Thomas said. 'What a delight, James. But don't such pleasures conflict with your ascetic life-style?'

'I sincerely hope you're teasing me. Now, Thomas. I have permitted us a little extravagance this evening – I thought it might facilitate our discourse. I have to admit I'm quite looking forward to it.'

'Mm. Jesus once said to me, that brother of ours – James – there's purpose in everything he does.'

'Really? It must be a family trait then. Now, sit you down.' James directed Thomas to a place exactly at the centre of the table, facing the city – and the summit of Golgotha. Thomas, realising the implication that this might have been Jesus' place at the Passover meal – as James intended – was uneasy.

James said, 'Why do you hesitate?'

'I think you know. Why here?'

James appeared amused. 'Only because I thought that – with you looking so like our brother – it might help to suggest lines of thought so far neglected. You can move, but for a moment stay as you are. Who knows, for you too it may be an insightful experience. In a while Mary will bring us our food. Then you can move if you want to.'

'Is it coincidence that I can see Golgotha? Where we were this morning?'

'No. No coincidence. I thought it might focus our minds on what we saw there. As I believe it once focused his, our brother's.'

'The summit is bare.'

'But if you look hard you can see the cluster of olives near the tomb. There, down to the left. Tell me, what were your first thoughts – on seeing it again?'

'That I'd been made to confront something I'd chosen never again to see.'

'Can you explain that?'

'No. Not yet.'

'Try.'

'Very well then.' Thomas drew breath. 'When I saw it – days after the crucifixion – there were many others there. It hadn't yet been sealed off, you see. Someone had put a folded linen cloth where they thought his head had rested. But there was no feeling of... expectation.'

'That's about how it was for me.'

'I remember going outside to cry.'

'As did many others, including myself.'

'As a brother I should have known him better.'

For the first time James showed hostility towards Thomas. 'No. I think you knew him well enough.'

Thomas could not contain a thought he'd tried hard to suppress. 'Enough to know he was sometimes a misguided fool.'

'Ah. I begin to smell the truth.'

'James. Don't pursue this. It's in no-one's interest.'

'But it is in mine. Faith is one thing, Thomas, but blind faith I cannot stomach.'

'Then in my own time, eh?'

While they had been talking the room had been getting steadily darker. Far away the city lights shone more brightly. Mary, still wearing a headscarf, entered carrying a tray with plates and cutlery. James motioned her to set a bowl in front of Thomas. As seemed to be her custom she kept her eyes averted.

Thomas said loudly, 'James, there's something familiar about your servant.'

Mary, on hearing this, put down the tray and stared at him. Then she drew closer to see him better. To James she said, 'Is this a trick?' She peered more closely into Thomas' face. 'No. It's no trick.' She fell to her knees beside him.

'James, the woman's demented.'

James knelt beside Mary. 'Child, what's upsetting you?'

'Who is this man?'

'Judas. Judas Thomas. Your master's brother. You're not alone in seeing a resemblance, if that's what's troubling you. Get up, Mary. Thomas means you no harm.' He guided her to a seat facing Thomas, whose face she continued to scrutinise.

'So like him. So like him.'

'But neither of you have recollections of a meeting? Mary, take off your headscarf.'

Mary did so, revealing her long black hair. For the first time Thomas could see that she had once been beautiful.

'So, my brother,' James said. 'Are you still going to stay silent?'

It was a while before Thomas could bring himself to reply. 'I never intended it, James. But events moved so fast, as if they had been ordained. I was too weak to stop it.'

Mary was staring at him hard. 'You. In the tomb. Standing there with the white shroud.' Bitterly she added, 'As if it was yours.'

'Hardly white, being soiled with…'

'But in the darkness might have seemed so.' James said.

'You have to forgive me, Mary,' Thomas continued. 'I took you for one of the urchins that prowl the graveyards looking for spoils. When you tried to touch me…'

'You pushed me away. He wouldn't have done that. Even if I had been an urchin… or a leper.'

'Mary, that was the difference between us – me and Jesus. At that moment I failed him.'

'Understandable,' James said. 'But what interests me is what you were doing there, Thomas.'

'Simple enough. I'd worked out, you see, what he intended to do in Jerusalem. James knows that, while we were close as brothers, we were as different as rock and clay. And for him that made me a kind of sounding board… for how the public would react to his ideas. If it works on Thomas it will work on them – something like that. The logic was in the bits from scripture that you gave me, James. I didn't believe it, then… but he did. I knew that death at the hands of the Romans was his intention.'

'But you did nothing.'

'Not so! I followed. But days behind. At each village I heard of his growing band of followers. I reached Jerusalem on the evening of the crucifixion. The faces of people returning, droves of them passing me, ridiculing. It sickened me. So, knowing nothing, I took courage in my hands and went to the procurator's office.'

James was astonished. 'You saw Pilatus?'

'There was a councillor there from Arimathea – well known to him obviously – arguing to move the body. Can you believe that? And at that moment I felt God's hand – me a sinner – on my shoulder. I told him – this Joseph – who I was. With his friend Nicodemus we went to Golgotha.'

'But why would they want to move it… the body?'

'Because the tomb couldn't be sealed. The rock wouldn't close. There were rats… and dogs. Maybe even a child could have crept in.'

'So you moved him to another. Let me guess. About thirty paces away, now hidden behind brambles and tares.'

'How did my astute brother deduce that?'

'I caught you looking when we passed it together.'
'That suggests to me you already suspected…'
'Yes. But for the moment go on with your story.'

Thomas continued. 'I had no knowledge of this house, then. Or where the Twelve might be. So I stayed with Joseph in the upper city, and remained there for the Sabbath.'

'But the following morning – why did you go back?'

'We replaced the original shroud when we moved the body, but in our haste stupidly left the first behind. Unscrupulous people might have… found value in it. So at daybreak…'

To Mary, James said, 'You almost beat him to it.'

'Had I known who she was…'

'… the course of history would have been different.'

Thomas walked to the front of the portico and looked out. 'It took me two more days to discover that my – our – mother was here.'

Mary began to cry bitterly. 'Oh, why was I hiding myself away?'

'Decision time, then,' James said.

'Exactly. Simon Peter – and I think John likewise – already had it in their heads that something… well… extraordinary had happened.'

'And you chickened out of telling them.'

'Yes. I thought it would all blow over – that I'd tell them when they'd come down to earth. Also I needed to get back to Galilee, where there was building work to finish.'

'But you had one more opportunity to come clean, didn't you?'

'James, as you seem to know everything, just tell Mary.'

'I think,' James said, 'that when Thomas left Jerusalem he intended to take the shorter – but more dangerous – road through Samaria. And on the way, by chance, he fell in with his uncle Cleopas and his son.'

'Who'd only known me as a boy. They told me who they were, how ecstatic they were about what Simon Peter and John had told them about the risen Jesus.'

'And again you stayed silent. Oh, Thomas.'

Mary was now crying bitterly. 'I waited so long for him to come. Now I know he never will.'

James placed his arm about her shoulders. 'That is not necessarily so, Mary.'

Noises were heard from outside, then below.

'Ah, that clatter in the street could be our food arriving. Mary, would you…'

'Yes, Father,' Mary said, leaving the room.

'What you've told us, Thomas, only raises further questions. You realise that?'

Thomas was amused. 'Now what's passing through that scheming mind of yours, James?'

'That we should complete the picture, as we're so nearly there.'

'I don't follow.'

'I think you never reached Samaria.'

'Hm. I knew it was risky. Just two miles beyond Emmaus I got waylaid. In fact very badly beaten. I made it back to the inn – fortunately no sign of Cleopas – and next day in darkness crept back to the city. I stayed with Joseph until… well… my face was presentable.'

'By which time most of the Twelve had returned.'

'I sought them out, intending to explain. I found them here in this very room…'

Mary returned with steaming dishes, which she placed on the table.

'I was telling Thomas about when the Twelve returned.'

'I remember,' she said.

'You were there?' Thomas asked.

'I watched them sit at the table. How they had when Jesus was with them.'

'But you weren't there when I came.'

'They hadn't let me stay.'

James asked, 'Was it dark in here?'

Thomas said, 'They'd forgotten to light the candles. They seemed to recognise me, then they didn't. They stared and stared, nudging one another, awed and frightened. They didn't understand what they were seeing. Only later did I realise they thought I was the risen Jesus.'

'You'd never met them?'

'They never came to Sepphoris, to my knowledge.' Thomas smiled. 'There was confusion, I remember, because the only vacant seat was where Jesus must have sat. In my ignorance I took it.'

'They still hadn't guessed – that you were Jesus' brother?'

'Why should they? Then a strange thing happened. They offered me food – fish it was – and as we began to eat it was as if a great burden had been lifted and a feeling of joy entered the room. Their faces became transformed... as if...'

'And then?'

'I couldn't cope. I'm afraid I got up and left.'

'Oh, Oh, Thomas. You could have told them. Instead you dug an even greater hole for yourself.'

'I was pleased to be back in Sepphoris. In the real world of workshops and animals and... real people going about their ordinary business '

'And it never occurred to you to think how it all might have happened?'

'Of course it did. I'd seen it before, you see. Don't you remember? In our youth it was his party trick. He'd gather us together and go round tapping our shoulders and somehow – I've no idea how – he'd seed our minds with an idea, or an instruction. Then, later, something would trigger that idea. One mealtime we closed our eyes and when we opened them – to his delight – there was our sister Salome with bright red hair. You don't remember?'

'Salome wasn't the only one.'

'Later,' Thomas said, 'I came to realise he put his talent to better use – helping people to come to terms with pain and disabilities. Things like that. It was impressive.'

'A gift from God, would you say?'

'It must have been.'

'I think so too.' He turned to Mary, 'Would you pass that dish there?' Mary placed the dish in front of him and he peered into it. 'That fish looks delicious.' Mary, becoming agitated, began to re-arrange the cutlery aimlessly.

'What troubles you, Mary?' Thomas asked.

'Not now, Thomas.'

'I think…'

'I said, not now.'

'No. I'll tell him,' Mary said aggressively. 'It was because of what I was. They would never accept me. He would tell them to, but when his back was turned…'

'Mary!'

'And when *he* came,' she said, pointing at Thomas, 'they all saw. Except me, pushed upstairs by that oaf…'

'Mary!'

'And the worst of it. After he'd gone they couldn't be bothered to tell me. If his wounds had healed, whether the holes in his forehead… The look on their smug faces as they went out.'

'Mary, you had no reason to feel excluded.'

'They relished it!'

'You were the favoured ones, you and John. Were you not the very first to see him?'

Mary pointed at Thomas. 'He's shown me I wasn't.'

'Mary, Thomas has shown you no such thing.'

'James,' Thomas said. 'You're confusing us.'

'You, Thomas, wonder why I asked you here. What was it that I realised when I met…'

'…your mysterious fisherman in Galilee? Who was he? What did he say?'

'Who he was is insignificant. What he told me was… that he'd seen you, Thomas.'

'Me?'

'You went there from time to time, did you not?'

'We had work there – repairing the quayside.'

'And got to know the locals.'

'Some of them.'

'And when the Twelve fled Jerusalem and returned to their villages along the shore where they would have known everybody and everybody knew them and what had happened here in Jerusalem… And you saw them on the beach, and invited them to join your meal…'

'It was a… momentary encounter.'

'Possibly. But some thought it confirmed what they still doubted… that Jesus was alive.'

'Including John the priest…'

'…who reported it to me when I came here, just before he left for Ephesus.'

'And gave me hope,' Mary interjected.

'Yes. Now look, our food will be getting cold. Pass me your plates.' James spooned some of the fish stew into their bowls. 'They say the fish takes only a day and a half to reach us from Galilee.'

'Surely it's quicker from the sea.'

'But then it wouldn't be the same, would it? Now, let's taste it together.'

They each raised a portion of fish to their lips. Suddenly Mary dropped her spoon, stretched out her hands and grasped Thomas' wrists, staring at them intently. Then she fell backwards in her chair and scuttled, whimpering, to the far corner of the room. Thomas, distraught by what he saw, was staring at his wrists. James looked on, concerned and thoughtful.

'You went too far, James.'

'I think you should make your peace with Mary.'

Thomas walked across to Mary, helped her to her feet and guided her back to the table. Once more Mary took Thomas's hands, this time gently, and examined them, turning them over with her own.

'They've gone,' she said'

'What have gone, Mary?'

'Where the nails were. Just for a moment.'

'Then be thankful that you've seen him. Now, I think you should rest.'

James rose, and Mary walked slowly from the room. After the door had closed James said, 'I have a task for you, Thomas – a kind of penance I suppose – but I think it will give you some satisfaction.' He left the room and returned carrying an open box. 'You see, since I came here I've been trying to recall our brother's teachings. What he actually said, human memory being so fallible. So I've been asking those who knew him to write down what they remember… and they have. He took out handfuls of the sheets and spread them on the table. They'll have you crying, Thomas, I tell you.'

Thomas took up one sheet after another and read them. 'Look at this. Blessed are the poor, for yours is the kingdom of heaven. Remember that? And this. They showed Jesus a gold coin and said to him, Caesar's men demand taxes from us. He said to them, give Caesar what belongs to Caesar, give God what belongs to God, and give me what is mine.'

James smiled. 'I was asked to interpret that only yesterday.'

Thomas continued reading: 'His disciples said to him, is circumcision beneficial or not? He said to them, if it were beneficial their father would beget them already circumcised from their mother.'

'Oh,' said James, 'not sure about that one. But Paul would be glad to hear it.'

'And here,' Thomas continued: 'The disciples said to Jesus, we know that you will depart from us, who is to be our leader? Jesus said to them, wherever you are, go to James the Righteous for whose sake heaven and earth came into being.'

'Praise indeed! But it took a while to happen.'

'And so on.'

'Enough I think, don't you? You say you'll be leaving tomorrow?'

'In the morning.'

'Time to walk up to the second tomb? To take a look? I don't believe it's ever been disturbed.'

'No... no, I don't think so.'

'And if I were to tell you for a fact it's empty?'

'Then I would tell you for a fact that that's good enough for me.'

James moved to the portico, where Thomas joined him. 'The light has left Golgotha. How splendid the city looks.'

'I wonder if it will always be so.'

'Who knows.'

THE RUNNERS OF AFTON JAIL

They sometimes ask – the thick black line of death having been crossed – why I would wish to revisit people and places so integral to my demise. Did expiation work? Or, in the great scheme of things, does it matter at all? I leave that to others of us to judge. Perhaps it is that we just need to carry over with us a compelling story.

It was not difficult to spot him, in Fenner's Café, staring ahead at nothing in particular, moodily stirring his tea. It was the same image I'd had of him in Afton Jail, sitting at a long table amongst other mobsters and the like, before the parole board had been persuaded, somehow, that he'd shown remorse. What he'd done didn't interest me; what linked us was his friendship – if that's the right word for cellmates thrust upon one another – with my brother. He was the only one Harry ever mentioned during my visits – those fraught, infrequent visits when we were allowed just twenty minutes to chew over past demeanours with – thankfully then but regretfully now – no time left to consider… well… deeper issues.

Without looking up or apparently seeing me, Grimston – I never knew his given name – stopped stirring. Perhaps in prison one becomes sensitive to approaching footsteps, as like as not spelling danger. Then he showed me a face bearing the mental scars of a potential lifer, unexpectedly cast adrift in an unwelcoming world. And I saw there the dregs of the same hopelessness that I'd begun to see in Harry.

'I got your message,' I said, taking the seat opposite.

'Yeah, well,' he said. His tone implied reluctant compliance with an instruction, as if he'd been thrust into an action that didn't come easily. 'You want a drink?'

'You said you had something of my brother's.'

He picked up a brown paper package from the seat beside him. I expected him to push it across the table but he just fidgeted with it. I judged his reluctance to part with it as having significance: a sole momento of someone who had meant something . And I couldn't imagine there had been many of those in his bleak life.

'He'd worked on it, y'see. Days at it he was, before his… before he came to grief. Never told me why. Made no sense.'

'May I see it,' I said.

He kept his hand on the parcel.

'Look when I've gone. It's nothing I can help you with. Give it to my brother,' he said. 'Make sure you give it to Michael. He'll understand.'

It didn't quite make sense. 'That suggests he knew something was going to happen to him.'

'Don't know how he could. Always kept his head down. I couldn't see anything coming.'

'And you don't know who did it?'

'Probably wouldn't tell you if I did. But nah, no idea.'

'And he had no enemies, that you know of?'

'Beaten up, a couple of times, long time ago. Respect thing. Meant nothing. It happens.'

'When they found him, were you there?'

'Soon after. On my knees, bloody crying.'

And indeed that was not difficult to imagine, for I could see his eyes were glistening. Suddenly he got up and made for the door. I called after him, 'If there's anything I can do for you…'

He stopped in the doorway and turned.

'Like you did for Harry? No thanks.'

Seeing me alone at the table the waitress – who had perhaps wisely kept her distance – came up to me. 'You want something?'

I felt like saying, my brother back, but that would have needed an explanation and she didn't look the type. 'A coffee,' I said. 'No milk.'

I fingered the brown package, then tore it open. I withdrew a notebook – of poor quality, with the Afton Jail stamp – that I imaging was issued to prisoners to fend off boredom. I felt the pulse at my temple quicken. A diary, I thought at first. But on turning the cover it was nothing of the kind. The few used pages were covered in what appeared to be calculations, and geometric shapes based upon the circle. Before his arrest he'd worked in a surveyor's office and my first thought was that they related to a building, for here surely was a dome. And yet… It made no sense and I replaced the notebook in the bag.

As the waitress bent over my shoulder I caught the drift of a perfume more subtle than her status suggested. 'Your coffee. You look as if you need it.'

'I do. Just lost my brother. He died in prison.'

Her eyes widened. 'Topped himself, did he?'

'No. Got attacked.'

'Know how you must feel. Mine was a suicide.'

'At Afton?'

'Yeah. Years ago though.'

'Your brother?'

'Me partner. Left me with two kids.'

I suddenly felt a desperate need to talk. 'Can you sit for a minute?'

'No, but we close in five minutes. When I shut the door you can finish your coffee and I'll join you.'

But under her searching eyes I still couldn't tell her my great secret, which from the moment I entered the café and saw Grimston had expanded within me like a flesh-consuming infection. Yet wasn't this girl a lifeline too valuable to throw away? 'Can I ring you sometime,' I said.

'Yeah, yeah, okay.'

Without invitation she wrote her number on the paper that had enclosed Harry's book. As she held the door for me our eyes engaged and I felt an unexpected warmth flow between us.

On the way to my mother's – our mother's – I passed St Peter's Church, where the funeral was to be. I saw myself in the pulpit spouting about loyalty and respect and family values. But how do you speak about someone with love and affection – even if that was the case – when you've sinned so much against them? I felt already the lump that would creep into my throat and the tremor in my speech, and imagined the accusations in the eyes of the congregation, even though no such thoughts yet troubled their minds. I had volunteered a reading, which I thought I could manage, but Mum had said, no, you owe it to Harry. And so I had agreed, knowing that embarrassment – and pain – would surely be my lot.

I was still grasping Harry's notebook and felt a compelling urge to study it, to get inside his mind during those last bleak days. Did I not owe him that – to understand? I retraced my steps to the church and went in. The sepulchral gloom seemed appropriate to the task and I sat at the foot of the pulpit, to contemplate my Armageddon.

The light was dim but I could see enough of the numbers and drawings to make more sense of them. Here was a circle, with arrows against it, as might represent the dome of a building subjected to the stresses of overlying concrete. And in the equations supporting this were surely coefficients relating to stress. A link with his former life, perhaps? A mental exercise to stimulate a soul reduced to immeasurable boredom tipping over into the intolerable?

I recalled my last meeting with him three months before, after the regularity of my weekly visits had tailed off – the effect of a trade-off between brotherly duty and hypocrisy. Yet the regret was on all my side. Nowhere did I see the resentment that was my due. He'd looked at me with those soft child-like eyes. Don't worry about it, Michael, it's okay, it's in the past. What's done is done and can't be undone. Now I just want you to live your life and be successful.

And successful I had been, if a big house, a wife and kids, and a Range Rover in the drive were benchmarks. And a business – if that's what you call a… well, let's say an activity in the pharmaceutical supply industry – as yet unlikely to be rumbled.

A faint cough from behind made me turn. The girl from the café was sitting two pews behind. 'I happened to be going the same way and saw you come in here. I'm a good listener, if that's what you want.' But it was still too early to tell. As she walked away I doubted if I would see her again.

In the kitchen my mother was cutting vegetables at the table. In her grief the image of Grimston in the café came to me and I could see there were elements in the tragedy they both shared. 'Grimston?' she said. 'Yes, he came here just after… I made him tea and he said how close he and Harry had been. It's a pity you didn't visit more often, Michael.

He once said he'd do anything for you. Did you know that? He was so proud of having a brother he could look up to. Made up for his own deficiencies, he said.'

I turned away, not able to look at her, groping for something to say. 'Did Grimston say why Harry had changed?'

'Well, it seemed to him Harry'd had a new lease of life. Which makes the thing so difficult to understand.' She paused to wipe away a tear. 'You know he'd joined a fitness class? He'd even started running when they let them do it in the yard. Quite good at it, Grimston said, considering he was never the active one of you two. And he'd even started writing. Michael, why couldn't they have left him alone, when he seemed to be doing so well? What had he done to deserve it?'

I couldn't show her Harry's notebook. Not yet understanding its contents I knew there was a risk if it ever got passed around. On the other hand I felt an obligation to seek an explanation for her. It was then that I went to the next room and telephoned the prison for an appointment with the governor.

Was it the forlorn hope of seduction or expiation of guilt that made me pass Fenner's Café, the next day, on my way to the station? She looked up from wiping a table as I approached the window, then opened the door, with that little half-smile I'd carried in my head from the day before; and what – if I was honest – had drawn me back now. But I was taken aback by her first words.

'You weren't straight with me yesterday, were you?'

'What do you mean?'

'You said your brother had killed a man.'

'I said…'

'He came back, you see. That bloke you were talking to.'

'Grimston?'

'If that's what you call him.'

My body chilled as she motioned me to a table in the darker depths of the café. 'This Grimston said your brother was innocent. That's not what you told me.' Then she said, 'I'll bring you your coffee.'

My thoughts raced. By the time she'd returned I'd rehearsed what to say. 'What I said was he'd been arrested for killing someone. It was never proved but his prints were on the knife. It was enough to convict.'

'But did he do it?'

What had Grimston told her, or for that matter known? I tried to adopt an explanatory tone. 'My brother told the police he had, under interrogation...' I said, looking down at the table.

'You believed that?'

'The bar was packed. In the confusion it was impossible to see what happened. The witnesses – if there were any – didn't hang around.'

'Shouldn't think they did, but that's not what I asked.' She lowered herself into the seat opposite me, elbows on the table, chin resting on her interlocked fingers, waiting.

Under normal circumstances I would have switched on the charm. But not now. 'Why are you so concerned?'

'I told you about my partner.'

'You did.'

'But not about my affairs, while he was banged up.' There was a brief catching of breath. She lowered he voice. 'So I know what makes people do such things... and the hell you go through after.'

I looked at my watch and jumped to my feet, suddenly relieved I could claim only just enough time to catch my train. 'Shall I see you again?' I said. 'That depends on you,' she replied. I looked back to see her still sitting there.

At two-thirty I rang that familiar and innocuous-looking bell at the prison gate. But instead of passing through the usual series of clanking doors I was shunted along a less forbiddingly grey corridor, into the beige neutrality of the governor's office.

'The thing that puzzles me about your brother,' governor Robinson said, 'is that he seemed to have no enemies. Bullied sometimes, maybe. Depended on what others were passing through. But certainly nothing recently. In fact about a month ago his demeanour seemed to change for the better. He got quite motivated when we introduced changes in the PE sessions and made a small running track around the yard. Brought out all their competitive instincts – and made them more subdued when they came back in. But Harry, he seemed obsessed by it. Not just in winning, but in bettering his own achievements.'

'Grimston said he'd started writing in his cell.'

'Ah, yes. Grimston, his cell-mate. Curious that. Considering the two were so pally it was odd that the change in your brother seemed to start when we announced Grimston's release. Perhaps Harry did it to take his mind off the prospect of another cell-mate. It gets to some of them that way.'

I thought a new line of attack was needed. 'Did my brother ever question the verdict that had sent him here?'

Robinson smiled sadly. 'I once looked through the transcript of the trial. If he hadn't pleaded guilty my guess is that the conviction would have been unsafe. In my opinion. But the matter was never raised.'

Into my head came an image of Harry pausing to look at me as he stepped from the dock: a little grimace – without malice – that said, don't worry about it Michael, I'll be okay.

But in the end it wasn't okay, after it must have seemed I'd abandoned him.

'I suppose you would like to see where it happened?'

The building seemed deserted and you could tell why from the shrieks from the exercise yard outside. We climbed the three flights of metal stairs to the uppermost corridor.

'The odd thing,' Robinson said, 'was why he was up here in the first place, seeing that his own cell was two floors below.'

I had visions of him being chased, terrified, up those bleak steps and along the corridor. Robinson saw my unease.

'The puzzle is that there were no witnesses that we know of and as you can imagine no-one's admitted to the attack.'

'Is that surprising?'

'No. But we have the rudiments of an intelligence system and so far that's drawn a blank.'

He led me along the top corridor, which ended in a blank wall faced with those brown glazed bricks one associates with pre-war public lavatories. He pointed to a spot about four feet from the floor.

'It must have been a powerful blow as the wall here – and the floor below – was splattered with blood. I can only think that someone felled him with a blow to the head while he was bending down. If you're up to it I can show you photographs when we get back to the office. The other strange thing is that there's been no trace of a weapon and I can't believe a fist alone could have opened up his skull like that. We've searched high and low, but found nothing.'

'Smuggled out?' I asked.

He gave me a withering glance at having challenged the integrity of prison security. 'I don't think so.' He looked at the ground. 'Won't please the prison visitor, though, when we can't come up with an explanation. Anyway, we ought to get back, before the prisoners return from their exercise.'

Things were beginning to come together in my head.

'Would you mind if I stayed just a moment,' I said. 'By myself, just to reflect. I did love my brother, you know.' I was about to add, for all his faults, but in those last few minutes something fundamental to my relationship with Harry's memory had changed. Whatever had been there before had become an amalgam of guilt and remorse.

'Of course. A minute then? I'll be waiting on the floor below.'

I watched him walk the length of the corridor, back to the stairs at the far end. I turned my attention to that shiny brown wall, imagining the red blood upon it, dripping to the floor, and poor Harry's body writhing in its death throes, splattering his blood around. I followed in my mind the pages of the notebook Grimston had given me – the skull-shaped dome at the centre of the calculations and the estimations of speed – of that I was now sure – and the forces that needed to be applied to it through the resilience of the only structure unambiguously available in that hellish place.

I slowly retraced my steps along the corridor, counting the paces; at the head of the stairs leading down I noted their number. It did not surprise me that it matched the figure in Harry's calculations: the distance in yards that would enable – for a fit and determined runner – to work up sufficient speed…

The governor looked up from the floor below. I smiled at him and waved, concealing as best I could the doubts that had now become certainties. As I did so the shrieks and howls from outside gave way to the banging of doors as the prisoners left the yard. The governor signalled to me to make haste, and then it was as if that malignant body of sound had suddenly been transplanted wholesale into the echoing emptiness of the building. It became a seething mass of raw masculinity, barbarous and threatening, without constraint. Against my will I was transported back to the bar of the Green Lion, and saw Harry's shocked and innocent face as I thrust the bloodied knife into his hand; and heard myself saying 'get rid of it for me' before pushing my way, unnoticed, out of the scrum. Within that crush of bodies no-one had seen, and when the stunned and now silent mass began to disperse, there was Harry, bewildered and still, blood dripping to the floor from the knife held at his side.

Into my head came again the number of paces I'd taken along the corridor – the same figure circled in Harry's notebook. The meaning of those calculations – of distance, and speed, and the consequences of impact – became icily clear. The governor's clattering footsteps towards me seemed only seconds ahead of the advancing cohorts behind him. There was no going back. I turned to contemplate for one last time the length of the still empty corridor, and focused on that distant, beckoning brown wall. Then I lowered my head to achieve the greatest speed, and ran…

THE WIDOWER

Greville was busy at his workbench when the doorbell rang. Not the usual location for a workbench, in the bow of his drawing room window, but it was here that the light was best, and the view over the Thames was never less than inspirational.

It hadn't always been like this. When Emma was alive he'd had to observe social norms. But since her death in a boating accident three years previously there had been no such restrictions, and he'd rearranged the house to please himself. So in that part of the room there were now lathes, electric drills, saws and goodness knows what else.

When he and Emma had started their distribution business out of a garage in Watford they could not have foreseen its takeover by one of the electronics giants and a windfall out of all proportion to its worth. That was what funded their move to a much grander house – Maple Lodge – overlooking the towpath at Strand-on-the-Green in Chiswick. And there, unencumbered by marital constraints, Greville had given free rein to his creative instincts – to be precise the development of miniaturised surveillance equipment that had already found a lucrative market with some of the more disreputable governments and, close on their heels, one or two of the scarcely more reputable multinationals. Above all, though, he enjoyed his work and wanted for little else in life, except that…

Except that his present lifestyle was not conducive to finding a replacement for Emma. Not that, towards the end, they'd enjoyed much of a physical relationship, but it had been enough to fend off temptation. Now, driven by self-determined abstinence, that need had grown.

Strangely, this was the thought foremost in his mind when, that bright autumnal afternoon, the doorbell rang. He'd forgotten the message from his niece Clarice to say she was calling by. She was his late brother Michael's child, whom he hadn't seen – nor frankly wanted to see – since Emma's funeral. He remembered her as a gawky, bespectacled teenager, only dimly aware that – if the TV credits of recent documentaries were anything to go by – she was beginning to make a mark in that industry. So, when he opened the door, he was surprised to see a demure young woman, smartly dressed, with no sign of spectacles. He must have looked confused.

'Uncle Greville, surely you remember me?'

'Of course I do. Come on in.'

Greville was savvy enough to know that the visit was no social call. He surmised – wrongly as it turned out – that it had something to do with his business: a documentary perhaps, or a new series along the lines of *Tomorrow's World*, a programme he'd followed avidly. 'Now,' he continued, 'before we talk I must show you this.' He held out a metal cylinder about ten centimetres long and slightly fatter than a fountain pen. 'It's what's got people buzzing at the moment. I call it an *inquiscope*. Look.'

He pointed the object towards a bird sitting on a twig of a distant tree. Clarice saw the magnified image appear on a laptop screen on Greville's workbench. And then, loud and clear, she heard the throaty warblings of the bird.

'That's impressive,' Clarice said.

'Then watch this.' Greville pointed the instrument at an elderly couple walking along the opposite river bank. The expressions on their faces were clear to see and their voices carried around the room.

'That's amazing,' Clarice said.

'I thought you'd be impressed. Something there for us to talk about? A TV programme, possibly?'

'Well, perhaps in the future. But you're right about a television programme. Which is why I wanted to show you this.' She handed him a neatly handwritten letter, which he began to read. 'Wayside TV Productions – my company – is making a series where long lost family members are reunited. Not very original, but it will draw in the audiences. When I received this I thought of you.'

The letter was from a young woman – so Greville presumed – called Samantha, now living in the UK but who had been brought up as a foster child in Australia. By chance she'd come across a note from her long-dead mother to a man apparently trying to absolve himself from being her father – and giving his family name. Samantha had seen Clarice's name – with the same surname – in a list of TV credits and this was her letter to the company. Clarice, dimly aware that an uncle had migrated to Australia as a teenager, had come to the conclusion they might just be related.

'So where do I fit in?' Greville asked.

'We thought you'd like to meet her – for one of our programmes.'

'Me? Why not you?'

'Being an employee rules me out. Besides, with all this fascinating stuff' – she swept her arm across the workbench with an expression of profound admiration – 'you would be... well... of much more interest to our viewers.'

Greville glimpsed another opportunity for the commercial exposure of his inventions. 'But what's she like?' he asked, foreseeing obstacles.

As if as an afterthought Clarice scrabbled in her handbag and drew out a photograph of a slim young woman with regular features and long, straight black hair.

'Doesn't resemble my brother,' Greville said. 'Was her mother English?'

'I wouldn't know. The question is, would you be happy to meet her?'

'In front of the cameras?'

'Of course.'

'There's a pub just along the towpath. Why don't we arrange to meet there? We could go there now to take a look.'

'How it will work,' Clarice said over beers in the City Barge, 'is that you'll meet for the first time here, before the cameras. We have to do it that way for spontaneity. Then we'll leave you both in peace for a few days to get to know one another – if that's what you want – then meet again for a second shoot to see how you've got on.'

Greville could see in his mind an image of this attractive young woman holding his surveillance device between finger and thumb alongside a set of gleaming white teeth.

Exactly one week later Greville was positioned at the same table, facing the door.

'We'll have a shot of you sitting there,' Clarice said, 'then go outside to follow Samantha in. Act normally but please look delighted to see her. After all, you've always wondered about your long-deceased brother.' Then she added, 'C'mon, cheer up. It won't be that bad.'

The whole episode so far had made Greville nervous. For

a start he had vague feelings that his life as a recluse – with all the advantages it offered – was about to be compromised. Having met this woman what was he supposed to do with her? Forget her? Send her Christmas cards – or money? She was, after all, only a niece, like Clarice – and he'd managed to push her almost completely out of his mind. But then, he thought, besides Clarice she was probably his only remaining blood relative.

The cameraman squirmed though the door ahead of Samantha, then moved several paces backwards to include Greville in the same frame.

Greville rose and stepped towards her. As she threw her arms around his neck the hand that was rising to shake hers unexpectedly found its way around her waist. 'I'm so pleased to meet you,' he whispered into her ear.

They sat opposite one another. Greville realised that the photograph Clarice had given him did not do Samantha justice. Perhaps that had been deliberate, so as not to build up his expectations. The face was more perfect, the eyes more dreamy, the long black hair glossier. He looked at the bare arms extended on the table before him and noted the pallor of his hands in comparison.

'If my brother Edmund was your father, who was your mother?' he asked.

'An oriental princess,' she replied, teasing him. 'Actually, my mother was Anglo-Indian.'

'Was?'

'My mother was… it was an honour killing, you see.'

'And my…'

'… which is partly why your brother committed suicide soon after.'

'Did he? I didn't know that. I thought he'd had a fall – an accident.'

'It was a fall, but we think it was deliberate.'

The cameraman having left, Clarice approached the table. 'I'll leave you two alone, but there is one last formality. I would like to take swabs from you both for DNA analysis – just to be absolutely sure. Our viewers are suspicious people, you see. There was a brisk scouring of each of their mouths with swabs, which she put into her bag. Then she was gone.

'I expect you'd like to see where I live,' Greville said.

Samantha looked at her watch and smiled apologetically. 'Maybe another time. I have an appointment in an hour. Perhaps the next camera shoot can be in your house.' She kissed his cheek perfunctorily and left the pub.

That evening Clarice telephoned to ask if all went well.

'Well, no,' Greville replied. 'She left soon after you did.'

'Oh, dear. I was hoping you'd hit it off. But she is rather shy. Why don't you give her a ring?' She reminded him of Samantha's telephone number.

That night he slept fitfully. Something was telling him to be careful, something that might upset the life-style he had painstakingly created for himself. He tried to analyse the situation. Why had she left so abruptly, having gone through the circuitous exercise of seeking out relatives in the first place? For sure something was not quite right. Yet… The following morning he dialled her number.

A male voice said, 'I'll get her.'

'I think it would be a good idea if we were to meet before they film us together. Are you free anytime this week?'

'No, but I could make next Tuesday.'

They met in the rotunda of Chiswick House – that gloomy icing cake of a Palladian villa – and sat in the cafeteria.

'I must seem an awful intrusion into your life,' Samantha

said. 'I'm sure when the television people have got what they want…'

'No, not at all. Sitting at my workbench day in day out can get quite monotonous. A small diversion is exactly what I need.'

'You miss your wife?'

'I miss having someone around – someone I can relate to. I'm not sure that's the same thing. She liked our new-found affluence, you see, but lacked the dedication to the cause.'

'If it's not too bold a question, what happened to her?'

'A boating accident in the Mediterranean, near Cannes, one holiday. Swimming from the boat. It's believed she was stung by a jellyfish. Allergic to the toxin, apparently. It happened so quickly.' He looked carefully for her reaction, but saw none.

They wandered away from the house and found themselves in the stone grotto beside the lake.

'You don't look old enough to be my uncle,' she said.

'Is that a compliment?'

'Well, no.'

'Your father, my eldest brother, was fourteen years my senior. I was an unexpected late addition to the family. He must have been still a teenager when he emigrated.'

'And I think he sowed his wild oats very early on.' For the first time he saw the hint of a smile. 'So there's not much difference between us after all.'

'I suppose not.'

Whether it was this deduction that caused her to rest her hand on his knee – perhaps not even being aware of it – he could not be sure. But he placed his own hand over hers. She turned her head away but did not withdraw the hand. The black hair over her slender body seemed to become even more lustrous. 'It's not far to walk back to my house – if you'd like to,' he said.

And that is what they did. They parted the following morning, having agreed – for the camera – to appear interested but otherwise cool towards one another.

That afternoon Clarice rang to say that the DNA tests had shown the expected match. 'Have you seen anything of her?' she asked casually. 'We met briefly for tea,' he replied, as calmly as he could, adding, 'I quite like her.' 'Well, don't get too involved,' she said. 'Remember you are related.'

That last remark set him thinking. He went to his computer and googled 'incest.' But legal restrictions seemed to stop at full siblings, parents and offspring. He grunted approvingly, failing to see the footnote advising that the law was about to change in favour of wider inclusivity.

A week later he was tidying the drawing room in readiness for the shoot the following morning. At first he placed the items on his workbench so as to be seen to best advantage. But as he picked up his inquiscope he froze. Suddenly it made sense that Samantha had shown no outward interest in his invention, had even seemed to avoid the subject when he tried to explain his work to her. It had disappointed him at the time, but now it began to make sense. Could it have been a deliberate show of disinterest to mask something that was precisely the opposite? That actually her presence here – and all that had gone before – was a plot to spy on him? For financial gain, even? He realised how little he knew of her background.

The shoot began at ten the following day. The bright sunlight through the window lit up not only Greville's workbench but also the sofa on which he and Samantha were seated. 'It would be nice if you could hold hands,' Clarice, said, 'then I'll ask each of you about your reactions to seeing one another.' Feeling the warmth of Samantha's fingers entwined with his, all Greville's doubts about her possible motives evaporated. 'Will your relationship continue, do you think,' Clarice asked them, and each smiled back in affirmation. 'Certainly,' said Greville. 'Of course,' Samantha agreed. The cameraman packed up his equipment and left. Clarice jotted a few notes on her clipboard. 'The viewers will love it,' she said. 'Now, when I'm done how about some lunch at Ronaldo's at Kew. It gets quite full but as we're early we should be okay.'

As soon as Clarice had finished writing Samantha rose from the sofa as if, Greville thought, a matter of some triviality had been transacted. The same cold fear he had experienced the night before returned. He watched the two women staring down at the glistening instruments on the workbench. Something passed between them but he could not hear what was said. Their bodies seemed unnaturally close together, suggesting an intimacy he had not expected. Then he rebuked himself inwardly for his suspicious mind; after all, they were cousins, for heaven's sake. Why should they not have developed a relationship outside his own.

Before following Clarice out of the door, Samantha cast one lingering look – or so Greville thought – over the items on the workbench. That decided him. 'You two go on ahead,' he said. 'I have a quick call to make.'

'What can we get you to drink?' Clarice asked.

'A G&T please.'

He watched them walk along the towpath. As soon as they were out of sight of the window he checked the charge of his inquiscope, then put it into his pocket. He folded up his laptop, set the house alarm and followed the path the women had taken.

From outside the restaurant he watched them being led to a table at the far end of the dining room. Once inside, instead of walking between the tables he took the stairs to the gallery above, where he knew from experience there would be tables free. And why did he know that? Why, because it was from a table overlooking the floor below that he had watched Emma, his erstwhile wife, entertaining the man he presumed was her lover. And it was here that the idea of the inquiscope was born – and what had driven the rapidity of its development so that it could be put to practical use.

Below him in the distance the two women were already seated. To Greville they seemed at ease with one another, though neither smiled. Hidden behind a plastic fern he connected the instrument to the laptop and discreetly pointed it at them. In seconds their faces appeared on the screen. Hastily he muted the sound and plugged in his earphones.

Below him the waiter appeared with their drinks, including his G&T. Then the conversation between the women became serious.

'Before he gets here,' Clarice said. 'You're quite sure you want to go through with it?'

'As sure as I've ever been. Having met the man, I think I can just about tolerate him. For a while.'

'You still have suspicions about your sister's death – about Emma?'

'More than just suspicions. It was a preposterous story – about the jellyfish.'

'I think so too.' A fleeting smile crossed Clarice's lips. 'But it's his imagination that has got him where he is. I mean, like with his clever instruments.'

'Aren't they just! No wonder he's made a fortune. You think he resented sharing it, with Emma?'

'No, I'm sure it wasn't that. After all, it was her capital that started their electronics business. No, I think it was more that she'd become an encumbrance.'

'We'll just have to see, won't we?'

'But in the meantime don't forget we have a deal.'

'Dividing the spoils, you mean?'

'Only fair,' Clarice said. 'I'm the blood relative.'

They raised their glasses and reached across the table. 'To our future spoils,' they said.

Clarice put down her glass. 'Now, to practicalities. Have you got all your new paperwork – passport, birth certificate, fostering papers?'

'Our Pakistani friends in Camden were most obliging.'

'Will you ever tell Greville – that you're actually his wife's little sister?'

A look of contempt crossed Samantha's face. 'When I look into his eyes for the very last time I'll wave Emma's letter in front of his nose. So it's the last thing he'll ever see.'

'Oh? What letter?'

'The one telling me she was frightened, that she was convinced something was about to happen to her. Sent the day before she… was drowned.'

'My God! I'm not sure I want to be part of this.' For the first time Clarice laughed. 'I thought we were into it just for the money.'

'Well, we're in too deep to stop now.'

The waiter arrived with their main courses. Their conversation drifted towards more womanly matters. Greville, still glued to his screen and listening, saw his hands were trembling. In spite of all the women had revealed something was missing. But for the moment he could not grasp what it was.

Instinct told him to confront them, to go below and end the whole sordid business. Yet… He watched Samantha's elegant and sinuous passage between the tables towards the door – and thought back to their night of passion at Maple Lodge. Anyone who could behave like that towards him in the face of the hatred she must bear deserved… well… his admiration. And he, knowing the score, had a challenge. Like playing a dangerous fish and bringing it aboard to its death while at the same time avoiding its sharp teeth. A delicious tingle passed down his spine.

As he was about to disconnect the inquiscope he noticed Clarice's forgotten handbag hanging from the back of her chair. They would be walking back to the house, wondering why he had not appeared. He would run after them with it and so begin the next phase of their… interesting… relationship.

He descended to the floor below, walked to the chair and grasped the bag. There was a voice at his shoulder.

'Excuse me Sir, but are you sure this bag is yours?' Greville turned to see the waiter standing there.

'It belongs to my friend who was here just now.'

'I'm sure that's right, Sir, but I must ask you to identify it.'

'In the wallet you'll see that…'

His voice tailed off as he saw the contents of the bag. The first item to catch his eye was a school class photograph in which Clarice and Samantha were standing side by side. The second was a thin plastic tube containing a swab, with Samantha's name on the label, just as he had seen it written before his eyes; Clarice, then, must have substituted her own one, to cover the lie. And that, he said to himself, made her a legitimate second target.

There was a spring in his step as he walked briskly back to Maple Lodge.

ENDURING LIGHT

The little church of Santa Maria Maggiore stands in a back street some two hundred metres from the Piazza Publica, where the great cathedral of San Marco casts its shadows over hordes of tourists taking coffee at the myriad tables. Those dazzled by the splendour of the cathedral generally have little time for anything else but resting their feet, restoring their fluid balance and heading back to their hotels – and certainly little interest in the lesser church, in spite of it possessing paintings by Titian and Veronese and a campanile taller and more beautiful than any other in the city. But it was none of these that first drew Theodore there; rather, a need to find tranquillity and darkness to help still a mind suddenly and unexpectedly troubled. For he had in his pocket the letter from the hospital containing the results of blood tests telling him that he had myeloid leukaemia and needed to return home as soon as was practicable to discuss treatment with his doctor. He regretted opening the letter at all, knowing that it could spoil his holiday. Yet, strangely, it had cleared his mind, in the sense that a need to establish order in his life had suddenly become a priority.

He had come upon the church by accident, its dark interior just visible through the narrow door, beckoning him in. He'd visited other Catholic churches before, but seldom stayed long, finding the decoration excessive and the messages of the paintings and statuary unbelievable. So, now, he wondered again if this was what the Christ-figure would have wanted; and whether he would have identified with the effigies strung up on crosses or bleeding copiously from spear thrusts and thorn wounds. For sure, he thought, from what he knew of the New Testament, the Jesus of history would not have approved of the gilt crucifixes, the fantastically elaborate wood carvings and other extreme paraphernalia. But he might have welcomed the cool interior, as he would have done in the synagogues of Galilee after days of humility and ridicule.

The stations of the cross afforded a guided tour of sorts, but the artist had captured nothing with which he could empathise. Instead he was drawn to an image of the head of the Christ-figure bearing a plaque that told him it was from the school of Leonardo. The enigmatic smile held his attention – was it asking or telling, inviting shared confidences or imparting judgement? So intense did the gaze seem to become that Theodore looked behind him to see if there was another person standing there as the subject of attention. But there was no-one. He walked on, then looked back to see the painting presiding over a gaggle of schoolchildren with no interest in it whatsoever. Suffer little children... He smiled to himself and walked on.

Against his intention he stopped walking. Something in the painting was drawing him back. He retraced his steps and again confronted the image. Then he saw that what he sought lay not in the face at all but in the background. There, surely, was the Jewish Temple, with its arches and colonnades. And if this was Jerusalem – and it could be no other place – then the Christ-figure, like himself, knew he was awaiting death.

These were not thoughts he should have had. They were thoughts that would have induced self-ridicule before that fateful letter had come. He looked about him. Small though the church was in the general scheme of things, for him, now, in the late afternoon light, with the frescoed ceiling becoming fainter, it assumed a vastness that made him feel no more than a tiny worthless speck of irrelevance.

A high segment of the great stained glass west window was still taking the strength of the sun. On the floor where the light fell a perfect circle had superimposed itself upon the reciprocating patterns of the floor. Theodore suddenly thought of it as a test. He tried to clear his head of all thought that might oppose receptivity, and stepped into the circle of light. Surely, if enlightenment was to come at all, it would come now. But about him all remained still. Nothing changed. A minute later, mildly disappointed but not surprised, he stepped out of the light.

He passed the door to the corridor leading to the campanile – the great bell tower standing slightly apart from the mass of the church, higher even than the window that had offered him its light. A notice beside the door directed him to the information desk where he might buy a ticket. The young man behind the counter – from his dress and long hair most likely a student – looked up as he approached. It was a neutral look, Theodore thought, or perhaps a concealing look.

'I would like a ticket for the campanile, please,' Theodore said, handing the man a banknote of a rather large denomination.

'I'm sorry, Sir. I'm afraid I'm unable to change that.'

'But that's ridiculous. You must have been given change all morning.'

'That is so, but at the end of the morning the priest in

charge comes to collect whatever has been given and takes it away. There's a shop next to the church where you can get change, and there are cash machines at several places in the Piazza.'

'But I don't have time,' Theodore said. 'The light is already going and I would like to see the campanile.'

'I'm sorry I cannot help you. I'm sure you will appreciate that I'm forbidden to allow visitors to ascend the campanile without a ticket.'

Angrily, Theodore left the church, passing the shop where – had he been so minded – he could have got change with just a small purchase. He walked into the Piazza and slumped into a chair outside one of the small cafés. He ordered a coffee and spent the next half-hour staring moodily over his cup. In the distance he could see members of his own group making their way to the hotel shuttle bus. This was his cue to get up and leave, to forget the church and its wretched campanile. He looked at his watch – still half an hour before it closed. He paid for his coffee, then stared in disbelief at the change in the bowl. There were banknotes, for sure, but on top of them were coins stacked to the exact value of the ticket for entrance to the campanile. Surely… He swept up what he might otherwise have left as a tip and walked back to the church.

Their eyes met. 'I found some change,' Theodore said sheepishly. And as he said it a burden of unreasonableness was lifted from him. The eyes across the counter lit up with an expression of relief and pleasure that Theodore might have guessed was beyond the possible. 'I was truly hoping you would return,' the man said.

And suddenly Theodore was seeing, not the face of a humble attendant, but that of the Christ-figure in the painting. He realised it was not meaningful to distinguish between those differing elements in the enigmatic smile, but instead accept that there was no conflict between conviction in the rightness of a cause and concern that it might not be fulfilled.

'I'm closing the desk now,' the man said, looking at his watch. 'But if you like I can accompany you to the campanile. From the summit I can show you many things.'

Together they climbed the succession of ever-narrowing staircases and, reaching the top, stepped into the bright evening light.

NOTES ON *A JERUSALEM TRILOGY*

Whatever one's interpretation of the story of the raising of Lazarus by Jesus, it is difficult to escape the conclusion that the event made it easier for Jesus' followers to accept the concept of the resurrection after the crucifixion and the disappearance of his body from the tomb in which it had been placed. If it is not accepted that the raising of Lazarus was a miracle (i.e. that Lazarus did not actually die) it is difficult to account for Jesus' grief, both on being told beforehand of Lazarus' 'death' and, later, at the tomb before he was called to 'come forth.' A possible interpretation without supernatural overtones is that Jesus himself was misled and that the perpetrators – albeit innocently and with Jesus' interests at heart – could have been Lazarus and his two sisters, Mary and Martha. In *Lazarus*, the story presented here, this conclusion is reached by a biblical scholar in Jerusalem, whose interest is kindled on seeing a copy of a letter by the second century church father Clement of Alexandria, discovered in the monastery of Mar Saba, near Jerusalem, by Professor Morton Smith in 1958. This letter quotes passages from an alternative version of Mark's gospel in which there is a reference to the raising of Lazarus. (In the New Testament an account of the raising of Lazarus occurs only in John's gospel.) Our scholar's insightful conclusion follows a visit to the supposed tomb of Lazarus in Bethany; described as early as the fourth century CE, this could well be the authentic site.

The traditional role of Judas Iscariot in Jesus' demise has led to his almost universal vilification. However, it is clear that by the time of the last supper Jesus knew of Judas' intention to expose him. If, as many believe, Jesus was deliberately pursuing a path towards his own destruction it is difficult not to conclude that there was at least a degree of collusion between them. Had Jesus wished to avoid the consequences of Judas' action he would not have awaited arrest in the Garden of Gethsemane.

The inconsistencies and gaps in the story of the resurrection of Jesus following his crucifixion have perplexed both theologians and historians to the present day. Whilst no-one has produced a convincing physical explanation for the disappearance of Jesus' body from the tomb in which it was first laid – an event witnessed by Jesus' entourage – it has to be recognised that something extraordinary happened to make Jesus' followers believe they later encountered the risen Jesus. This was, after all, the cornerstone of the faith of both the messianic community in Jerusalem led by Jesus' younger brother James and by the envoy Paul, who took the message to gentile communities elsewhere.

The idea that the person encountered by Mary in the tomb early on the Sunday morning – the foundation of the initial rumour that Jesus had risen – was not Jesus but someone such as a brother having a resemblance to him is not new. However, there does not seem to have been any attempt to cast such an explanation in a form that takes account of the salient landmarks in the gospel accounts. There is strong possibility that Jesus had several siblings, including brothers James, Joses, Simeon and Judas, and a sister Salome. The story presented here, *Judas Thomas*, makes the fourth brother, Judas, the one that Mary encountered in the tomb. He is called here Judas Thomas, or just Thomas, this name meaning 'twin' in Aramaic. Here it has been given to Thomas as a nickname because of his physical resemblance to his elder brother. There are references in the early literature to Jesus having a twin brother, the most well-known being the 'Gospel of Thomas' – one of a collection of early Christian writings unearthed at Nag Hamadi in Egypt in 1945. This text begins: 'These are the secret sayings which the living Jesus spoke and which Didymos Judas Thomas wrote down...' It is not known whether this Coptic gospel was based on writings of a true brother of Jesus or is attributable to Jesus' disciple Thomas, who was one of the Twelve but most likely a different figure altogether. The former interpretation is assumed for the purpose of the story.

The location of the house in which the last supper was held – probably on the Thursday evening before Jesus' arrest – cannot with certainty be identified with the house of John the Priest (the most likely candidate for the 'disciple whom Jesus loved') but this must be a strong possibility. It was on the recollections of this John that John's Gospel – attributable to another John – was based. In this gospel it is reported that he was among those who believed they had witnessed the risen Jesus on the shore of the Sea of Galilee.

The true fate of Mary of Magdala (in later Christian parlance Mary Magdalene) after the crucifixion of Jesus is not known, but is seems not inconsistent with James' character that he should have taken her in when he arrived in Jerusalem to assume leadership of the messianic community there. James was to hold this position for at least two decades. He died at the hands of the high priest Ananias in 62 CE, by which time Christian communities had been established – often with the help of Paul – in various cities throughout the eastern Mediterranean.

Finally, it is not widely realised that the hillside village of Nazareth lay only three miles or so from – and in sight of – the large town of Sepphoris, the administrative capital of Galilee. Although Sepphoris is hardly mentioned in the Bible it cannot be doubted that Jesus and his family would have known it well. In this story Judas Thomas is an artisan in the town, carrying on there the business of Jesus' family.